Sarah Anne's Faithful Friends

Book 4 of the Unshakable Faith Series

By

Cathy Lynn Bryant
Jessica Marie Dorman

BRYANT & DORMAN
BOOKS†

Copyright © 2016 by Cathy Lynn Bryant with contributor Jessica Marie Dorman

BRYANT DORMAN BOOKS†

Bangor, Maine 04401

bryantdormanbooks.com

Cover model Jessica Marie Dorman

Interior photo model Jessica Marie Dorman

Printed in the United States of America

All Scripture references are from the KJV

Library of Congress Control Number: **2016912353**

ISBN: **13: 978-0692562987**

First Edition:

The book is comprised of historical figures intermingled with fictional characters.

Authors Cathy Lynn Bryant and Jessica Dorman have again captivated their readers with their newest novel titled *Sarah Anne's Faithful Friends*. The Authors seamlessly reunite their readers with Sarah Anne as if we have only briefly parted, taking us back to sweet, simpler traditions of times past. Sarah Anne's internal battle with tragic circumstances from her past explodes with haunting reminders throughout the story. How she comes to a resolution will keep you turning the pages of this delightful twist of a tale. This beautifully written novel will ignite a newfound perspective of a faithful God, as well as the love of family and treasured friends, as we observe Grace and Forgiveness in this young woman. Welcome back Sarah Anne. We have missed you.

Author, L.A. Muse
http://www.orphancrusade.com/

Prologue

The year 1735, Amesbury, Massachusetts Bay Colony

It had been nearly a year since that tragic day. Sarah Anne could scarcely believe Alexander was gone. What took but a moment, would change her life forever. From that time on, the distraught young woman had been busying herself to the point of exhaustion, hoping to put the awful event behind her; but the memory remained as vivid as ever.

Chapter 1

Early spring, the year 1735, Boston, Massachusetts Bay Colony

Upon the arrival of Sarah Anne Swyndhurst and Mr. Hoyt, Daniel Thompson ushered them into the house. Once he had made his guests comfortable in the rather spacious parlor, Daniel went to his bedchamber where his wife was currently resting to inform her that her father and Sarah had safely arrived. The family had been expecting Mr. Hoyt and hoped he would persuade Sarah to come, too. While looking closely at his beloved wife, Daniel sensed that something was troubling her.

"What is it, Joanna?" he inquired with concern.

"Daniel, I am at a loss as to what to say to Sarah. How can someone so young have had to suffer so much? Until her birthday next month, she is not yet five and twenty." At this point, Joanna had tears welling up in her eyes.

At ten years Sarah's senior, from the time they had first become acquainted, Joanna had always been a little protective of her friend. Sarah's father, Joseph Goodwin, had passed not long before his daughter's marriage to Alexander Swyndhurst. Now that Alexander was gone as well, Joanna felt her protective instincts for Sarah even more acutely.

Besides having their faith and a great love of children in common, both women had fathers whose Christian name was Joseph. Since Sarah's father was no longer living, Joanna was very glad that her own father had all but adopted the young woman as his own.

Daniel approached the bed and made himself comfortable next to his wife. "You are right. She seems to have suffered one tragedy after another—having been twice captured by Matthew Raymond and all that entailed. But for her to lose her beloved husband—that was the worst of all."

"Indeed, and she was right there watching as the wagon—" Joanna could not bring herself to say the words. "How her heart must yet be breaking—they loved each other so dearly. And because of that despicable Matthew Raymond, they lost several months together when she came to us, believing her husband would no longer want her after what had happened. If only we had known Alexander at the time, we certainly would not have agreed to keep her whereabouts a secret from him."

Grabbing his wife's hand, Daniel responded, "When

she comes in to see you, allow her demeanor to guide the conversation. Regardless of whether or not she wishes to talk of Alexander, it is my belief that being here, assisting with the boys and taking care of you whilst you rest shall do her the most good."

"I pray you are right, Daniel. However, I am also concerned that the birth of our child may remind Sarah of the loss of her own son, and that owing to her injuries from her fall, she will likely never have another child of her own—that is, if she again weds. She mentioned in a recent missive that the Strout children are no longer even with her after their mother's remarriage."

"Yes, well, as for the Strout children, I always believed it was asking a bit much of Sarah to keep them, in particular after Alexander's passing. I was indeed astonished to hear Alice Strout had taken them to Ipswich, for I felt certain she had abandoned them to Sarah's care forever. And as evidenced by her love and concern for those children and our boys, she shall certainly be overjoyed when she meets our new little one."

"I hope you are right. If you wish, you may send Father and Sarah in now. I believe I am ready," Joanna said while adjusting her bedcoverings over her legs and swelled middle, and pulling her long brown hair over her shoulder so it could be re-tied with the ribbon that had slipped out while she was resting. She watched as her husband moved toward the door, and sighed. She had never grown tired of his kind nature and, to her, his looks had not diminished a bit, even with the few silver strands now weaving through his blonde hair. And given her tall stature, he was one of the few men to whom she had to look up.

Within a few minutes, Sarah and Mr. Hoyt appeared at Joanna's bedside. As they made themselves comfortable on the chairs Daniel had provided, which were situated on either side of the bed, Joanna's father reached over and took hold of his daughter's hand.

"Joanna, it is wonderful to see you looking so well. My dear, is all of this necessary? The bed rest, I mean?"

While squeezing her father's hand with one hand and placing her other upon Sarah's, which was resting next to hers on the opposite side of the bed, Joanna responded. "You may remember, Father, I had a rather difficult time of it with Joseph. Daniel merely wishes to avoid any complications."

Mr. Hoyt leaned forward and then silently prayed all would turn out well with both Joanna and the baby when the time came for her to deliver.

A few minutes had passed when Sarah noticed Joanna staring at her with a troubled look; therefore, to set her friend's mind at ease, she stated, "Joanna, your countenance appears to be one of concern. There truly is no need to be anxious over me. Now that I am here with you and your family, all will be well. Getting away from Amesbury was just what I needed. Staying in the home where there are so many memories of Alexander has made it difficult to stop myself from thinking about him, not to mention his things are about the place in nearly every room."

Joanna smiled at her younger friend. "Sarah, you never were one to conceal your thoughts. I appreciate your frankness. You may regret coming here at this time, though, for Daniel is sure to put you to work."

If Joanna had been privy to Sarah's thoughts at that moment, she would have known that this was Sarah's hope—to be kept busy so as to distract herself from her thoughts. The images of Alexander and that fateful day were still so frequent and vivid, and try as she might, she had met with little success at pushing them from her mind.

After a time, Sarah and Mr. Hoyt noticed Joanna appeared fatigued. They soon left the room, allowing her to rest.

When Sarah was directed to the same lovely bedchamber she had previously occupied, she found her belongings next to the bed. She then glanced around at the familiar surroundings. The bed still had the lovely lace pillows and colorful quilt upon it. What she had always loved most about the room was the window from which she could see the sparkling stream just beyond her favorite bench. Making her way over to look out, her eyes quickly fixed on the bench under the shade tree. The memories of an earlier visit came flooding in, bringing with them a torrent of varied emotions. Her last visit had been during a very turbulent time in her life. Turning back from the window, her eyes went to the settee on the opposite wall.

She decided it was time to sit and pray for a while.

Later, when the boys came in from doing their chores, they were delighted to see Sarah. They had grown to love her when she had last stayed with them. Though it had been some time since they had seen her, in their view she looked nearly the same, with her long hair the color of chestnuts. Her tiny frame, however, at present, appeared somewhat smaller to the young men.

Sarah's deep blue eyes beheld both of the young Mr. Thompsons standing before her. How much they had changed. The last time she had seen them, Daniel was just shy of eleven, and Joseph was not yet nine. At now twelve and ten, the boys had grown immensely. Sarah noticed the boys still resembled their mother, with similar hair and eyes to hers. As she continued to study them, she realized the eldest had to tilt his head down a little to look at her, and Joseph was now nearly her height. Daniel, Jr., was also quick to correct her when she called him Daniel. It seems he had decided he wished to be known as Dan, so as not to be confused with his father. As for Joseph, happy to have been named after his grandfather, he did not feel the need to shorten or alter his name. Sarah was glad for she loved the name Joseph, as it reminded her of her own dear father.

After hugging them both, Sarah sighed. She was right; this was precisely what she needed. Before long, the boys convinced her to come out of doors with them. Because of the way she had taken part in their activities on her last visit, they often seemed to have forgotten she was actually a grown woman and not merely a chum.

While Sarah was out in the yard with Dan and Joseph, their father and Mr. Hoyt watched out the window. The boys had tied something over Sarah's eyes and at present were spinning her around. Daniel and his father-in-law had a good laugh over this.

"I see nothing much has changed between Sarah and the boys," chuckled Daniel. "It is as if she never left."

Out in the yard, as Sarah whirled round and round, she called out, "All right! I am getting dizzy now, boys."

Dan grabbed hold of her arms to steady her. He then backed away and said, "Sarah, now see if you can catch us."

In this game, the boys were not to be more than an arm's length away. Sarah had to try and capture one of them, which was no easy task, given that she was currently blindfolded. The boys both laughed as she stumbled around. She soon began to chuckle as well. The game went on for several minutes before Sarah finally caught hold of one of their arms. Pulling the covering from her eyes, she found that she had captured Joseph. It was now his turn. The game continued for a while. Sarah hated to disappoint her young friends, but she was feeling quite spent. When she had given them a few more minutes, she finally voiced her need for a rest.

In the kitchen, Mr. Hoyt told Daniel that Sarah was probably tired from their trip. They had arrived only a few hours before. Hearing his father-in-law's words, Daniel made his way over to the door to beckon to his sons.

Chapter 2

Early the next morning, Sarah arose feeling rested for the first time in weeks. After a long afternoon the previous day of spending time out of doors with the boys and seeing to Joanna's regular duties, she had been completely worn out. As she thought about how much she had already enjoyed her time with the Thompsons, she was glad she had decided to come. She had not felt so needed in a very long time.

Coming into the kitchen, Sarah found four sets of all male eyes on her; however, she was not the least bit intimidated by any of these particular gentlemen. They had always treated her like one of the family. "Good morning, everyone," she said smiling brightly.

Daniel and Mr. Hoyt were delighted to see that Sarah appeared joyful. Daniel returned the greeting, "And good morning to you, Sarah. Did you have a restful sleep?"

"Oh, my...did I ever! I have not rested so comfortably in, well—" She had no desire to revisit the reason she hadn't been sleeping. She was determined to press on and focus on the Thompsons and enjoying her time with them.

After observing the pensive look upon Sarah's face following her shortened response, while holding out a chair for her, Daniel called her over to the table. Out of respect, the Thompson boys and Mr. Hoyt also stood and waited for her to be seated.

Daniel had already breakfasted with Joanna but had decided to join them anyway. He had always placed great importance on taking meals together with his sons; that is, when his doctoring did not get in the way. At times he was called away and couldn't take his meals with his family. He so disliked that part of the life of a physician.

After tidying up the kitchen, Sarah went in to visit with Joanna. As the friends talked, Joanna revealed her fears with regard to the birth of her third child. Until now, she had not disclosed to Sarah how difficult Joseph's birth had been.

With understanding, Sarah reached over and grabbed hold of her friend's hand. She, more than most, knew about difficult births, for she had lost her one and only child very soon after his birth. "Joanna, you have Daniel here to see you through this, and I shall be right by your side."

Joanna was reluctant to talk about this with Sarah for fear of reviving her friend's heartrending memories of her child, but she felt she needed to talk to someone. She had no desire to distress her husband. "I am ready to go if the Lord calls me home, Sarah. My only concern is for my family."

"Joanna, you are not thinking clearly. Daniel has no such worries, of that I am certain. Now you must push such thoughts from your mind. Let us talk of happier things, such as what you intend to call the baby when he or she arrives."

Joanna knew she should not be borrowing trouble. "You are so right, Sarah. Pay no attention to my babbling." Reaching over to the little table beside her bed, Joanna retrieved a list she had written of potential names for the baby. Her first two children had been easy. She had always known she wished to name a child after Daniel, and when the second one arrived, she was delighted for him to be her father's namesake. But this third one was a bit difficult. She had one brother, but it seemed he was always bent on getting into trouble. She had no wish to name a son after him. To her, passing down a name was similar to bestowing a blessing, which she hoped would bring about a desire in the child to carry on the godly character of the one after whom he was named. Consequently, she could not bring herself to consider her brother George.

At present, she had no desire to reveal her thoughts about George to Sarah. She disliked speaking evil of anyone, especially her own brother. She hoped that this time the baby would be a girl, for it would solve the problem of what to name the child. She had a number of feminine names listed.

"Daniel and I have come up with several possibilities. Take a look and tell me what you think," she said as she handed the list to Sarah.

Sarah read each name and then remarked, "Joanna,

this list is in want of any names for a male child. I thought at the very least the list would contain your brother's name. Did you not tell me his name is George?"

Even with the current state of her relationship with her brother, Joanna loved him deeply. She recalled then how happy she had been when her parents brought George home shortly after his birth. A great deal had changed between them since that time. It seemed that whenever they were together now, they had a tendency to argue; thus, to Joanna's great disappointment, her brother rarely visited. *I so wish things were different*, she thought.

Feeling a little discomfited that her friend might find fault with her for not considering her brother's name, Joanna replied, "As you see, I am quite hopeful this time it shall be a girl." Then, attempting to change the subject, she asked, "Have you seen the quilt I made for the baby?"

Although her friend had indicated that the reason for the absence of her brother's name was because she hoped for a girl, Sarah felt she had initiated an unwanted topic of conversation. Not wanting to press the issue, she allowed her friend to direct the discussion away from what to name the child. "No, Joanna. I have not. Shall I fetch it for you? I would dearly love to see it."

Catching a glimpse of the strange look upon Sarah's face, Joanna realized her friend had perceived her quick change of topic. With a flushed face for making Sarah uncomfortable, Joanna directed Sarah's attention to the corner of the room. "I believe I left it over there on the chair."

Sarah went to retrieve the little quilt. With eyes wide as she lifted it, she exclaimed, "Oh, Joanna, it is simply lovely!"

A smile stretched across Joanna's face at her friend's approval of her work. "Do you really think so, Sarah? I have never been mistaken for an accomplished seamstress."

"That makes two of us," Sarah chuckled. "But to look at this, one would never guess. It is just wonderful," she responded while continuing to study the quilt.

Daniel came in then and found his two favorite ladies having a marvelous time together. Sarah stayed a few minutes longer before slipping out, leaving the couple alone.

After making her way to her bedchamber, she gathered up her Bible and a small lap quilt. She then headed to the old, familiar bench under the lovely shade tree, which was nearly in full bloom. From there, she listened to the flowing water in the stream a few yards away. If anyone inquired as to her favorite place on the earth, she would surely say it was where she was presently sitting.

With the wind blowing through her hair, Sarah was reminded of another windy day, the day Alexander found her in that very spot. She had been gone from home for many months. Following an attack by Matthew Raymond, she learned that she was with child. When Alexander discovered her whereabouts, he came for her and made known his deep love for her and the child—whom he assured he intended to raise as his very own. She recalled how stunned she had been that he would accept her child as his own.

All of a sudden, Matthew Raymond's fierce face flashed before her. Sarah shivered at the thought of the despicable man who had not only forced himself upon her, but had also caused the death of her child when she gave birth prematurely. As if to rescue her from the dreadful image, Alexander came to mind. She then thought about how terrible her husband had felt for leading the despicable man straight to her. He had learned, after his arrival, that Matthew Raymond had followed him from Amesbury to Boston.

Glancing over at the trees along the edge of the yard, she recalled Matthew Raymond hiding there watching her with her husband. At this remembrance, the comforting images of Alexander and the peace she had always felt while sitting on this particular bench suddenly slipped away. Unable to shake off the memory of that day, she envisioned her captor creeping up behind her while she was alone on the bench, after Alexander had gone into the house. She could almost feel his rough grasp as she thought about how he seized her for a second time.

Tightly closing her eyes, Sarah attempted to push the images from her mind. But try as she might, they continued. She saw herself falling out of the back of her captor's wagon. She could almost feel the pains that began soon after the fall. Her mind then carried her to the room in which her son was born and, shortly after, died. By this time, she felt wetness on her cheeks.

A feeling of deep sadness settled over her, making it difficult to remain where she was. She decided not to give in to her grief, as it had a tendency to be all consuming. Reading from the Psalms had always served to lighten her mood thus she thumbed through her Bible until she came to where she had last read. After a time, she felt a calmness pervade her being. Growing tired now, she leaned back against the bench and closed her eyes, allowing the few rays of sun that were peeking through the greenery from the shade tree to warm her face.

While peering out the window, Daniel observed Sarah resting in her favorite spot. At the sight of her, his thoughts went to a similar place as Sarah's had only moments before. He recalled what had happened the last time she was on that very bench—Alexander speaking with her for the first time in months, and Matthew Raymond abducting her for a second time. As he stood there, his heart ached over all that his young friend had suffered. *How one so small and delicate could have so much courage, I shall never know. It had to be in God's strength that she endured it all. There truly is no other source for that kind of fortitude.* "Lord, help her stretch here to be a time of healing, as it was once before."

Chapter 3

The Thompson boys worked alongside Sarah in their mother's garden for most of the day, weeding and planting. Sarah felt that in doing this, the house would remain quiet for the boys' mother to rest. She had also reasoned that it might relieve her friend's mind that her garden was being tended. Just as she was about to go in, Mr. Hoyt called out to her. Hastening in to see what he needed, she found that Joanna's pains had begun.

"We came none too soon, Sarah. Here it is only the third day since our arrival, and already the birth of my third grandchild is upon us."

Sarah smiled at the delight in her elderly friend's eyes.

Late in the day, Daniel came home to find that Joanna's labor had been going on for some time. Sarah informed him that if he had been much longer, she would have sent Mr. Hoyt to fetch him. His wife had insisted that there was plenty of time, knowing the visit he had to make that day was necessary. With their boys, her labor had been quite long. Unbeknownst to him, however, as the hours passed, Joanna had begun to grow a little restless, sensing that something was different than the other two times. Her heart was beating so fast that she felt short of breath.

Daniel and Sarah kept vigil throughout the night, both hoping the child would come before daybreak; however, as the sun peeked through the window the following morning, an exhausted Joanna—still with child—seemed to be struggling for every breath. Daniel was concerned that something was dreadfully wrong. He recalled that ever since she had been ill with a high fever a few months earlier, she seemed to tire easily. He had hoped it was merely the fact that she was with child. He had seen instances where, after just such an illness, the person suffered from a weakened heart, often permanently.

A few hours later, his concerns were validated when his wife began to have pains, not only what was normal for birthing a baby, but discomfort in the region of her chest and left arm as well. Once she finally brought forth the child, the physician-husband's heart sank when he realized the baby had died. The umbilical cord was tightly wound around her tiny neck. He may have been able to save her had the delivery not taken so long, but there was nothing he could do now.

His wife, very weak, with tears streaming down her cheeks, held out trembling hands to him. She wanted the child placed next to her. As Daniel studied his wife, he saw that her lips appeared a bluish color and she could scarcely talk or even breathe.

Sarah had slipped out the moment she realized the

child was gone. Though her concern for her friend persisted, she knew the couple needed to be alone with the lifeless child. And at the remembrance of her own baby, she could not manage another moment in that room. It was all too reminiscent of what she had suffered.

As she closed the door behind her, the tears began to flow. She remained on the other side of the door to take a moment to pray for her friends. She then made her way to the parlor to be with Joanna's father and boys, hoping they would not ask about the baby, for she had no intention of revealing that the little girl had died. It wasn't her place. She would also keep her concerns for Joanna to herself.

In Daniel and Joanna's bedchamber, Daniel struggled to save the life of his beloved wife. As he prayed, he heard Joanna's faint voice whispering to him. She told him what she suspected, that she was dying, and that she wanted to discuss her family's future with him. He knew once she revealed what was on her mind, she would then allow herself to grieve the loss of their child, whom they both believed she would soon follow.

"Daniel, if...I pass from this life—" Joanna had to catch her breath before she could continue.

Barely able to hear his wife, her voice was so weak, Daniel strained to listen. He needed to stay focused on what he was doing, but he also wanted to know what his wife had to say. "Joanna, I am listening, my love."

"There is something I want you to know before it

is—" With great difficulty, she continued, "too late."

"What are you trying to say, Joanna?"

Looking intently at her husband, her voice faint, Joanna said, "Daniel...I want you to consider...taking Sarah as your wife. The boys will need a mother. Sarah loves them deeply, and they...her. I know she will," continuing to struggle for air, she went on, "take great care of them. And you shall also need a—"

Joanna then fell silent. Daniel noticed her head had fallen against the pillow and her eyes were fixed as though observing something above her, but of course she was not able to see a thing. She was gone. Grabbing her wrist, he checked for a pulse. Finding none, he attempted to revive her. When he realized there was nothing he could do, he leaned his head on her chest and wept. His wife and baby daughter had passed in the space of less than an hour.

In the parlor, both Sarah and Mr. Hoyt thought they heard Daniel weeping. Mr. Hoyt tilted his head toward the doorway for Sarah to take the boys out.

With tears in her eyes, she complied, not knowing if it was for the baby alone that Daniel wept, or if something had happened to Joanna as well. After what she had seen while she was still in with her friend, she thought it was a real possibility they had lost them both. She had never seen anyone with lips as blue as Joanna's, who also seemed to be having trouble breathing.

Once they had made their way out, the boys questioned Sarah. Having heard their father crying, they wondered what was happening in their parents' room. They were very frightened and in need of comfort. Sarah walked them toward the bench at the far end of the yard. The last time she had been seated there, she had been overcome with dreadful memories. She would not allow that to happen today. Taking a deep breath, Sarah continued to guide Dan and Joseph to the bench, where they then seated themselves on either side of her. Grasping their hands, she began to pray.

After a time, Mr. Hoyt, with red eyes, came out to fetch his grandsons and Sarah. With one look at her elderly friend's face, Sarah knew that, just as the baby had, Joanna had died. At least she was fairly certain that was what had happened. In confirmation of her questioning expression, Mr. Hoyt slowly nodded his head. After taking a quick glance at Joanna's sons, Sarah closed her eyes, wanting to shut out the truth of the situation. She knew the pain the boys would experience when they learned what had happened to their mother.

Chapter 4

It had been a week since Daniel lost his wife and daughter. He had shared with his father-in-law the last conversation he would ever have with his wife; consequently, without revealing the reason for his request, his father-in-law had asked Sarah to remain in Boston for a while, knowing that if she returned home, Joanna's dying wish would likely never happen. Although his father-in-law, as with everyone else, was still in shock over what had happened, he had clearly understood his daughter's concern for her family, knowing that she would not be there to look after them. He told Daniel that if he had anything to say about it, he would make certain her last wish was fulfilled.

Daniel, on the other hand, had no intention of following through with what Joanna had requested. His wife had only been gone a week. He couldn't fathom taking another wife at this point, or ever for that matter.

Furthermore, if he were to marry Sarah Swyndhurst simply to honor his wife's wish for their sons to have a mother, he would be putting the young woman in another marriage that was merely for convenience. He could not bring himself to do that to her. She had already had a marriage of that nature with Alexander—at least it was at the start. Sarah had once informed him that she and Alexander had wed to honor her father's last request, not for love. Oh, he knew that the couple had come to love each other deeply, but that would certainly not happen with them, of that he was sure. Joanna had been his one and only, and Sarah was much the same as a little sister to him.

Sarah had been helping out with the cooking and cleaning for the Thompson men and Mr. Hoyt. Though her heart was breaking over the loss of her friend and the Thompsons' baby, she had pushed all of that aside to be there for Joanna's family. She knew she could not stay forever, but until Mr. Hoyt was prepared to leave, she would continue looking after everyone. She had also been thinking about how lonely she would be when she returned home. When she was last in Amesbury, she had been able to correspond with Joanna by way of missives. Her friend was gone now. When she returned to Amesbury, she would not be coming back. It wouldn't be appropriate to pay the Thompsons a visit without Joanna there. With all of this in mind, she was in no hurry to go.

◊◊◊

Daniel was grateful Sarah had stayed on for a time looking after things. Since that terrible day, he had not been much good for anything, other than going out on house calls. His father-in-law had not pressed him with regard to fulfilling Joanna's wish that he marry Sarah, but Daniel knew Joseph thought it was a good plan. Whenever he had observed his sons clinging to Sarah, he wavered a little with regard to the marriage idea, wondering how they were going to manage without her; nonetheless, he knew he had to prepare himself and his sons, for she would not be staying on much longer. His father-in-law had mentioned remaining for only a few more weeks. When the time came for the older man to go, Sarah would be returning with him to Amesbury.

◊◊◊

A month had passed without alteration. Sarah and Mr. Hoyt were still at the Thompson home looking after things. The distraught physician continued to do little more than see to the needs of the townsfolk.

Daniel had not pressed church attendance with his sons so upset over the loss of their mother, given that he was in much the same state, but he knew it was time they resumed their attendance. He had also struggled with the idea of going for the reason that there would likely be well meaning people coming up to speak with him about Joanna and the baby. He was not prepared for that. Truth be told, he probably never would be; nonetheless, he and his sons could not stay away from church forever.

The next Lord's Day, with his sons, Sarah and Mr. Hoyt in tow, Daniel set off for church. Designated seating had recently eased. People now sat wherever they wished. Upon their arrival, Daniel made his way to the far end of a bench. His sons followed. Mr. Hoyt then ushered Sarah in and took a seat next to her on the opposite end of the bench from his son-in-law.

Sensing that many eyes were fixed upon her, Sarah felt uneasy. She had also heard whispers she knew were about her, given that a couple of women actually pointed in her direction. At the end of the service, she couldn't get out of there fast enough. On her way out, she overheard one woman say that she was trying to win the good physician, and this with his wife's body scarcely in the ground; as a result, Sarah nearly ran to the wagon.

Mr. Hoyt had also heard what the woman had said about Sarah. As he watched her sitting stiffly in the wagon on the trip home, he knew he had to share what was on his mind with his son-in-law, as well as what he and, he was quite certain, Sarah had overheard.

As soon as they had arrived at home, Sarah alighted from the wagon and went directly to her bedchamber. She had already prepared the food for the family's afternoon meal. Knowing they could manage serving themselves, she remained in her room. When Mr. Hoyt knocked on the door for her to come and eat with them, she declined—stating that she was not feeling well. Reluctantly, the elderly gentleman left her to herself and returned to the kitchen.

Once the meal was over, the boys went to the barn to set about doing their chores. While Mr. Hoyt and Daniel were alone, the older man explained what had happened at church. Daniel felt terrible. He had been wondering why Sarah seemed rather quiet on the ride home. After hearing this, he could not blame her.

Mr. Hoyt decided it was time to discuss the matter of the marriage between his son-in-law and Sarah. Daniel quietly listened as Joseph made a case for going along with Joanna's wish. From the start, the grief-stricken man had decided against it. He reasoned with himself that Joanna could not have known what she was asking. But after listening to his father-in-law, he was seriously considering it. *What could be so terrible? We would go on as we have been—just friends, living under the same roof with her caring for the boys and the home. Having Sarah here would be the best thing for the boys. And it would break their hearts if she were to leave. And she has no one to go home to, other than her servants.*

After mulling it over, Daniel told Mr. Hoyt he would think on it awhile longer before making a decision. He was astonished at himself for even considering the arrangement.

Mr. Hoyt warned that he not wait too long, for he had a feeling that after what had happened at the church, Sarah would want to return home very soon.

Chapter 5

Following his conversation with his father-in-law, Daniel had difficulty sleeping as he pondered the idea of wedding Sarah and how he would go about asking her. Additionally, since his wife's passing, he hadn't as yet grown accustomed to sleeping alone. After making his way to the kitchen, lamp in hand, he caught a glimpse of something, or someone, moving in the shadows by the window. Lifting the lantern higher so he could see more clearly, he found that it was Sarah.

"Sarah, what are you doing up at this hour? Were you having trouble sleeping?" he inquired with concern. He then observed her head quickly turn away from the glow of the lantern, but not before catching a glimpse of tears spilling from her eyes.

As she stared out the window at the moonlit yard, she softly replied, "Yes, just a bit. I didn't mean to wake you." Unaware that he had already detected that she had been crying, as she spoke she surreptitiously wiped her tears on her sleeve, hoping to dry her face before he noticed. She was up trying to think of the best way to let the boys and Daniel know that she needed to go home. Her heart felt so heavy at the thought of leaving, she had been sobbing for some time now. The Thompsons were like family. With the passing of her friend, her connection to the Thompsons had come to an end.

"Let us sit awhile." Moving towards her, he gently took hold of her arm and directed her over to the table. When they had each taken a seat, he grasped her hand. "What is it, Sarah?"

Hoping to maintain her composure, she cleared her throat before responding. "Daniel, I need to go home. I feel terrible leaving the boys, but it cannot be helped. My being here is bringing shame upon us both." Not wanting to bring up that it was no longer appropriate for her to be there with Joanna gone, in particular with gossips everywhere, she merely said, "In the circumstances, it is best that I take my leave as soon as possible. What is more, I shall not be returning. I hope that whenever you are in Amesbury to visit Mr. Hoyt, you will bring the boys to see me."

There it was, exactly as Joseph had warned. Sarah was planning to leave, most likely as soon as arrangements could be made. He had no choice. He had to ask her now, or she would soon be gone. His boys needed her, so he would do it for them. Feeling uncomfortable with what he was about to request, Daniel had to force himself to speak. "Sarah, there is something I must ask you. It is difficult, however, as my request may render you speechless."

"What is it, Daniel? By the serious look on your face, it must be something dreadful."

In hearing her words, Daniel felt awful. He had no wish for her to think marrying her would be a dreadful thing. "It is nothing of the sort. Still, I hope you shall not misunderstand my reasons for asking." Not knowing any other way to broach the subject, he spoke the question straightforwardly. "Sarah, would you consider marrying me so you might remain here with us? Joseph told me what happened at church. None of us want you to go. This would be the only way to go on as we have been." After asking Sarah such a ridiculous question, he paused—hoping for an answer—but not really believing she would consent.

Stunned, Sarah swallowed hard. "What? No! I could never do that to Joanna. Anyway, since we are friends, it would be rather awkward for us both."

As much as he expected that kind of a reaction, Daniel still hoped he could convince her. "Sarah, you may not believe this but with her last breath Joanna requested that we marry. She believed that you would care for the boys much as she would have—with love and tenderness."

Eyes wide, not fully comprehending what Daniel had said, for clarity she questioned, "This was Joanna's wish, then?"

"Yes, Sarah, it was. I was not for it at first, but I now see the wisdom in it. As you say, we are friends, good friends, are we not?"

"Well, yes, Daniel, but—"

"I know it seems rather strange to us now, but you have married for practicality's sake before. It wasn't so terrible, was it?" He then remembered what he had thought the first time he realized what kind of marriage

Alexander and Sarah Swyndhurst had entered into at the start, though it later changed to a loving relationship. At the time, he couldn't fathom ever doing such a thing. But here he was, suggesting precisely that kind of a marriage to Sarah.

Looking thoughtful, she responded, "No. But, Daniel, that was different. I hadn't even met Alexander until shortly before our wedding day. You and I have known each other for some time now. And your wife was my very best friend. To be married to you...it would be so...well, it's just absurd." She couldn't think of a suitable way to describe how she felt about his request.

Daniel had been uncertain about the prospect of marrying Sarah, but now he sensed that Sarah would see the arrangement for what it was—merely an understanding between friends. She wouldn't expect anything more. Now he just had to convince her that it was the right thing to do.

"Sarah, nothing would have to change between us. We could go on exactly as we have been. I need someone to look after the boys, and you are alone, apart from your servants and Alexander's father—who, from what you have said, will return to England one day. Moreover, I believe Alexander would wish for you to be here, safe with us. Not to mention your father, who never wanted you alone and unprotected, as evidenced by his having arranged a marriage of this kind for you before."

Sarah was beginning to give way. *It does seem*

practical. I could look after the boys while he is out on calls. And I would have a family, of sorts. As I am never to have children of my own, I would dearly love to help finish raising two such wonderful boys. Daniel is not going to expect anything more of me than what we have now—a friendship.

"Daniel, if we do this, you would never change your mind and expect...ah...traditional marriage, would you?" She was fairly certain he never would, but she had to be sure.

Daniel could see that Sarah was seriously considering his offer. He understood her fears about things altering after they were wed, for that had happened in her marriage to Alexander. In their present situation, though, it was different; neither would want that to take place. "Sarah, I believe we are likeminded on this issue, so that will never be a concern. In fact, I wish more than anything that we could remain as we are, but as you say, it isn't proper. If you are to remain, we must wed."

"Very well, Daniel. If you're sure this is what Joanna wanted, and you sincerely desire it, then I shall pray about it. If God leads me to consent to your proposal, then I surely will. By week's end, I shall have an answer. If, however, I believe it is not what God has in mind for me to do, then I shall be leaving soon after."

Daniel nodded to acknowledge her decision to pray about his offer of marriage. Even though he had not wanted to ask this of Sarah, he himself had taken the matter to the Lord. Until he had been pushed into a decision, with Sarah planning to leave, he had avoided what he believed to be the answer to his prayer; this was God's plan.

Before Sarah returned to her room, Daniel asked if he could pray with her over the matter. When they had finished, they each went to their separate bedchambers.

Chapter 6

The following morning, Mr. Hoyt sensed that something had happened between his son-in-law and Sarah. He wondered if Daniel had asked her to marry him, as his daughter had urged. After making his way over to the table, Mr. Hoyt sat down with Daniel and his grandsons. Sarah soon approached with a loaf of bread in one hand and a trencher loaded with sliced fruit in the other.

When Sarah was seated, she bowed her head as Daniel thanked God for providing for them. Hearing his voice reminded her of his question the night before. When she had returned to her bed following their conversation, still unable to sleep, she had spent some time in prayer. She had promised Daniel an answer by the end of the week. As she glanced at Dan and Joseph, her heart melted. She dearly loved them both. With their mother gone she wondered how she could ever leave them.

Daniel watched as Sarah looked lovingly at the boys. He smiled, for he could see that her countenance clearly demonstrated that she would say yes to his proposal. Her love for the boys was so great, he was fairly certain she could never leave them. He then thought about Joanna and his smile faded. Even if Sarah remained, nothing would ever be the same for his family. His darling wife was gone forever.

Mr. Hoyt had also been observing the two adults at the table. He beamed at Sarah's tender expression when she looked at his grandsons. If her tender gaze offered any indication of how she would answer his son-in-law, if he had indeed mustered up the courage to ask, she would be staying on with Daniel and the boys.

Just as Daniel had a moment ago, the older man felt a wave of sorrow at the thought of his daughter and that on this side of eternity he would never see her again. Remembering his age, he reassured himself that this side of eternity, for him, was not so very long; he would be seeing her again soon. And knowing Joanna would be pleased to know Sarah would be looking after her sons served to ease his sadness.

Once the boys had finished eating, they went out to the barn to begin their chores. Without his grandsons present, Mr. Hoyt decided to broach the subject of whether Daniel had asked Sarah to marry him. "You two appear to have had a conversation; one about marriage, I take it."

With surprise, Daniel's head turned toward Joseph, and he blurted out, "How did you know?"

Smiling, the older man responded, "You would not know it to look at me, but I am rather intuitive." He was delighted when his son-in-law and the young woman chuckled at this, for he sensed they had been far too somber about the whole business. "Truth be told, in looking at the two of you, I knew something had happened.

Is it settled, then?"

As she thought over the fact that the question had come from Mr. Hoyt, Sarah felt ill and soon excused herself from the room. This was Joanna's father asking whether she intended to marry Daniel. In her eyes, Daniel was still Joanna's husband, and always would be.

With Sarah gone from the room, Daniel explained that he had asked, but that she had not yet given an answer. "She requested that I allow her time to pray about it, which is as it should be. She said she shall inform me of her decision by the week's end."

"If I may inquire, what prompted you to ask at this time? I wasn't even sure you had settled upon the idea."

"It was as you had said. I found her up during the night. When I came upon her in the kitchen she had been crying. She explained that it was not proper for her to stay here any longer. She even reminded me that this would be her last visit. Knowing you and Joanna were right about the situation—the boys needing a mother, and Sarah lacking a family—I decided I had better ask while there was yet time. Initially, she reacted as though it would be a betrayal of Joanna if she were to accept—that is, until I informed her that it was Joanna's wish."

"She must have been surprised both by the question and then to learn that Joanna had wanted the two of you to marry."

"She was indeed. As I had indicated, her first response was a definite *no*, which was exactly what I had expected. I am of the opinion, however, that just knowing Joanna wanted it this way made her willing to at least consider my proposal. Even as we speak about this, I still cannot fully accept that Joanna is truly gone. Though it may be the right thing to do, proposing to Sarah still feels wrong somehow."

"I understand, Daniel, but this needed to be dealt with while Sarah is still here. Joanna showed real wisdom in making the suggestion that Sarah become a part of our family. Let us pray that our young friend accepts your proposal."

◊◊◊

As Sarah reclined on her bed, she felt uneasy about her future, a future that might include Joanna's family. Was she really prepared to marry Daniel? She had no fears where he was concerned, but she wondered if it was truly the right thing to do.

Taking the matter to the Lord, Sarah began, "Not that I ever intend to marry again, but what if, in time, I wish to be wed? If I consent to Daniel's proposal, I shall never have an opportunity for a real marriage with someone else. Daniel will love me as one loves a sister; therefore, ours will never be a traditional marriage. Neither of us would want it to be. But when I look at Joseph and Dan, I know I can make the sacrifice. In fact, I am quite certain it would be more of a blessing. What would you have me do, Lord?"

For the remainder of the week, Daniel did not

mention the topic of marriage again to Sarah. He had no wish to pressure her. Furthermore, he required time as well to adjust to the idea. He was grateful the whole thing felt like a business proposal; otherwise, he could not have conceived of going through with it. On the final day, the day she had said she would have an answer, he decided to approach Sarah. When they had a moment alone, he sat her down and inquired, "Sarah, have you come to a decision?"

Still a bit stunned that he had even asked, she dropped her eyes to her lap. "Daniel, after praying about this I have a peace about it. I do believe that, for the boys' sake I can do this."

Daniel noticed by Sarah's demeanor she was now uncomfortable in his presence. She had accepted for the boys and the boys alone. He was relieved at that thought, but also uneasy about how she was reacting to him now that they would soon be married. He never intended to lose her friendship. He decided to address the issue. "Sarah, clearly you are uncomfortable around me now. You needn't be. There is absolutely no reason for things to change between us. We are still friends, are we not?"

Sarah understood that what he had said was true. Nothing would have to change between them. "I apologize, Daniel. I guess I am a little dumbfounded by all that has happened. Yes, we are still friends."

Smiling, he took hold of her hand. "We best speak to the boys." He felt that the sooner they had this marriage transaction behind them, the sooner they could get back to the way things had always been between them. What is more, he still needed time to accept that Joanna and the baby were truly gone. With his boys' future on his mind, he had been unable to allow himself to grieve properly.

Sarah suddenly felt a flutter in her stomach. "What if they do not understand why we are doing this and are angry with me?"

Hearing the fear in her tone, Daniel assured her. "Sarah, you shall see; the boys will be happy about this. They love you very much."

While making their way out to the barn, Daniel kept hold of Sarah's trembling hand. Though he had told her that the boys would be happy about their decision, he was not completely certain of that. As they entered the barn, the boys caught sight of them and hastily made their way over. With his sons approaching, Daniel quickly let go of Sarah's hand.

Wondering why Sarah and his father had come to the barn, Joseph inquired, "What is it, Father?"

Daniel noticed that Sarah was fidgeting and thought perhaps he should have kept hold of her. He had intended to tell the boys to come straight in doors when they were through so he might speak with them, but he could not put Sarah through the torture of prolonging the whole affair. "Boys, take a seat over there on the bench. We have something we wish to tell you."

Once he and his brother were seated, with Sarah and their father standing directly in front of them, Dan bravely stated, "We are prepared to hear whatever it is you have to say to us, Father. By the look on your face, we seem to have done something to anger you."

A little apprehensive, Daniel glanced down at his sons and replied, "No, Dan, you are not in any trouble. Sarah and I merely have something we wish to tell you. As you know, I shall be going out on calls, as always. Besides you boys, there is the house and the garden to manage." Not exactly certain how to begin, he babbled for a few more minutes.

Dan spoke up. "Father, you are not making any sense. What exactly are you trying to tell us?"

Daniel decided to speak plainly so there would be no misunderstanding. "Boys, it isn't proper for Sarah to remain here any longer with a house full of men." He had no desire to mention the loss of their mother.

Joseph, with tears in his eyes, blurted out, "No, Father! Sarah must stay here with us! You cannot let her leave. We need her!" Dan also had tears in his eyes.

Daniel hated to see the pain on his sons' faces, but he was delighted they wanted Sarah to stay. Knowing this made what he had to say all the easier. "Boys, Sarah can only stay if she and I were to marry. For it to be proper, there is no other way."

All at once, both boys cried out in unison, "Then marry her!" Having lost their dear mother, neither one wanted to give up Sarah. She was the next best thing.

Delighted at their reaction, Daniel and Sarah

glanced at each other. They had worried for nothing. The boys jumped up then and took hold of Sarah, each asking her to stay and marry their father.

"Boys, Sarah has already consented to be my wife."

Pleased, the young men both hugged Sarah. Sarah hugged them right back. Their response had confirmed for her that she had made the right decision. "Your father and I shall remain as we are—purely friends. We are only marrying that I might stay on here with all of you. I shall never try and take the place of—"

Seeing tears in Sarah's eyes, Dan broke in, "Sarah, we know you loved our mother and that you are only marrying Father because of what those women at the church said about you. This is the only way for you to stay."

Stunned that the boys had heard and, what is more, had understood what the women had implied with their comments, Daniel looked at Sarah. They were both equally surprised the boys had comprehended theirs was going to be solely a marriage of convenience.

Chapter 7

The following week, Sarah and Daniel, after meeting with their pastor, were in front of the magistrate. They had received a special license from the very man who would be presiding over the ceremony; therefore, they could forgo the three weeks of the posting of the banns.

Daniel's sons and father-in-law were the only people in attendance. Even though everyone was delighted that Sarah would be staying on, this was a rather solemn day, in particular for Sarah and Daniel, for their marriage was another reminder that Joanna and Alexander were gone, never to return.

Amidst his sadness, just as Sarah's father and father-in-law had done during her marriage to Alexander, Mr. Hoyt prayed that one day Daniel and Sarah would come to love each other. Although it hadn't been that long since his daughter had passed, he understood that a marriage devoid of love would be a very lonely place, especially once Dan and Joseph were grown. The boys had no such concerns. For them, this day simply meant that Sarah could stay.

When the ceremony had ended, everyone piled onto the wagon for the ride home. As they rode along, Sarah came to the realization that she was now Sarah Thompson.

A little sad to be losing the name of the man she had dearly loved, she turned her head away from the other occupants in the wagon. While attempting to rein in her emotions, she prayed that God would help her to put all thoughts of Alexander behind her so she could forge ahead with her new family.

Daniel also felt sorrow at the knowledge that his marriage today had somehow put a barrier between him and his past—a past that included Joanna. As he glanced at Sarah, he detected a strained expression upon her face and surmised that she was feeling much the same as he.

◊◊◊

Upon the family's arrival at home, the boys hastily climbed down from the wagon and made for the barn, where they found Zechariah—a farm hand that helped on occasion. He had already done most of the chores, leaving the boys only a few things to finish up. Dan and Joseph worked as fast as they could, for they wanted time with Sarah before the day ended. As they were missing their mother terribly, Sarah was a timely and much-loved alternative.

Daniel helped Sarah down from the wagon and then escorted her to the house, with Mr. Hoyt following close behind. However, as they approached the door, Mr. Hoyt decided to join the boys in the barn to allow Daniel and Sarah a few moments alone. "I shall be in shortly. My grandsons may need my assistance."

Glancing over his shoulder, Daniel responded, "Very

well, Joseph. I am certain they'll appreciate the help. They seemed rather anxious to be done."

Sarah gave a weary smile, and then continued toward the house. After making her way to her bedchamber to change into a work dress, she returned to the kitchen to prepare the evening meal.

Daniel had also exchanged his Sunday best for everyday clothes. He then decided to join Sarah in the kitchen to see if he could be of any help. "Sarah, put me to work. Whatever you need, just say the word," he stated, trying to lighten the mood.

Forcing a smile, Sarah handed him a knife and a few potatoes to cut up for the pot of stew she was preparing. They had worked companionably for almost an hour when the boys returned to the house and made their way to the table.

Their father spoke the moment he clasped eyes on them. "You boys know better than to be seated before cleaning yourselves up. Go and wash. The food is almost ready."

Mr. Hoyt came in next. After washing up, he returned to the kitchen, prepared to help set the table. As he looked over at the newly married couple, if their appearance gave away their true feelings, they had worked through whatever somber emotions the day had brought on; but he was certain there would be many more days ahead when one or both would be feeling precisely as they had earlier.

Later that evening, when it was time for Dan and Joseph to turn in, they asked their father if it would be all right if Sarah read to them. She had done this on many occasions, both before and after Joanna's death. Giving his consent, Daniel then turned his focus back to his work. He had been writing notes concerning one of the people he intended to call upon the following day. The visit was to be with a woman who was nearing her time. It had been a rather difficult confinement. Daniel hoped all would go well when the time came to deliver the child. Just the thought of ever delivering another lifeless child caused him to sigh from the grief that was still ever present.

While in the boys' bedchamber, Sarah beamed at the fact that, even at their ages, they still wished for her to read to them. Sitting on the edge of Joseph's bed, she began reading from the Old Testament. The story about David and Goliath had always fascinated the young men, so she continued on from where she had left off the last time she had read to them.

A short time later, Sarah quietly made her way out of the boys' bedchamber. Mr. Hoyt happened to be passing by as she turned around after closing the door. While smiling at the young woman standing before him, he reached out and wrapped his arm around her shoulders. As he walked her to her bedchamber, he noticed that she wouldn't look him in the eye.

"Sarah, you mustn't feel bad about marrying Daniel. If I have not already told you, just as Joanna had, I think this match is a good thing. You are like a daughter to me, Sarah. Knowing that you will be here under Daniel's protection relieves my mind. And I am happy that you shall be here helping out with my grandsons." He knew now was not the time to tell her he hoped she would grow to love Daniel, as she had his grandsons; otherwise—as had been on his mind for much of the day—once the boys were grown, his new daughter-in-law and Daniel would be left to themselves in a loveless marriage.

Daring a quick look in his direction, Sarah softly replied, "Are you certain you truly feel this way?"

Studying her face, he answered, "Yes, my girl. I am quite certain. And you would do well to put the words of those malicious women at church out of your mind. I caught what they said in your hearing. They are exactly the sort to stir up trouble."

With her eyes focused on the elderly gentleman who had correctly guessed her thoughts, she confided, "It is true; I hoped I hadn't hurt you in marrying your daughter's husband. And you are right; I was a little bothered by what those women said. I still am, in fact. What will they say now that I have gone and married Daniel?"

Pulling her close, he replied, "Forget about those busy bodies. What they think should be of no consequence. And as for my feelings, Sarah, I loved my daughter exceedingly, but she is no longer here. You and Daniel must go on for the boys' sakes, as well as your own. I am of the opinion that someone of my years sees things a little more clearly. We are all here but a short while. One by one we make our way to our final destination. My daughter made the decision to receive Christ's sacrifice for her a long time ago. I know where she is. What is more, it shan't be long before I join her there. So, as for how I feel about your marriage, allow me to state it plainly so there shall be no confusion from this time forward; I am delighted that you and Daniel have married. As I said before, you have been much the same as a daughter to me, almost from the first moment we met. And with Joanna gone, my life would be quite empty without you."

Reaching her bedchamber, Sarah hugged Mr. Hoyt's neck. "It means a lot to me to hear you say that."

After kissing her forehead, Mr. Hoyt made his way to his own room. It had been a long day. His body was in need of rest. Before he went to sleep, he thanked the Lord that things had gone as his daughter had wanted. His grandsons would have a woman in their life to love them, and Daniel would not be going it alone. Even if he and Sarah remained only close friends throughout their lives, they would at least be companions for each other.

Chapter 8

The following day, Mr. Hoyt convinced Daniel to take Sarah along on a visit with an expectant mother. His daughter had often gone with the physician on just such visits. Sensing that Sarah was a little hesitant to go, he wondered at the reason. Perhaps it was her intention to avoid being alone with Daniel, even when it came to accompanying him on calls.

As Daniel had always appreciated having a woman along on his calls with expectant mothers, he was delighted at the idea of having Sarah join him. "Sarah, I really could use your assistance with Muriel Shaw. Being as this case has been challenging, she tends to be anxious when I am there. With you present, it might set her mind at ease."

Sarah studied Daniel's face for any sign that he was asking merely out of obligation, now that his father-in-law had made the suggestion. His countenance revealing a genuine interest, she reluctantly agreed. A short time later, they were on their way. Sarah positioned herself as far to the opposite side of the bench from Daniel as possible. The physician had noticed the space between them and could not hold back a grin. Thankfully, Sarah was purposefully studying the countryside, never chancing a look in his direction; otherwise, she may have detected the grin.

After a few minutes, feeling that this was too ridiculous, Daniel spoke up. "Sarah, you seem a little uncomfortable with the idea of being alone with me."

With heat rising in her cheeks, looking straight ahead, she attempted a casual response. "Just a bit, yes." Knowing he had noticed her discomfort, she decided to explain herself. "It is...well...this is something Joanna used to do with you. I feel akin to a usurper."

While smiling at her, he remarked, "Sarah, there are likely to be many things we do together that Joanna and I experienced. You shall have to get over feeling this way. Nothing has changed. We are friends who happen to be married."

"You are right, Daniel. I am being foolish. Pray forgive me."

"There is nothing to forgive. I completely understand how you feel. To be honest, I have had similar feelings. However, I have decided not to allow such sentiments to ruin things we might do together, as friends." He smiled at her and then turned his attention back to the horses.

The rest of the ride was made with the two conversing in a relaxed manner. By the time they arrived at Muriel Shaw's house, Sarah was feeling completely at ease and ready to do whatever was needed.

Once Daniel had helped her down from the wagon, they made their way to the door.

Muriel's husband, Michael, opened the door to the

sound of someone knocking. As he had hoped, it was the physician. "Do come in. My wife has been having regular pains for nearly an hour. I was about to come and fetch you. But you are here now. I am glad for it, for she did not want to be left alone."

Daniel made his way in to see Muriel, with Sarah close behind. As soon as he clasped eyes on her, his mind went back to Joanna and his own child. Feeling ill, he made his way to a chair by the door.

Sarah had witnessed Daniel's face drain of all color the moment he saw Muriel. Though not experienced in these matters, she decided to go on as though nothing had happened. She quickly approached the bed and took Muriel by the hand. "How are you doing? It seems your pains have indeed begun. What a blessing it shall be when at last you see your child's face."

Sarah's demeanor served to put Muriel at ease. As she studied the young woman, Muriel thought she remembered seeing her at church not long ago, accompanied by Daniel Thompson and his family. "Sarah, is it not?"

Smiling nervously, she responded, "Indeed it is." Glancing over her shoulder to see if Daniel had regained his composure, she was delighted to see that he was coming toward her, his cheeks full of color once more.

As Daniel approached the bed, he chided himself for making such a display. The vision of the woman lying in bed, about to give birth, was all too reminiscent of his wife and baby. Since it was only nearing two months since that tragic day, the sorrowful images were still fairly vivid. As he glanced down at Sarah, he whispered, "I am grateful to you."

While moving out of the way, his wife offered the expectant mother a reassuring look. The physician went right to work assessing the woman. He directed Sarah to fetch a cloth and then pointed to the washbowl next to the bed. Sarah understood that he wanted her to mop the woman's brow.

All the while, Mr. Shaw waited near the door, afraid to come too close. This was his first child. He had no idea what to do or expect. Thankfully, his mind had been so preoccupied he had not observed the physician taking a seat for a few minutes.

If Daniel had thought the scene when he had first arrived was strangely similar to his last moments with Joanna, as the hours passed the comparisons between the two births had grown even more alike. Something was clearly wrong. A few hours later, though he and Sarah had given it their all, the child had died. Unlike Joanna, at least this time the mother had survived.

It was Sarah's turn to feel faint. Looking at the lifeless child reminded her of her own baby; the one she had lost. There were never two people with more understanding for the couple's anguish than she and Daniel.

A few hours later, Daniel and Sarah were on their

way home. It had been a long day and night. The sun was beginning to rise. Once they arrived, Sarah made her way to the backyard and somberly strolled down to the stream. As she stood there gazing at the rippling water, her heart hurt for Muriel and her husband. With tears streaming down her face, she prayed for the grieving couple. A few moments later, Daniel found her. As distracted as she was, she had not heard him approaching. When he said her name, she started at the sound of his voice.

Seeing Sarah's alarmed reaction, he said softly, "I didn't mean to frighten you. I thought you might be here, by the water." He had put the horses in the barn and then gone into the house. When he could not locate Sarah, he knew right where to look.

She peered back at him, and then fixed her eyes on the rippling water once again. "This must have been difficult for you as well."

Moving in close, he wrapped his arms around her from behind. "Indeed. I am much obliged to you for taking over when we first arrived at Muriel's home. Hers was the first delivery I have had since—"

Feeling Daniel's arms holding her tight comforted Sarah. Ordinarily, she would have been uneasy at the thought of having him so near. But after all that had happened, she was not her usual self. Still facing forward, she grasped the arms that were holding her. "Yes. I wish you hadn't had to go through this, so soon anyway." The pair stood where they were for a few more minutes. When

Sarah said she was ready to go in, they turned in the direction of the house.

Mr. Hoyt had heard the sound of the wagon approaching. Not having seen Daniel when he briefly entered the house, Joseph wondered what was keeping the couple. With concern, he rose from his chair and peered out the window. Unable to see either of them in the front yard, he went to the kitchen to look out toward the yard behind the house. Spotting Daniel and Sarah coming from the direction of the stream, he surmised that something must have happened with the mother or her child. He was aware that when Sarah was bothered by something she had often sought solace down by the water. Taking a seat at the table, Joseph waited for them to come in.

Before long, the pair found Mr. Hoyt sitting in the kitchen. With the boys still in their beds, the couple disclosed to Mr. Hoyt all that had happened. Since he was well aware of the losses Daniel and Sarah had each suffered, he understood how terribly the day must have affected them.

Chapter 9

Late summer, the year 1735, Boston, Massachusetts Bay Colony

Things had been going on unaltered for a few months. One morning as Mr. Hoyt observed Sarah and Daniel, he thought about their friendship and how it had grown a little wooden, given their situation. He was concerned that they were establishing a pattern that would be difficult to break. After thinking on it for a time, he decided that if he took his grandsons with him to Amesbury for the winter, leaving his son-in-law and Sarah alone, it might alter the couple's daily routine. In his view, Daniel would be forced to see Sarah as more than merely a surrogate mother for his boys, and Sarah would be free of the distraction of caring for everyone else.

When he felt the time was right, Mr. Hoyt suggested to Daniel that his grandsons come along with him to Amesbury for the winter. By his son-in-law's reaction, Mr. Hoyt sensed that the younger man needed a little convincing; therefore, the next time he was alone with his grandsons, he encouraged them to do a good measure of pleading with their father. They could be very persuasive when it was something they really wanted to do.

Reluctantly, Daniel agreed to the plan. Sarah had been listening to the entire exchange, hoping the boys' father would frown upon the idea. But to her chagrin he had given his consent. Feeling panicked at the notion of being alone with Daniel, she suggested that she go along as well.

Mr. Hoyt had privately cautioned his grandsons not to ask Sarah to go with them, stating that he did not want to leave their father alone. Although they had not fully comprehended their grandfather's true intentions, they had agreed not to ask Sarah to join them. They would, of course, miss their father and Sarah, but spending the winter in Amesbury with their grandfather sounded like a great adventure to them.

In hearing Sarah's offer to go with his sons and father-in-law, Daniel suspected that Sarah was not happy with this arrangement. He couldn't blame her; nonetheless, he kept silent.

Mr. Hoyt answered, "Sarah, Daniel may need your assistance with his calls—especially since two of the ladies are near their time. Besides, the boys and I can manage fine on our own."

Not wanting to press the matter with the elderly gentleman, Sarah gave up trying to convince him. While fidgeting with her sleeve, as she often did, she inquired, "When will you go?"

With compassion for the young woman, he took hold of her hand. "Sarah, I hope to be on our way in a few days. Not to worry, we shall return once spring arrives."

Offering a halfhearted smile, Sarah slipped her hand out of his, and turned in the direction of her bedchamber. She needed to be by herself to adjust to the idea. Things were going to feel very awkward once she and Daniel were left by themselves.

For the remainder of the week, Daniel had second thoughts about allowing his sons to be away until spring. Not only would he miss them, but precisely as Sarah had been feeling, he believed that it would be strange to be alone for so many months with Sarah. After all, the chief reason they had married was so that she might assist him with the boys.

The week passed without Daniel disclosing that he had been having second thoughts. In the end, he allowed the boys to go with their grandfather. He knew his father-in-law was still hurting over the loss of his daughter, as was he, but he had his work to occupy him. Mr. Hoyt would be returning to an empty house with little to distract him unless Dan and Joseph were to go along.

◊◊◊

Daniel and Sarah stood waving to the boys and Mr. Hoyt as they left. Sarah then hastened toward the house. Making her way to the kitchen, she began preparing food for later in the day. But as she worked, she thought about being alone at the table with Daniel when it came time to eat. With her mind racing for a reason to take her food to her room, she continued the meal preparations.

Daniel had been busying himself in his study. Just now he wished someone would have need of his services. It was going to be uncomfortable conversing with only Sarah for the remainder of the day.

When it was time for him to come to the table, Sarah peeked in to tell him the food was ready. After putting aside his work, he meandered toward the kitchen.

As he entered, Sarah made an excuse to go to her bedchamber, advising him to start without her. When she didn't return, he ate his meal alone. While he sat there, it occurred to him that Sarah had obviously felt as uneasy as he had about eating together without the others. He decided it would be a long autumn and winter if they didn't move beyond feeling tense about being the only two in the house. When he finished his meal, he went to her bedchamber and knocked on the door.

Startled, Sarah called out, "Just a moment." Taking a deep breath, she made her way to the door. Opening it scarcely enough to peek out, she inquired, "Yes, what is it?"

"Would you come to the parlor? I have something to discuss with you."

Wondering what it was that he wanted to speak to her about, she nervously replied, "Certainly. I shall be there directly."

Daniel then went to the parlor to wait for Sarah. Within a few minutes, looking quite flushed, she entered the room.

"Sarah, please be seated," he said, directing her to a

chair to the right of him. Once she was settled, he began. "It seems we both are feeling ill at ease at being alone with each other."

She lowered her eyes as she listened.

"We need to come to some sort of an understanding. As for me, I don't expect that anything should change because it is only the two of us now. We ought to still eat together as well as keep to our usual schedules for everything else."

Feeling a little relieved by what Daniel had said about things remaining the same, Sarah responded, "Very well, Daniel. You are right." To be certain she had heard him correctly, with a little grin she questioned, "You felt uncomfortable, too, then?"

Amused by her reaction to what he had said, he replied, "What is wrong with us? We are acting like perfect strangers. I realize it is not going to be easy, but we must behave in a relaxed manner with each other, or it shall be a rather miserable few months. Before marrying, we were at ease in each other's company. Were we not?"

Still smiling, Sarah responded in the affirmative. For the remainder of the evening, Sarah and Daniel talked companionably, just as they had before their marriage.

The next morning Daniel waited for Sarah in the kitchen. Not long after he had taken a seat, she came in, still fiddling with her hair. "I trust you slept well," he said as he observed her frustration over her matted hair. Hearing a soft reply indicating that she had, he asked, "May

I be of assistance? I am well practiced at untangling hair. Joanna's looked much the same as yours on many a morning."

Though she wanted to say yes, she shook her head no. "I can manage it on my own, but I thank you all the same."

By now, Daniel knew Sarah would never give her consent for things of such a personal nature; for that reason, carrying his chair, he made his way over to her. After placing the chair behind the small woman, he took the comb from her hand, sat himself down, and began gently working the tangles out. Seeing her flushed face, he decided to distract her with conversation. "Would you like to accompany me today? I believe I mentioned a young man who fell from a tree. The injuries he incurred required a few stitches."

Pleasingly diverted from the hair combing, Sarah responded, "Yes, I do recollect you mentioning something about it. And if you think my coming along may be of any benefit, I would be happy to go with you."

Not quite finished with combing out the tangles and seeing the delighted look upon Sarah's face about accompanying him, he continued. "The young man was a little hesitant to allow me near him on my recent visit. The whole process took longer than necessary. Given your way with children, I believe you may be able to coax him into letting me have a look at his wound to see that it is healing properly."

With the hair now hanging perfectly straight, Daniel ran his hand down the locks. "I believe you are now liberated from every tangle."

Feeling Daniel's hand stroking her hair, she quickly pulled away and thanked him for his trouble. She then asked, "When do you plan to leave?"

"Whenever you wish," he answered as he stood and then carried the chair back to the table. "I have already eaten, but you take your time. When you are ready, come to my study."

A short time later, Sarah and Daniel were on their way. Though there had been a few awkward moments while Daniel combed her hair, things between them still seemed greatly improved. As they rode along on the wagon, they discussed many things—including the fact that they both, at times, continued to experience intense grief over the loss of Joanna, the baby, and for Sarah, Alexander had also never been far from her thoughts.

By the time they arrived at the boy's home, they had decided to be more open with each other in the future with regard to their grief, reasoning that there shouldn't be any problem with two friends talking about such things.

Chapter 10

O ver the next few weeks, Sarah accompanied Daniel on many of his visits. Each time, Daniel had admired the kind and proficient manner in which his new wife had conducted herself on the calls. In the instances where the person he was looking after was ill at ease, she had quickly calmed them. Additionally, when an extra set of hands was needed, she had risen to the occasion no matter how unpleasant the task. With her love and care of others, she reminded him more and more of his beloved Joanna.

The day came for one of the physician's expectant mothers to deliver. As soon as it was made known the woman was with child, the midwife caring for her had asked for the physician's help. The mother had experienced complications with the births of her first three children. Daniel was always prepared to help out in these instances, and even though the midwife would be present, he still brought Sarah along. If nothing else, he knew she would at least look after the other three children, for in his experience, fathers were often too distracted to do the job properly.

The birth had taken an inordinate amount of time. When the Thompsons later set off for home, they were both utterly exhausted.

As they rode along, Daniel noticed Sarah's head bob a few times. Not wanting her to fall from the wagon, he pulled her over close to him so that she could rest against him. As tired as she was, she did not protest. By the time they arrived at home, Sarah was sound asleep.

Bringing the wagon to a halt at the front door, Daniel then lifted Sarah and made for the house. He observed that, in moving her, she had not even stirred. Finding success at opening the door without dropping his precious load, he then carried her to her bedchamber. Once he had laid her down, he grabbed the candle next to her bed and went in the direction of the parlor. There were still a few embers in the fireplace with which to light the candle. As soon as he had returned to Sarah's room, moving toward the table, he placed the candle in its usual spot.

Glancing down, though Sarah stirred a little, Daniel noticed her eyes were still closed in sleep. Reaching to the foot of the bed, he pulled off her shoes and then covered her with a quilt. As he stooped to move her hair away from her face, he again noted how youthful she looked. "It's not a wonder that you are completely done in with all that you accomplished today—what with taking care of the children, preparing food and such. On days like today, I am truly glad we married." Leaning in, he placed a kiss upon her brow and then turned to leave, extinguishing the candle on his way out.

As he went out to stable the horses, he thought

about what a help Sarah had been with the children that day. Not for the first time did he consider what a wonderful mother Sarah would have made had she been able to have a child of her own—one that had lived, that is. His mind lingered for a moment on her baby boy; the one he delivered. The child had lived but a few minutes. Daniel had so many memories tied to that time with Sarah and her first husband, Alexander. The memories brought Joanna to mind. He had always thought that Sarah seemed so different from Joanna, but the more time he spent with her, the more he realized they were similar in many ways.

When Daniel had finished in the barn, he went back to the house. After washing up, he changed his clothes and climbed into bed. Before falling asleep, he thanked the Lord that all had gone well that day.

◊◊◊

Early the next morning, with autumn well under way, Daniel decided to start the preparations for securing his home for winter. Amongst other things, to help keep out the cold he had a habit of piling hay around the base of the house. As he worked in the yard, he observed bear tracks. Though it was not all that unusual, he wanted to be sure to inform Sarah not to be out of doors until he was certain the animal had moved on.

Later that afternoon, while the couple was sitting at the table having tea, Daniel told Sarah there had been a bear near the place. He then warned that, until he was certain the animal was long gone, she should remain in the house unless he was with her. Not all that concerned, she went back to drinking her tea.

Sarah was grateful that Daniel was never one to press his will on her; as a result, she reasoned that if she needed to be out of doors, she would be sure to keep an eye out for the bear, but would go out just the same. She then thought about how Alexander, though she had dearly loved him, had been a little severe at times; however, she had to admit that he had been right on more than one occasion, and she would have done well to have listened. Her mind then went to the terrible night she was attacked after ignoring her husband's wishes. She shivered at the images that came to mind.

While Sarah was absorbed in thought, Daniel quietly observed her, noticing that she went from calm to an almost panic stricken look upon her face. Believing she was frightened at the idea of a bear lingering near their home, he stated, "Sarah, as long as you remain indoors, you shall be safe. The bear cannot get to you in here."

Sarah jolted at the sound of Daniel's voice. Coming to herself, she realized her face must have shown fear at the remembrance of the attack. "Oh, of course, Daniel. I am certain you are right." She left it at that. Though she was not overly afraid of the bear, she had no desire to explain what she had been thinking about.

As they ate, they discussed the rapidly approaching winter. Sarah remembered from when she had previously stayed with the Thompsons—long before Joanna's death—

that it had been challenging, on occasion, for Daniel to get out and call on the sick. Joanna had shared with her that she had often worried about him when he was away, particularly during a storm.

Breaking in on her thoughts, Daniel decided to apprise her of his plans for the following day. "Sarah, as I don't have any calls to make tomorrow, I will be going to town. Would you like to come along with me?"

"No, Daniel. I have plenty to do here. We have been gone so often of late, there are a few things that require my attention. I thank you for asking, though."

As Sarah had expected, Daniel left early the next morning. He would be gone a few hours. When she had finished tidying up in doors, she made her way out to the backyard to clear out the remnants of the garden.

As she worked, she piled everything alongside the garden to haul away when she had finished. After a couple of hours, she decided to begin dragging away arm loads from the pile. On her third trip into the woods to dispose of the garden remnants, as exhausted as she felt, she was glad she was nearly done.

The moment she was about to drop her load, she heard a loud cracking sound like that of a large branch breaking. While quickly glancing over her shoulder, she remembered Daniel's words from the day before. When she spotted the source of the noise moving in her direction, she wished she had heeded her husband's warning and remained in the house.

With hair standing up on the back of her neck at the sight of an enormous bear moving toward her, dropping her load, she turned and began to run. In her haste, however, she tripped over the pile, landing hard on her wrist and shoulder. Thinking she was about to be the creature's lunch, she cried, "Why don't I ever listen?" As she attempted to rise to continue her getaway, she heard a loud blast. With her heart racing, she peeked behind her and spotted the bear sprawled out on the ground and a large man hastening toward her.

As alarmed as she had been of the bear, she was almost as frightened of the stranger who was rapidly approaching. Before she could rise, she felt the man's hands scooping her up off the ground.

With an intense gaze, the man inquired, "Are you injured, ma'am?"

Her heart still pounding, she shook her head no, but she wasn't exactly certain what she had said was true. Presently, her wrist and shoulder throbbed. There was also a stabbing pain in her left ankle.

"That bear almost had you for supper. What were you doing out here all alone?"

As she stared at him, she remembered scolding herself only moments before for paying no heed to her husband's warning about the bear.

All at once, memories of Matthew Raymond and that terrible night came to mind. She began violently shaking in the arms of the stranger. To her knowledge, she had never before set eyes on the man. She wondered what he intended to do with her. No one even knew where she was.

Seeing the fear in the young woman's eyes, and realizing it wasn't only the bear that frightened her, the man introduced himself. "I am Simon Findley, an acquaintance of your husband's; that is, if your husband is Daniel Thompson."

Simon observed a slight tilt of the head. Though she did not give her name, he was pretty certain he had heard it was Sarah.

"Let's get you home. Daniel must be worried about you. More to the point, what was he thinking, letting you come out here alone?"

At the thought that the man was a friend of Daniel's, and that he meant to take her home, relief started to pervade her entire being. She had escaped the bear with the help of this stranger, and she was now quite certain he intended her no harm.

"Well, actually...Daniel has no idea of my whereabouts." She remained uncertain about whether to disclose that Daniel had gone to town, but as she looked into the man's eyes, once again she understood he meant her no harm. "Truthfully, he warned me there was a bear and that I should not come out of doors, at least until he was sure it had moved on."

Simon was glad she no longer appeared frightened of him. As he listened to Sarah he admired her pluck. *She obviously was not concerned about the bear until she came face to face with it. And she clearly does as she pleases. I wonder what Daniel thinks of this independent, albeit tiny woman.*

As he walked with Sarah in his arms, he inquired as to how she managed to be out of doors without her husband having noticed. He presumed her response would be that Daniel was not at home.

Sarah was about to answer when they moved out from the trees to her backyard. Spotting Daniel, his countenance one of alarm, hastily moving in their direction, she felt a flutter in her chest.

As Daniel approached, he shouted, "Simon! Sarah! What has happened? I heard the gun blast as I was arriving."

Sarah felt terrible that she hadn't listened to Daniel and had caused such a fuss. Unable to form any words of her own for fear of the wrathful look upon her husband's face, Sarah then heard Simon clear his throat. Though she was glad he was about to respond for her, she wished he would put her down. She was sure she could stand on her own two feet, and being held like an injured child was only making things worse. She wanted Daniel to see for himself that she was all right.

"Well, my friend, this little wife of yours found herself in a great deal of trouble. I am glad I happened to be out hunting today, or she may have been a meal for a rather large bear."

Daniel's eyes flashed in his wife's direction. "Sarah Anne, what were you doing out here? Are you injured?" As he looked her over, he reached out for Simon to place her in his arms.

"I do apologize, Daniel. I was merely clearing away the dried remnants from the garden. I believe I can walk on my own. You may put me down."

Still holding her, he responded angrily, "I warned you there was a bear in the vicinity! What were you thinking, being out here like that?"

Simon was beginning to feel uncomfortable at being present for a quarrel between Daniel and his new wife, so he lightheartedly said, "It was good to meet you, Sarah. I believe I shall be off now. I have a bear to skin."

Daniel stopped questioning Sarah long enough to thank Simon for saving his wife's life; after which the man tilted his chin in Sarah's direction and then turned to go.

Before he had taken two steps, Sarah blurted out, "I am much obliged to you, sir."

Turning back, he replied, "Do not give it another thought."

Before she could say more, the man turned again and was soon gone from sight. Alone with Daniel now, she peeked up at him. "Pray forgive me, Daniel. I was not thinking. I should not have come out of doors."

Daniel's anger lessened a little as he listened to Sarah's apology. He remained quiet while moving toward the house.

"Did you get what you needed in town? Perhaps I should have gone with you after all. I believe I can walk now. There is no need for you to carry me." She babbled on nervously, for she was not used to Daniel speaking to her in such an angry manner. Even though, at times, she believed he thought of her much as a child, he had never treated her with anything less than the respect owed an adult. Conversely, she had always known that Alexander had thought of her as a grown woman; nevertheless, he had often spoken to her as if she were a child.

When Daniel attempted to place his wife on her feet as she had requested, she buckled. "What is it? Your ankle?" After hurriedly taking hold of her wrist to steady her, he heard her cry out in pain. Lifting her again, he stated he would carry her the rest of the way, for it was clear she had injured herself.

Unable to walk on her own, his wife made no argument. As they moved toward the house, they fell silent. Once they had entered the kitchen, Daniel placed Sarah on a chair at the table. While observing her, he could see dirt smeared on her face, hands, and clothes. Still silent, he went over to the basin of water, which sat upon the cupboard. Grabbing a cloth, he carried the basin over to the table and proceeded to wash Sarah's face and hands.

"You are in need of a fresh frock. The one you are wearing is completely soiled."

While observing Daniel, Sarah sensed that his anger, at this point, had completely dwindled. Still feeling awful for not having listened, she apologized once more, to which her husband replied that the matter was closed.

Once Daniel had cleaned her up, all but her clothes, he conveyed her to the room in which he performed his examinations. After having a look at her wrist, he was certain she had cracked a bone, so he not only wrapped it, but splinted it as well. He then took a look at her ankle before showing her one of the crutches he had fashioned for just such an occasion. He had in fact made several different sizes to suit from the very small to the largest of persons.

Sarah listened as her physician husband explained that her ankle was just slightly injured and that she could put some of her weight on it, but that the crutch should help her to step lightly. Fortunately for her, she had injured only one of her wrists. She was therefore able to make use of one crutch. Daniel then clarified that in order for her wrist to heal, she needed to keep from using her hand.

To be sure she understood, he summed up the situation for her. "Sarah, your ankle should be fine in a few days. But as for your wrist, that shall take some time."

Daniel helped Sarah to her bedchamber so she could change into a clean frock. After laying one out for her on the bed, he stated that she need only call out if he was needed. He was fairly certain she could manage getting into it on her own, but may require his help with fastening it. Once she had changed, she slowly made her way to the parlor, where she found that Daniel had already placed a trencher of food for her on the table next to the settee.

Before taking a seat, reluctantly, Sarah asked her husband to fasten her frock. As he approached, she turned around. Once he had completed the task she thanked him and made her way over to the settee.

At the thought that she would now be unable to carry much of anything, Sarah became frustrated. "Daniel, I am sorry. It seems I have caused you additional work, as I shall be practically useless until my injuries have healed."

"Nonsense," he replied, smiling. "Your company is enough. If not for you, with the boys away I would be rattling around in this house all alone. Furthermore, you have been diligently taking care of all of us. It is time someone did for you for a change."

Sarah knew Daniel was simply being kind, but she said nothing more on the subject of having caused extra work for him. Not long after she had eaten a little of her meal, her eyelids grew heavy. She decided to make her way to her bedchamber.

Daniel followed after Sarah to see that she made it safely. When he had finished helping his wife ready herself for bed, he returned to the kitchen to tidy up; after which he took himself off to bed. It was quite some time before he could sleep, for thoughts of what might have happened to Sarah if Simon had not come along filled his mind.

Chapter 11

The following morning, Daniel knocked on Sarah's door to see if she needed his assistance. He was fairly certain she would. Hearing her respond in the affirmative, he opened the door.

As Sarah waited for Daniel from where she was sitting on the edge of her bed, she felt uneasy. She wished she did not require his help, but of course she did with her hand and ankle injured.

While making his way into the room, Daniel observed that Sarah appeared apprehensive; as a result, with the manner in which he cared for his patients, he calmly moved forward and laced up and fastened everything that needed it from her head on down to her feet. When Sarah was dressed and ready to begin the day, Daniel helped her to the kitchen where he set to work preparing something for them to eat.

As they ate, Daniel discussed Sarah's injuries and what kind of assistance she would require while on the mend. They decided to ask their neighbor, Mrs. Findley, if she would mind coming over each morning to help. The former Mrs. Thompson had employed her on occasion to assist with the cooking and cleaning.

While they were discussing the neighbor, Sarah

asked if Mrs. Findley and Simon were related since they had the same family name. Daniel responded in the affirmative. "I wish I had known. I acted so foolishly toward Mr. Findley, not knowing he was related to our neighbor."

"I am certain he understood," Daniel offered reassuringly. Then he stated that he would ride over to speak with Mrs. Findley before setting off for the day.

Sarah was grateful that a woman would be the one helping her dress, at least part of the time. When they had finished eating, Sarah attempted to help clear the table but was finding it difficult. Daniel turned around and found her leaning over the table to grasp a dish while trying to balance herself on one foot.

"Sarah, even if you could manage to load up one armful, you wouldn't be able to walk over here to me. Please, just take a seat. I can manage on my own."

Sighing, Sarah dropped back down into her chair. "If only I had listened to you none of this would have happened. Having to take care of me on top of everything else is too much."

Daniel smiled at her frustration. He knew she was right—if she had just heeded his warning, she would not have been injured. Then his smile faded when he thought once more about what had happened. *Things could have been much worse if the bear had gotten ahold of her.* The image that thought brought to mind caused Daniel to shudder.

Before long, he had straightened up the kitchen. He then helped Sarah to the parlor. After she had taken a seat, he lifted her legs up onto the cushioned settee.

"Sarah, it would be good if you kept your ankle elevated as much as possible."

Looking up, she inquired, "How long shall you be gone?"

"As I have only two to see today, I shan't be too long; nonetheless, I dislike leaving you here like this, unable to do for yourself. When I call on Mrs. Findley about helping out for a time, I shall ask if she might come and sit with you until I return."

"I hate to cause such a fuss. I'm certain I can manage on my own."

"I have explained your injuries. You must know you cannot get on by yourself for the foreseeable future. If nothing else, for my peace of mind, allow me to at least inquire of Mrs. Findley whether she is available to come."

"Very well. If it will make you feel more at ease, do ask."

Once that was settled, Daniel turned to go. Mrs. Findley arrived a short time later, explaining that with her present schedule she could afford to come by each morning for an hour or so; however, today she could stay longer. She sensed that Sarah felt foolish for requiring assistance.

"Oh, I am sure that will be fine, Mrs. Findley."

"Let us see what can be accomplished whilst I am

here, shall we?" For the remainder of the morning, the kind neighbor did what she could for Sarah as well as to ease the burden on Mr. Thompson.

By afternoon, Sarah found herself alone. Mrs. Findley had left food and something to drink next to where she was sitting, hoping that would be all she would need until Daniel returned. As Sarah reclined, reading a book, her eyelids grew heavy. When she awoke, she discovered Daniel, sitting across the room, half asleep.

When Daniel noticed Sarah had opened her eyes, he spoke to her. "I returned as soon as I could." Studying her, he noticed she still appeared rather sleepy.

"There really wasn't any need to rush." Glancing toward the window, Sarah observed with surprise, "It looks dark out. I must have slept a few hours."

"You must have needed the sleep. May I do anything for you before I see what there is for us to eat?"

"I feel just awful about all of this, Daniel. You have worked hard all day, tending to patients, only to come home to more work."

"Sarah, it cannot be helped. And besides, I think Mrs. Findley prepared something for us. If not, it really is no bother." With that, he gathered up Sarah's empty dishes and made his way to the kitchen. He returned a short time later, holding two trenchers rounded with food, one of which he placed on the little table next to his wife. Once he had taken a seat, he thanked the Lord for His many blessings.

After they had eaten and conversed for an hour or so, Daniel neatened up the kitchen before helping Sarah to her bedchamber. He then took himself off to bed, relieved the day had gone well for his wife.

◊◊◊

The following morning, Daniel was up just after sunup—Sarah awakening an hour or so later. After helping her ready herself for the day, he made certain she had everything she needed and then, with haste, set off for his morning calls. He hoped the day's visits would be brief since Mrs. Findley would be unable to look after Sarah on this particular morning.

Late in the afternoon, Joanna's brother, George Hoyt, arrived unexpectedly. Sarah was surprised and a bit frightened by the strange, albeit fine-looking man with large blue eyes that greeted her while she was reclining in the parlor. She had assumed it was Daniel arriving.

From the parlor doorway, George detected that his brother-in-law's new wife was injured, for she had her foot propped up and one hand bandaged. He also noticed she was quite striking. But neither her beauty nor her injuries moved his heart toward the woman who had maneuvered her way into his sister's family. Truth be told, that she was even more beautiful than his sister served to intensify his ire. As he sauntered in, he glared at her.

Frightened, Sarah watched closely as the stranger made his way into the room. Briefly making eye contact, she detected he didn't appear any too happy.

Enjoying the fear that he saw on the young woman's face, he took his time in revealing his connection to the Thompson family. Besides his annoyance at the very presence of this woman in his sister's house, he was also vexed with Daniel for not sending word of his marriage and for taking another wife so soon after his sister's passing. George's father had sent a missive to his home explaining what had happened to Joanna, but he had heard nothing since. It was not until a friend from Boston happened by his home in Salem less than a fortnight ago that he first learned of Sarah.

Once the man disclosed who he was, though still quite uneasy about being alone with a stranger, Sarah forced herself to smile and invited him to take a seat. As they sat there, staring at one another, she struggled for something to say. Not only did her heart hurt for him over the loss of his sister, she also felt awkward about filling the role of Mrs. Thompson.

"Mr. Hoyt, Daniel will be delighted you have come." At that point, she wondered if Daniel knew and hadn't said anything to her about his brother-in-law coming for a visit.

As George listened to Sarah, he grew even angrier. *Who does she think she is, telling me how my sister's husband is going to feel about my having arrived?* Not wanting to respond to her comment, he changed the subject. "I had hoped to find my nephews at home. It has been quite some time since I've seen them."

Grateful for any sort of conversation to fill the time

until Daniel returned, Sarah responded, "Oh, yes...well...they went with their grandfather to Amesbury for the winter."

After hearing this, George's fury could no longer be contained. "How convenient. I cannot imagine Daniel agreeing to send his sons off. This was all your doing, ridding yourself of the boys, was it not?"

While carefully observing the tiny woman for a reaction to what he had said, he thought about his father and the role he had played in allowing the newlyweds alone time. His relationship with his father had been difficult for as long as he could remember; however, he had always attributed the strain to the fact that he was not the man's natural son. *Well, it looks as though his connection to his real daughter holds no meaning for him either.*

Stunned at the directness of the man, Sarah began to tremble. She dared not look at him and wondered how she was going to go on conversing with him, for he had an obvious disdain for her. She could not blame him. She had often felt the same way about taking Joanna's place in the Thompson home. But what was she to do now? Daniel might not return for hours.

As silence fell over the room for the next half hour, Sarah kept her gaze directed away from Joanna's brother. The longer he sat there, glaring at her, the more she shook. Finally, she heard a wagon approaching, and prayed that it was Daniel.

Chapter 12

As Daniel entered the room in which Sarah and his brother-in-law were presently sitting, he was astonished to see George. He had wondered who owned the wagon out front, never expecting it to be his brother-in-law.

As George rose to his feet and greeted Daniel, Sarah wondered what rude thing he might say to her husband about the fact that they had married. But what she heard left her dumbfounded. The man was as nice as ever a man could be, even feigning happiness at having made her acquaintance.

Daniel had been a little apprehensive at the thought of George finding out about Sarah; therefore, he delayed in sending word of their marriage. At present, he was surprised by his brother-in-law's warm tone and thought perhaps he had worried needlessly.

"Well, then. I am delighted the two of you have met."

George looked over his shoulder at the young woman. "Yes, we have had a nice little visit. Would you not agree, Sarah?"

Sarah's mouth hung open at the exchange between the man and her husband. She could scarcely believe this was the same person that had spoken so harshly to her before Daniel arrived. *I hope he is not planning to stay, for I certainly cannot tell Daniel about what was said. The man is his brother-in-law, Joanna's brother. I mustn't come between them.* With all of this on her mind, she had not heard George's question.

As Daniel studied Sarah, while awaiting her response to George, he noticed she appeared rather pale and hoped his brother-in-law had not behaved inappropriately with her, as was his tendency with the ladies. This thought caused him to question how long George intended to stay. If it was to be an extended visit, he would quickly move his wife's belongings into his room. He was concerned that his brother-in-law might see it as an opportunity to bother Sarah if he were to learn that her bedchamber was separate from his.

Hoping to learn what his brother-in-law planned to do, he inquired, "George, how long shall you be with us?"

Since he wished to be as disruptive as possible to the newlyweds, he replied, "If it is all the same to you, I should like to stay on for a few days, or perhaps even a week or two."

Daniel's heart sank at the news. He wondered what to do about going out on calls, leaving Sarah alone with a man who was much too fond of women, all women. He and Joanna had never even wanted to leave their boys, George's own nephews, alone with him for fear of them learning his ways. He chanced a look at Sarah to see her reaction to the news. If he had to guess what she was feeling at that moment, he would have to say it was most likely alarm, for her eyes had grown large and she appeared even paler than she had before. *What has her so alarmed? Has he already made advances toward her?*

Having no desire to be denied a lengthy visit, before Daniel could answer, George stated that he needed to retrieve his satchel from his wagon.

Coming to himself, Daniel nodded in his-brother-in-law's direction. The moment George was gone, the concerned husband hastily said, "Sarah, I shall explain later. Right now, I am going to go and quickly gather some of your things and bring them to my bedchamber. While George is here, you will need to stay in with me. When he returns, distract him for a moment." With that, Daniel swiftly left the room.

With her heart pounding, Sarah sat there rigidly, listening for the door to open. With dread, she thought about the fact that she may have to put up with the offensive man for up to two weeks. Soon, Sarah heard the front door open and then close. Taking a deep breath, she braced herself for the man's return.

George came strolling into the parlor and set his satchel down. "Where is Daniel?"

Attempting to conceal how nervous she was, she replied, "Oh, he is around here somewhere. Do sit down. I am sure he will return momentarily."

Scowling, George made his way over to the chair directly next to Sarah. Taking great delight in setting her nerves on edge, he whispered, "Do not get too used to living here with Daniel. Before I go, I mean to see you gone from here."

No matter how hard she had tried to brace herself for whatever George might do or say, she was still unprepared for his mean-spirited remarks.

"Have you no response?"

Sarah knew she needed to keep him in the room with her while Daniel conveyed some of her belongings to his bedchamber, but she wondered how she might engage in a conversation of this nature. Deciding to change the subject, and hoping the man would allow it, Sarah said with a tremor in her voice, "You must be famished. Daniel will prepare something soon."

George pounced on the opportunity to mistreat her once again. Leaning close, he hissed, "What good are you? With Daniel out on calls, the least you could do is prepare dinner for him. But no! You sit here, reclining like a princess."

By now, Sarah was shaking violently. As George studied her profile, he noticed the trembling. Realizing how fast he would be thrown out if Daniel knew the things he had said to her, he attempted to calm her. In this, they were allies—neither wanting Daniel to know she was upset.

"Well, you best get control of yourself before Daniel returns. You would not wish to be the cause of problems between Joanna's husband and brother, would you?"

Sarah had resolved within herself that very thing—not to come between George and Daniel. But she knew it would not be easy, for it seemed that Joanna's brother had figured her out. She would never reveal anything concerning his plan to be rid of her to Daniel. And to that end, he could say and do whatever he wished. That thought made her cringe. Risking a glance in his direction, she detected a smirk upon the evil man's face and wondered how he could be related to dear, sweet Joanna.

While George sat there waiting for Daniel, a similar thought to Sarah's came to the mean-spirited man; he was at liberty to speak unrestrained to Daniel's new wife. *I can do and say whatever I wish to the little waif, and as she has already demonstrated, she shall never say a word.*

When Daniel finally returned, he was a little out of breath from running back and forth between his and Sarah's bedchambers. Since Sarah had yet to return to Amesbury to collect the remainder of her belongings, he had been able to gather up the little she had, hoping George wouldn't detect that anyone had been staying in that particular bedchamber.

To be certain George would not have the opportunity to look around in Sarah's room, Daniel decided on the best place to put his brother-in-law. "George, you may stay in the boys' bedchamber since they are not here at present." He felt this was the safest option. After visiting for a time in the parlor, they all turned in for the night.

Chapter 13

As the couple entered Daniel's bedchamber, Sarah's stomach was in knots. She hadn't been in this room since they had lost Joanna and the baby—not even when she was tidying up the house. Besides the feelings of loss the sad memories generated, she was also uneasy about sharing a room with Daniel—particularly this room.

While observing his wife, Daniel perceived her hesitation. "Sarah, I know it is difficult for you, sharing my room, but it cannot be helped. Once you are settled in bed, I shall explain why I have moved you in here. Furthermore, you may have noticed the daybed over there by the window," he said while pointing to it. "That is where I shall sleep."

As Daniel recalled the reason he had crafted the daybed and had it moved into his room—which was to allow Joanna more space in the bed for proper rest during her lying in phase—he felt a sadness passing through his entire being. Then, with great difficulty, he pushed aside all thoughts of Joanna and their child and escorted Sarah over to where she would be sleeping. "You see, my brother-in-law's character is in question, where women are concerned."

As his wife listened, she merely nodded. In truth,

after what she had observed of the younger Mr. Hoyt, she needed no further explanation for why she had to be moved. And with the man's obvious contempt for her, she was quite certain he would not approach her, at least not in the way Daniel meant. After slowly lowering herself down on the edge of the bed with the aid of her crutch, she sighed, for though she was uncomfortable at being in her friend's room with her friend's husband, she also felt a little relieved; George couldn't say or do anything to her without Daniel's notice when she was in this room.

As the couple sat on their respective beds, Daniel spoke more about his reasons for having Sarah moved to his bedchamber.

This must be why Joanna did not want to name a child after him, she thought. Even though her husband had felt the need to share this information with her, she had no intention of revealing the mean things George had said.

Over by his wardrobe now, with the door standing open to block Sarah's view, Daniel hastily readied himself for bed. As he was setting his day clothes aside, he remembered Sarah having mentioned that she had experienced something similar with Alexander. On account of an illness, she had stayed in her first husband's bedchamber even though, at the time, theirs was also a marriage of convenience. "Sarah, being moved into your husband's room is something that happened when you were married before, was it not?"

Feeling embarrassed by the question, she had no

wish to discuss it; thus, she only nodded.

While peering around the open door of the wardrobe, Daniel observed Sarah's uneasiness. "I do apologize for this. If I felt that you were safe in your own bedchamber I certainly wouldn't have moved you and your belongings to mine. The moment George is gone, we shall simply put everything back the way it was before."

Sarah's eyes met Daniel's. In seeing his apologetic expression, she replied, "It truly is all right, Daniel. And as you say, it shall not be for long."

Daniel had one concern that continued to weigh upon him. What was he to do when he had to go out on calls, leaving Sarah alone with George? He couldn't take her with him, for bouncing around on a wagon, while injured, would be detrimental to her recovery. Not wanting to frighten her about being alone with his brother-in-law, he kept it to himself.

Both Daniel and Sarah slept little that night. Sarah was worried over spending time alone with George when Daniel wasn't home. And unbeknownst to her, her husband had similar worries.

When morning came, Daniel awakened to find Sarah sitting on the edge of her bed, dressed and attempting to fasten her frock. As she had since she had been injured, she required his help. Though he knew she was still a bit uncomfortable about having him help her with such personal things, he was grateful that at least his having previously been her physician made it a little less awkward.

A short time later, the couple made their way to the parlor. Once Daniel was certain that Sarah was settled, he began preparing something for everyone to eat. He would take his breakfast along with him when he left, for having several people to see before the day was over left little time for a leisurely meal.

Before long, the physician was headed out the door. Calling back over his shoulder loud enough for Sarah to hear from where she was in the parlor, he stated that he would be stopping by Mrs. Findley's to ask her to come by for a few hours. He hoped that, seeing as his brother-in-law was only a few steps behind him, in hearing this, he would behave himself.

Sarah was feeling panicked at the thought of being alone with George. But as her husband had said a moment ago—as he was leaving, their neighbor would almost certainly be paying a visit. Knowing this caused her to calm a little.

In an attempt to keep busy so that George would leave her be when he returned from walking her husband out, Sarah collected items from the table next to where she was sitting to write a missive to her head-servant. She had yet to tell her elderly friend that she had married Daniel Thompson. With Mr. Hoyt and the boys presently in Amesbury, however, she believed her servant-friend had most likely been made aware of the marriage; regardless, her missive would not contain such news, as she felt that it should be given in person.

There was also one other she needed to inform, but she dreaded the thought of doing so. She and Mr. Swyndhurst, Alexander's father, were very close. He had been at the Amesbury estate since before his son's passing. She hoped that when he learned of her marriage, he would not be hurt by the news.

Just as she had commenced with her writing, the very man she hoped to avoid came strutting into the room. Although she tried to stay focused on what she was doing, she was altogether unsuccessful. Hovering over her parchment, eyes down, she listened to every step he made in her direction.

Suddenly, George began scornfully laughing at her. As nervous as she was, she jolted at the sound of his voice, which made him laugh all the more. Though she endeavored to ignore him, he would have none of it. Coming over to where she was sitting, he planted himself directly next to her.

"Well, it seems we are alone. What shall we do for the remainder of the day?"

Even though his words were spoken in an almost normal tone, Sarah did not answer. Eyes still focused on her parchment, she nonchalantly moved a little to her left, away from the tall figure sitting beside her.

George detected the slight move of the tiny woman's body and wondered if he was carrying things a bit too far, for he had no desire for his actions to be reported to Daniel before he had accomplished his goal.

Deciding to bide his time and wait for the perfect opportunity to present itself, one in which Sarah would be gone so quickly Daniel would have little opportunity to prevent her departure, he rose to his feet, stating he needed to see to his horses.

His brother-in-law had a farmhand that helped out, when needed, and had said as much to George, so there really was no need for him to go. He went anyway. He needed to think about how he was going to manage pushing Sarah hard enough to make her leave, but not so hard that she felt the need to tell his sister's husband.

Once she was alone, Sarah heaved a heavy sigh. "I do not know how I am going to stand this, Lord. I cannot tell Daniel, but George scares me, not a little."

Chapter 14

On this day, while Daniel was away from the house, his mind remained fixed upon Sarah. He hoped the neighbor had been able to have a long stay with her. Wishing to get home as quickly as possible, the physician had not lingered at any of the homes he had visited.

Glancing up at the sky, he realized he would make it home just after dark. Since Mrs. Findley had said she would prepare the meals whenever she visited, he was certain she had. As tired as he was from rushing around all day, he was happy to have the kind neighbor's assistance while Sarah was on the mend.

◊◊◊

Mrs. Findley had been a good distraction for Sarah that morning. More importantly, while she was there, George hadn't shown his face. It had now been a couple of hours since Mrs. Findley had taken her leave. Sarah reasoned that George must not have noticed for he had yet to return from the barn. She dreaded the thought of seeing him. To her chagrin, her time to be by herself soon ended.

Coming into the parlor, George quickly resumed his taunting ways. "Well, my brother-in-law will be home soon. Owing to that old woman, this time there will be something prepared for him to eat, no thanks to you."

While attempting to conceal her fear of being alone with such a terrible man, Sarah remained silent. And she couldn't argue with what he had said. She knew he was right; she had not been much help to Daniel of late.

Not gaining the response he had hoped for, George sulked his way to the seat he had previously occupied, the one right beside Sarah.

Sarah reached over to the table next to her and retrieved her Bible. Somehow just holding it brought her comfort.

Observing her as she opened it to read, he sneered, "You do not fool me, little missy. Anyone can see that reading that book has done little to improve your character, given that you insinuated yourself into my sister's family—a woman who, from what I have been told, was supposed to have been your friend."

As before, George had hit a nerve, for this was exactly how Sarah saw herself—as a usurper. With tears threatening, she turned her head away. All at once, the occupants of the parlor heard the front door opening.

George hastily moved to the other end of the settee. Sighing with relief, Sarah quickly schooled her expression in order to appear relaxed.

Upon entering the room, Daniel was reassured to find Sarah and George in the parlor together, which caused him to wonder if perhaps he had worried over nothing; however, as he took a closer look at Sarah, he thought she appeared troubled by something.

Sarah noticed the questioning look upon Daniel's face and forced herself to smile. Though she had tried to conceal the way she was feeling, her husband had noticed that something was wrong. She had to convince him otherwise. "You are home. What a long day you have had. Mrs. Findley left plenty of food for everyone. In fact, George and I were about to partake of some."

In hearing Sarah's lighthearted tone, Daniel wondered whether he had indeed caught a glimpse of something amiss in her expression only a moment before. He now thought that perhaps he was mistaken.

George was surprised at how well Sarah hid her feelings, for he was certain she was anything but calm. He smiled to himself as he comprehended that this was going to be easier than he had imagined—getting rid of Sarah without Daniel knowing he had done anything to her.

When Daniel observed Sarah rising from her seat, he instructed, "Sarah, you remain where you are. I shall bring your dinner to you."

Knowing what George's reaction would be to Daniel having to take care of her, Sarah couldn't help but steal a look in his direction.

Daniel had already turned toward the kitchen when, as she had expected, George gave her a look that aptly communicated his belief that she was worthless. She watched as the unpleasant man followed Daniel out of the parlor, wondering again how she was going to endure having him there for the next week or two.

That evening, when Sarah and Daniel were alone in their bedchamber, Sarah's resolve to keep him in the dark regarding George was put to the test.

Once they were settled in their beds, with the candle still lit, Daniel said, "Sarah, I believe I may have given you the wrong impression of George. When I returned today, the two of you looked as if you were getting on marvelously. It seems I worried needlessly. My brother-in-law may not be as bad as I thought."

Fearing Daniel might read the truth in her expression, since he knew her so well, Sarah lowered her gaze. "Ye...yes, I am sure you are right. Everything has been satisfactory with George." Not wanting to continue the conversation, as lying had never come very easy to her, she leaned over and blew out the candle.

With satisfaction that he could now come and go from the house without worrying about Sarah being left alone with George, Daniel soon fell into a deep sleep. Sarah, however, lay awake for most of the night, dreading what the next day might bring, especially since Mrs. Findley, with too busy of a day ahead, would not be stopping by.

The following morning, Daniel awakened, rested and ready to begin his day. Sarah, on the other hand, had no desire for the day to commence.

Looking across the room at his wife, Daniel noticed she had dark circles under her eyes. He assumed her injuries had kept her awake. "Sarah, it looks as though you had a sleepless night. Were you in pain?"

"No, no. I have trouble sleeping, on occasion."

In hearing his new wife say she occasionally had sleepless nights, Daniel felt her words seemed to suggest it had nothing to do with her recent injuries. He then wondered if Sarah had been thinking of Alexander and the accident, which would, of course, explain her inability to sleep.

"Why not stay in bed for another hour or so? I will ask George to bring in something for you to eat later."

"I believe I shall. Actually, with my ankle a little tender from being up and about yesterday, to give it a rest, I may even stay in here for most of the day. And since I am not very hungry as yet, there really is no need to send George with food. Later, I shall go to the kitchen myself."

Daniel became suspicious. He quietly questioned whether George had been bothering Sarah, as he had originally feared. Before he could ask, she put his mind at ease by stating that she was merely tired.

When Sarah saw the worried expression disappear from Daniel's face, she knew she had settled his mind where she was concerned. She had no desire to raise suspicion by stating that she intended to stay where she was for the day, but neither could she force herself to face George. And she certainly didn't want him coming to her room with food.

When Daniel set off a short time later, he felt satisfied that Sarah would be well looked after, for their guest had reassured him he would see to her every need.

Chapter 15

Sarah was unable to sleep following Daniel's departure. She was also beginning to grow hungry. While patting her stomach, she thought, *I do not care how hungry I am. I would rather starve than go out there where George is lurking about. Though his sister was one of the kindest people I have ever known, in conduct and manners her brother is nothing like her.*

Just as she had finished that thought, she heard a knock on the door. With her heart racing, she called out, "Who is it?"

Laughing, George responded while opening the door, "Who do you think it is—with only the two of us at home?"

Alarmed, she asked sternly, "What are you doing in here?"

Making his way over to her, he held out a tray of food. "Daniel asked me to be certain you had your meals. He informed me that you often go without food for various reasons, such as being overly busy, which is obviously not the case today." Though George hated the thought of Sarah being a member of his sister's family, he had no desire to see the woman starve. In his opinion, she was already too slender.

Wanting the man out of her room as quickly as possible, in a shaky voice she responded, "You needn't have gone to the trouble. I can make it to the kitchen just fine on my own."

Since George had caught on to Sarah's intentions of hiding herself away, wanting to have the opportunity to continue pestering her, he stated, "No...no. I wouldn't hear of it. Daniel asked me to look after you, and look after you I shall. More to the point, even though you concealed your feelings admirably yesterday, my sister's husband still suspects that you are upset about something thus I shall do my best to have you looking well fed and rested when he returns."

Once George had set her tray down on the narrow table next to the bed, he took a seat on the other side of the room. From there, he closely watched Sarah for a few moments. Then, glancing next to him, he grinned when he noticed bedcoverings neatly folded at the foot of the daybed. The revelation regarding the couple's sleeping arrangements delighted him immensely. Though quite happy it would likely bother Sarah that he had grasped the situation, he decided to wait to use this bit of information until it would have its greatest effect.

Sarah was oblivious to what George had detected concerning her relationship with Daniel. And as unsettled as she was at having him in the room with her, her hunger had completely subsided. She wasn't about to let the detestable man know that he had shaken her, so she leaned over to the little table and began to eat the food he had prepared. With her heart racing, stomach in knots, each bite took great effort to swallow.

George had learned enough about her to know she wouldn't allow him to see how rattled she was by his presence. This made him chuckle to himself. He had to admire her stubbornness. And as he continued to survey her, not for the first time, he noted that she was actually quite attractive, which only caused him to wonder why she had attached herself to Daniel—a man who, naturally, still loved his sister, as evidenced by the fact that he wasn't even sleeping in the same bed with his new wife. *I am certain that tiny woman is nothing more than a live in maid. After all, someone has to look after the home and the boys while Daniel is out caring for the sick.*

Unable to force down another bite, Sarah leaned back against her pillow and closed her eyes, hoping that when she opened them again George would be gone.

"What? Not even a thank you?"

Sarah's eyes popped open at the sound of his voice. Sitting up, but not really looking in his direction, she answered, "Oh, yes, I do thank you." The way in which he had presented the food, in her opinion, was so ill-mannered it little warranted appreciation.

"That is more like it. Well, I believe I shall return your tray to the kitchen." As he stood, he noticed Sarah appeared relieved that he was going. Not wanting her to get too settled with the idea of being alone, he stated, "Do not be concerned. I will, of course, return momentarily."

George left the room with a satisfied look upon his face. Sarah, still shaking from the whole ordeal, rolled over and closed her eyes, thinking that maybe if she could actually fall asleep, he would leave her alone.

Soon, George returned to the room in which Sarah was resting. As he entered, he was surprised when he observed that she had fallen asleep. He decided to see what he could do about the evening meal. As upset as he was at Daniel for remarrying so soon, he still cared about his brother-in-law and wanted to do what he could to help out.

Throughout the remainder of the day, George checked on Sarah several times. Each time, she was still in a deep slumber. He had considered waking her in order to continue on with his badgering ways, but had thought better of it. If she was that tired, she must truly need the rest. It was not his desire that she should fall ill from lack of sleep.

When Daniel returned late in the afternoon, George had fixed something for him to eat. He had also tidied up.

After seeing that George had prepared the meal and the house looked in better shape than it had earlier, the tired physician smiled at his brother-in-law. "I am much obliged to you, George."

"That is what I am here for, to help you out now that my sister is—"

Neither man wanted to finish that thought, so

Daniel replied, "Yes, well, though Sarah is not at her best right now, she has been a great help to me and the boys."

Having no desire to acknowledge his brother-in-law's comment concerning Sarah, George proceeded to set the table.

Daniel went to look in on Sarah. She was waking when he poked his head in. "George has set the food on the table. Are you hungry?"

Sarah was delighted to see the friendly face peeking in. While moving into a sitting position, she replied, "Oh, perhaps in a little while. How were your visits today?"

Seeing that Sarah was now fully awake, Daniel made his way over to the bed. "Everyone I called on seemed to be doing well. As tired as you looked this morning, I am very glad you had a restful day."

It was true that she had been feeling tired early on, but a full day in bed had not really been necessary, and unbeknownst to George, more than once she had pretended to be sleeping when he had come to check on her. Sarah had no wish to divulge to her husband the real reason she had remained in bed, which was to stay clear of George. "Yes, I don't seem to be worth much these days, so staying out of the way is probably best. I cannot wait until I have fully recovered."

"You shall be back to your old self in no time. Would you like for me to help you to the parlor before I go?"

When she heard the word "go" her heart began to race. Before she had time to calm herself, she blurted out,

"What? I thought you were home to stay!"

Hearing the almost desperate tone in Sarah's voice, Daniel quickly responded, "I simply meant that I would help you to the parlor before returning to the kitchen. As I said, George has prepared dinner."

With heat rising in her cheeks, Sarah lowered her eyes. "Oh, of course. No...no. I believe I shall stay right here. But you go and have your dinner."

Daniel felt that something was amiss. "Sarah, is there anything bothering you?"

With her eyes still fixed on her lap, she replied, "Everything is fine. Go on. Your food must be getting cold."

"Very well. If you need anything, you only need to call out." With that, Daniel turned to go. Once he was out of Sarah's view, he paused to think a moment. *Something is definitely wrong. I wonder if George has been up to his usual practices. If that be the case, why hasn't she said anything?*

While the men ate together, Daniel asked a few questions regarding how the day had gone. George responded in such a cheerful manner that Daniel dismissed the idea that his brother-in-law was somehow responsible for Sarah's strange demeanor.

Chapter 16

The following day, after Daniel had gone, Mrs. Findley came to call on Sarah. Although she was aware that Joanna's brother was currently staying with the couple, she still came as often as time allowed, believing her injured friend would fare better with a woman's attention.

George opened the door and invited the neighbor in. Mrs. Findley went directly to see Sarah. Knowing the woman would be there for a few hours, to stay out of her way, he went to his bedchamber.

As soon as Sarah saw her neighbor's sweet face, she nearly cried. For at least part of the day she would not have to be alone with George. Once her neighbor had helped her dress, the ladies made their way to the parlor. After making sure that Sarah was comfortable, Mrs. Findley went to the kitchen to prepare something for Sarah and George to eat, as well as food for later.

George eventually made his way to the parlor where Sarah was currently reclining, reading a book. While Mrs. Findley was in the house he had been conducting himself in a gentlemanly manner. Late in the afternoon, when the neighbor came to tell Sarah she would soon be leaving, George grinned at the expression on Sarah's face. Though she had smiled at the lady, to him she appeared tense.

The moment Mrs. Findley was out the door, George started in on Sarah, calling her pitiful for needing someone to look after her. Unbeknownst to the despicable man, however, Mrs. Findley had returned to fetch the gloves she had absent-mindedly left behind. As she entered the kitchen, she heard George's wrathful words, which were directed at Sarah. Stunned, she quietly listened. For the next five minutes, George never let up. The kindly neighbor didn't know whether to intervene or quietly take her leave. She decided on the latter, but she had every intention of questioning Sarah about what she had overheard at the first opportunity.

When Daniel returned later that day, he searched around the house for Sarah, eventually finding her in his bedchamber. Coming to her, he asked about her day. As usual, she reported that everything had gone well. When Daniel offered to convey her to the parlor, she declined, stating that she was tired and would be turning in soon.

"Sarah, Mrs. Findley prepared a meal for us. Have you already eaten?"

To avoid having to offer an explanation for why she wasn't hungry, even though she knew it would be a lie, Sarah nodded. Not having to speak the lie somehow made it easier.

"Oh, very well. Perhaps George will join me. I shall leave you to yourself, then."

Sarah sighed with relief the moment Daniel left. It

was becoming more and more difficult to make things appear as though she and George were getting on well together. And with every passing day, her apprehension at being alone with George intensified, making it difficult to eat much of anything.

When the two men sat down together to eat, George asked where Sarah was, but the moment he had asked, he realized his mistake, for Daniel flashed a questioning look in his direction.

"She told me she had already eaten. Is that not the case?"

"Well...ah...she must have. I have been rather busy."

"I see. I wanted to be certain she did indeed have something. She cannot afford to miss a meal."

George looked down at his food. In truth, he knew Sarah had not been to the kitchen. He hoped she wouldn't fall ill because of him.

◊◊◊

Mrs. Findley tossed and turned all night. She could not get Sarah and what she had overheard off her mind, wondering if her young friend had been enduring that kind of ill-treatment ever since Daniel's brother-in-law had come. She questioned what to do about it. Should she tell Sarah what she had heard George say, or go directly to Mr. Thompson concerning the matter?

Upon Mrs. Findley's arrival at the Thompson home the next morning, she felt ill at ease the moment she clasped eyes on George. Hastening past him, she went

106

directly to Sarah's bedchamber where, upon entering, all at once she was reluctant to address the situation between Sarah and George Hoyt. While observing Sarah, she detected dark circles under her eyes. She also noticed that her cheeks appeared rather hollow. Deciding to be direct, she flatly stated what she had overheard. "Sarah, shortly after leaving yesterday, I returned to retrieve the gloves I had forgotten. You see, I heard the terrible things Joanna's brother said to you. Has this been going on like that the entire time he has been staying with you?"

Sarah's eyes darted in Mrs. Findley's direction. She didn't know how to answer. If she told the truth, Mrs. Findley would almost certainly tell Daniel. "Oh...ah...no! Of course not! I think he was simply in a foul mood yesterday. Not to worry, Mrs. Findley."

Mrs. Findley continued, "I little care about what kind of mood he was in, Sarah! There is no excuse for his behavior."

Sarah became flustered as she tried to convince her neighbor there was nothing about which to worry. "I do so appreciate your concern, Mrs. Findley, but there really isn't any cause for concern."

It was beginning to dawn on the older woman that Sarah, for whatever reason, had no wish to hold George Hoyt accountable for his actions. She determined that if she saw any sign of George mistreating her young friend again, she would go immediately to the young woman's husband.

Knowing she might not be present if there was a

repeat occurrence, she pleaded, "Sarah, I know what I heard. I will let it go for now, but if he ever speaks to you that way again, you must promise to tell me or your husband."

With relief that Mrs. Findley would allow the matter to drop for now, Sarah nodded and then changed the subject. The older woman began the task of helping her into her clothes. Once her kindly neighbor had brushed and pinned her hair, the two ladies went to the kitchen, each hoping George had gone off somewhere.

George had noticed the cold manner in which the neighbor had greeted him upon her arrival. As he was mulling over the possible reasons for the change in the older woman's attitude towards him, the ladies entered the room. He watched as Sarah was escorted through the kitchen to the parlor by Mrs. Findley, who then returned to the kitchen a moment later. As the woman entered, her countenance confirmed that she had indeed given him a reserved greeting.

George observed her setting right to work, preparing food, without even a glance in his direction. He decided to go to the parlor to speak to Sarah, hoping to glean something about what she might have said to the neighbor for her to be acting this way towards him.

Keeping her eyes focused on her book, the young woman never even looked up when he entered and made his way over next to her. Whispering, he asked, "What have you told that woman about me? Clearly, she is trying to avoid me."

Sarah felt her hands begin to shake. Not wanting George to notice, she set the book down and replied, "I have not said a word to Mrs. Findley about your rude behavior."

"I find that difficult to believe. She is angry with me about something."

Sarah wasn't exactly sure why, but she had no wish to divulge that Mrs. Findley had overheard their conversation the night before.

Mrs. Findley made excuses to return to the parlor every few minutes. With Sarah and George alone, she worried what the man might say to her young friend. When it came time for her to take her leave, she feared abandoning Sarah to the loathsome man.

"Sarah, I must be on my way." While scrutinizing Mr. Hoyt for a reaction to the news that he would be left alone with Sarah, she thought she detected a slight grin. "I'm certain Mr. Thompson shall be home very soon," she informed in an attempt to compel the man to behave himself once she was gone.

Sarah gave as bright a smile as she could muster to conceal her trepidation at being left alone with Joanna's brother. "I am much obliged to you, Mrs. Findley."

Then George walked Mrs. Findley to the door. She left without saying a word to him.

When George returned to the parlor, he observed Sarah endeavoring to stand on her bad ankle. While waiting to see what would happen, he noticed a satisfied look upon her face. *Her ankle must be nearly healed. She shall not be requiring as much assistance.* This thought delighted him.

"I see you are able to stand. Your ankle must be well."

Sarah made no reply as she turned to go. When she entered Daniel's bedchamber a few moments later, she resolved to remain there until her husband returned.

Chapter 17

Early winter, the year 1736, Boston, Massachusetts Bay
Colony

Two weeks had passed since George's arrival at the
Thompsons' home. As much as he had pushed for
Sarah to leave, the brave little woman had not seemed to
waver in the least in her resolve to remain. Though it was
time for him to go, he had every intention of returning to
finish the job of ridding the Thompson home of Sarah's
presence.

Watching Daniel wave to his brother-in-law, Sarah
noted that his countenance revealed his joy at how well he
believed the visit had gone. As he came toward her, her
heart sank, for she knew she could never ask him to make a
choice. And although she tried to appear calm, she knew in
her heart that she couldn't take another visit with George
Hoyt. When Daniel had gone out to the barn for a few
minutes that morning, the wicked man had grabbed hold of
her, warning her to be gone before he returned or he
would not be a part of his family's lives any longer. In other
words, it was either her or him.

With some difficulty, she talked in a lighthearted
manner so Daniel wouldn't detect how troubled she was.

She was convinced that if he knew what George had said before he left, as well as all that he had done to her while he was there, Daniel would refuse to allow him to return. Sarah couldn't let that happen to Joanna's brother. She forced a smile as Daniel took hold of her arm and directed her toward the house.

As they entered, Daniel sighed. "George's visit went quite well. If only he had been this agreeable when Joanna was—"

Sarah sensed that Daniel was saddened at the thought of Joanna missing out on time with her brother, now that he seemed to have changed for the better, at least in Daniel's view. Things had always been so strained between brother and sister, not by any fault of Joanna's. Sarah also had noticed, of late, that Daniel had stopped talking about Joanna as much in her presence. She wished she could bring herself to let him know that he needn't speak less of her friend on her account, but how to begin a conversation of that kind, she did not know.

Changing the subject, she replied, "Yes. And as I now have use of both ankles, I am perfectly able to prepare something for us to eat."

Smiling at her, he responded, "Yes, I see that you are managing without the crutch. It won't be long before your wrist is back to normal as well."

◊◊◊

Later that day, Daniel carried Sarah's belongings back to her bedchamber. As he was finishing up, he felt a little saddened at the thought that he would be alone in his room from now on.

With her one good arm, Sarah put her things away as Daniel brought them into her room. When he indicated that this was the last of it, she thanked him. Catching each other's eye, for a moment they stood there, staring at one another. Suddenly feeling awkward, Sarah turned away.

Clearing his throat, Daniel said, "Well, I will leave you to it, then."

Nodding, she continued on with the task of putting her things away. When she had finished, she sat down on the edge of her bed, her head was spinning with thoughts of George, Daniel, the boys, and even Alexander. *If only Alexander had not died, I wouldn't be here. I would be at home where I belong. What should I do? Should I return to Amesbury—allowing George to win, or should I stay? If I stay, how shall I tolerate another visit from that horrible man? If I go, I shall miss Dan...or rather the boys.* She could not admit to herself that she would also miss Daniel.

The following morning, Daniel inquired as to whether Sarah wished to accompany him on his calls. He watched as her countenance changed to one of joy. With her injuries, Sarah had not been able to make his visits with him in some time thus he was not surprised at her delight at the idea of being out and about again.

"I take it by the look on your face that you will be coming along with me today."

"Yes, Daniel, I would dearly love to come with you."

"I thought as much," he said with a grin.

A short time later, once Sarah had positioned herself atop the wagon, Daniel tucked a blanket around her. As he looked down, he chuckled at the large grin on her face.

Sarah heard the little burst of laughter and looked up. "What is so amusing?"

"You are. If you could but see yourself."

"What? Why? Do I have something on me?" she inquired while wiping at her face.

"No...no, your face is perfectly clean. It is solely that I have not seen you smile very often lately. Today, however, you appear to be in good spirits."

Having no desire to discuss the reason for her recent somber mood, since it had everything to do with his brother-in-law, Sarah directed the conversation elsewhere by asking questions about the visits they would be making that day.

Once Daniel had explained how he expected the day to proceed, he expressed his gratitude for her willingness to assist him.

Sarah's heart melted a little at the thought that, with her injuries almost healed, she was useful again. But she also silently cautioned herself not to get too attached to Daniel, for she believed that one day soon she would be returning to Amesbury—that is, unless George had a change of heart, which in her opinion was highly unlikely.

Daniel and Sarah arrived at their first stop. As they

made their way to the door, the physician began to quietly warn Sarah about the man who lived there; but just then the door opened, effectively cutting off their conversation before he had the chance to finish. A rather large man greeted them and ushered them in.

As they entered, Sarah glanced around, hoping to learn something about the occupants of the home. Daniel went on without her to check on the man's wife who had fallen a few days before and injured her leg.

The physician felt the injury wasn't all that serious and would heal in no time; however, the woman's husband, an overly protective sort, had insisted that his wife take to her bed until her leg had fully healed. The concerned husband had become a widower at a very young age and had no desire to lose another wife. Daniel understood all too well what the man was feeling. If nothing else, losing Joanna had taught him a deep understanding for what the man had suffered and his need to keep his present wife safe.

As Daniel approached the bed, he looked back, expecting to see Sarah. The room empty besides himself and the injured lady, he shrugged and moved forward.

As Sarah inspected her surroundings, she started at the large figure moving toward her. Looking up, she recognized the man standing before her as the one who had escorted them in.

"Oh, pray forgive me. I was distracted by all of the lovely quilts."

"That is quite all right. Yes, my wife is a wonderful seamstress," he responded proudly.

Feeling uncomfortable that she had lingered, Sarah cleared her throat. "Well, I better go and see how Daniel and your wife are doing."

The pair proceeded to the room where the physician was currently assessing his patient's injury.

Sarah moved in close. "May I be of any assistance?"

"No, I think we are just about done here." Looking up at the worried husband, Daniel stated, "There really is no need for her to remain in bed. In fact, a little exercise will help to strengthen her leg." Knowing that the woman had little say when it came to her health, Daniel had not directed his comments to her.

"If you are certain her leg is better."

Daniel nodded his head in the affirmative. He then turned and winked at the man's wife, who—when it had only been the two of them in the room—quietly expressed how tiring it had been to be in bed for so many days. Like Daniel, she knew it had not been necessary.

After Sarah and the physician said their farewells, the couple thanked them for coming. Once they were out of doors, Sarah apologized for not following right behind him when he went in to see to the woman.

"There is no need to apologize, Sarah. As I was hoping to explain before we went in, Mrs. Miller's injuries were not all that bad. You see, Mr. Miller lost his first wife so he tends to be exceedingly protective of his current wife for fear of losing her as well."

Similar to Daniel, Sarah could fully appreciate such sentiments. "Oh, the poor fellow."

"We understand all too well his concern for his wife, do we not?"

Sarah nodded as they made their way to the wagon. The pair spent the remainder of the day calling on two others who required a visit from the physician.

When evening came, since they would no longer be sharing a bedchamber, the couple was reluctant to turn in for the night thus they sat in the parlor for a while, discussing the day.

Chapter 18

During the night, Daniel and Sarah were awakened by a loud knock at the door. Daniel rushed from the room in the direction of the noise. Sarah peered out of her bedchamber just as he was passing by.

Upon opening the door, Daniel observed a close acquaintance from church. He had been to the man's home on more than one occasion, not only to visit but also to see to an injury or an illness. Daniel ushered Mr. Coffman over to a chair.

"What is the trouble, Michael?"

"Daniel, you must come straight away. My little Lydia is extremely ill. She is burning up and seems to be having difficulty breathing." Mr. Coffman leaned forward as he spoke, looking as though he himself could collapse at any moment.

"I shall fetch my bag and then set off straight away."

Mr. Coffman quickly acknowledged the physician and then nearly bounded from his chair, and was out the door before Daniel had taken a step. Sarah came into the room as the worried father was hastening out the door.

"What is it, Daniel?"

"The Coffman's youngest daughter, Lydia, is ill. I shall be setting off momentarily."

"Give me a minute to dress and I shall come with you."

Shaking his head, Daniel replied, "No, you mustn't. There is no need to risk your health."

"You may need me, and I am not concerned about becoming ill for having gone with you."

Daniel could see that Sarah was going to continue arguing, so he decided to procure her help with their neighbor, whom he had, in truth, planned to look in on the following day. To keep Sarah occupied, he would send her in his stead. "Sarah, I had intended to visit Elizabeth Brown tomorrow. Would you mind going for me? Since she lives alone and is up in years, I am concerned about her going for very long without someone looking in on her. Furthermore, now that your injuries have all but healed, I'm certain she would be delighted to see you. She asked after you the last time I was there."

"Of course. I would be happy to go. While I was on the mend from my foolishness with the bear, she must have felt quite neglected."

"Since I explained the situation to her, she completely understood your absence. Moreover, it was not for long. You dutifully called upon her before that."

Sarah, still feeling bad about not having been to their neighbor's house recently, merely nodded. "Is there anything I should do for her, other than the usual chores?"

Daniel had no desire to inform Sarah of the seriousness of Mrs. Brown's situation. "Actually, relieving her of some of her duties will be most helpful; however, you must not overdo or your injuries, though they have mostly healed, may become troublesome yet again."

"I shall be careful."

Hurriedly, Daniel then gathered his things and set off for the Coffman's house. His wife made her way back to bed for a few more hours.

In the morning, after Sarah had eaten, she prepared a basket of food for Elizabeth. A short time later, she arrived at her neighbor's door.

Lightly tapping a couple of times, with no response, Sarah poked her head in and softly called to her elderly neighbor. Still not hearing anyone about, she entered and looked around. As she approached Elizabeth's bedchamber, she heard coughing. While knocking, she called out, "Elizabeth, it is Sarah. May I come in?"

Between coughs, Elizabeth called her young friend into the room. "Well...Sarah." The coughing resumed before she could finish her sentence.

"Elizabeth, how long have you been feeling this way? Oh, there is no need to answer. I shall fetch you some tea. Have you had anything to eat today? You need only answer with a shake of the head."

Sarah observed the ill woman's response was no, but Elizabeth was also motioning with her hand that she had no desire to eat. As Sarah continued to study Elizabeth, she became quite concerned, for her complexion was extremely pale, almost greyish. She approached the bed and placed her hand upon Elizabeth's brow. "Oh my, you are burning up." *I wish Daniel were here.*

"Elizabeth, I am going to fetch some tepid water. We must bring your fever down." With haste, Sarah made her way from the room. She returned moments later with her hands loaded down with a pitcher, basin and cloth. She went right to work wiping down Elizabeth's face and arms.

Remembering what Daniel had always said about high fevers, she knew she also needed to get Elizabeth to drink; accordingly, she returned to the kitchen to make sack posset, which was known to be beneficial for the sick. As she looked around, she was glad to find that Elizabeth had everything she would need: sugar, dry sherry, nutmeg, cinnamon, and eggs. The final ingredient was milk, which Sarah had brought with her, fresh from earlier that morning.

Sarah spent the next few hours striving to bring down Elizabeth's fever but to no avail. She had also had little success in getting her elderly friend to drink any of the sack posset or even a mouthful of water. As the hours slipped by, she became more and more concerned.

Elizabeth knew in her heart that her time was coming to an end. Though she was glad she was not alone, she hated to have her young friend see what was to happen. Glancing over at Sarah, in a weak voice she said, "Sar...ah, you need...a rest. I shall be," gasping for air she continued, "just...fine."

Sarah wouldn't hear of it. She would stay by her

friend's side until she was well again.

When the sun gleamed through the window the next morning, in addition to being completely exhausted, Sarah's worry over Elizabeth had only increased. Throughout the night, she had been right by the ill woman's side. She had sensed, as the hours passed, Elizabeth was getting worse. *Should I go and fetch Daniel? No, no. I cannot. He is looking after a sick child. If he had returned home, he surely would have come. I must manage this on my own.*

Elizabeth was finding it difficult to even open her eyes, and she continued to struggle for every breath. As Sarah attempted to lift her friend's head enough to get her to drink, she felt fearful that she might lose her. Tears came to her eyes as she laid the sick woman back against her pillow.

By nightfall, Elizabeth's skin had cooled, but she had not spoken a word in hours, and her breathing seemed even more labored. Sarah's concern had not diminished, even a little. Yes, her ill friend had conquered the fever, but she knew Elizabeth was still in real trouble. What Sarah had not understood was the diminishing fever had occurred because her friend was close to passing from this life to the next.

Chapter 19

As Daniel bounded along on his way home, he thanked the Lord that the sick child he had been looking after had recovered. It had taken three days of constant care and very little sleep, but it was finally over. While struggling to keep his eyes open, Daniel thought of Sarah, wondering how she managed with Elizabeth.

When he reached home, he hoped that his farmhand, Zechariah, was about the place, for he was too tired to put up the horses himself. Making his way to the barn, he was pleased to find that, as he had hoped, Zechariah was there. After thanking his farmhand, he went to the house, fully expecting to see Sarah there. Upon entering the kitchen, he called out to his wife. It was early in the evening. The sun was beginning to set, so he thought he would see the glow of a candle coming from the parlor, or even Sarah's bedchamber. Once he had searched every room in the house, he was a little alarmed that Sarah was nowhere to be found. Quickly returning to the barn, he inquired of Zechariah as to his wife's whereabouts. His farmhand was distressed to learn Daniel had no knowledge of where his wife was, for he had no answer for him.

Daniel then remembered that he had asked Sarah to look in on their neighbor. "Perhaps she is still at

Elizabeth's. If that be the case, there may be something wrong. I must go there at once."

While the physician went to the house to fetch his medical bag—which he had set in his examining room only a few moments before—Zechariah readied one of the horses. He had only just put the animal in its stall. As he led the horse back out, he said to the animal, "There won't be any rest for you at this time, my friend." Within minutes, the worried husband was off.

Upon his arrival, Daniel observed that, just as it had been at his home, there was not a glimmer of even a single candle. Standing in the doorway, his heart began to race with thoughts of what he would do if Sarah wasn't there.

Daniel hated to wake Elizabeth, but he felt he had no choice. After entering the house, with the moonlight shining through the window, he caught sight of Sarah quietly sitting in a chair, staring straight ahead, unaware of his presence.

"Sarah, I am here." He made his way over to where she was sitting and pulled a chair up next to her.

As she looked in his direction, though the moon provided very little light, he could see tears streaming down her face. He quickly reached over and touched her arm. "What is it, Sarah?"

Closing her eyes, she answered, "El...Elizabeth...is gone."

Daniel patted her hand and said, "You stay here. I shall go and see for myself." As Daniel rose from his chair, he thought about Elizabeth and how much worse she had seemed on his last visit. She had been suffering from a weak heart for some time now. *Perhaps I should have warned Sarah.*

As he passed by the fireplace, he stopped to light a piece of kindling wood to carry in with him. After entering Elizabeth's room, he lit the candle next to her bed. He then reached down and touched her face. "Yes, Elizabeth, you are with our Lord now. In fact, it seems to have happened several hours ago, or even yesterday. I wonder why Sarah did not just go home." He spoke as though Elizabeth were listening.

As he made his way back to the sitting room, he thought about Sarah and the fact that she had stayed at Elizabeth's a long time after their elderly friend had passed.

Sarah looked up as Daniel approached, wishing with all of her heart that he would say she had been wrong and Elizabeth was only sleeping.

Daniel nodded his head as an indication that, as Sarah had said, Elizabeth had passed. Kneeling down in front of her, he reached for her hands, which each had cloth covering them almost to the tips of her fingers. Upon closer inspection he observed that Sarah was wearing what was apparently one of Elizabeth's nightgowns. Even though the situation was a somber one, he smiled at the way the gown engulfed her tiny frame; however, after pushing back the gown so as to caress her hands with his thumbs, he knew in an instant that she was ill. Her skin was almost hot to the touch. He had to get her home where she could rest comfortably.

With Daniel's confirmation that Elizabeth had died, Sarah began to weep all over again. "It is all my fault. I tried to remember everything I had seen you do for someone with a high fever, but I must not have done it correctly. I tried, Daniel, truly I did."

Daniel reached up and stroked her cheek. "Sarah, you did all you could. Even if I had come sooner, I could not have saved her. Elizabeth has had a heart condition for a long while now. I should have told you. In truth, she probably lived this long because of all that you have been doing for her since your arrival in Boston."

All at once, Sarah felt her last bit of strength drain from her body, causing her to slump forward into Daniel's arms. She could barely hear her husband as he spoke her name.

Fearing for her, Daniel scooped her up, grabbed the quilt on the back of the settee and headed for the door. He would send someone to see to Elizabeth tomorrow.

As exhausted as he was, lifting Sarah up onto the horse took great effort. Once he was seated behind her, he wrapped the quilt around her and they set off for home.

Upon their arrival, he alighted from the horse and then slid a swaddled Sarah down into his arms. Glancing to the side, he noticed Zechariah, with a pleased expression, was approaching.

"I see that you found your wife."

"Thankfully, yes. She was where I suspected she might be, at Elizabeth's. I am sorry to say that Elizabeth is no longer with us. She passed while Sarah was there."

Zechariah was saddened by the news. Realizing that Daniel was not only exhausted but had a distraught and perhaps even sick wife to tend to, he offered to make the necessary arrangements for Elizabeth.

"I would be most grateful, Zechariah." Confirming for his farmhand that his wife was ill, he then stated, "I really ought to stay with her."

Zechariah nodded as he grasped the reins and turned toward the barn.

Once Daniel had Sarah settled in bed, he stretched out beside her, too tired to go to his own bedchamber. The pair slept for several hours before Daniel startled himself awake. He had dreamt he was searching everywhere for Sarah, but to no avail. His slumbering mind had carried him back to when Sarah was taken, while sitting on a bench in his backyard, by Matthew Raymond; that was when he jolted himself awake.

With his heart racing, he quickly looked beside him for reassurance that Sarah was still in the bed. Sighing with relief, he reached over and felt her forehead. *She is still a little feverish. I better see to her.*

Sarah stirred at his touch. As she opened her eyes, she observed Daniel rising from the bed. It still seemed rather odd to be so near her friend's husband, especially in the same bedchamber.

Feeling weak, she remained where she was. As she looked up at Daniel, their eyes met. Since she persisted in her belief that Elizabeth had died because of her, she lowered her eyes.

Daniel had known Sarah long enough to read her expressions thus he was quite sure that she continued to blame herself for Elizabeth's passing. "Sarah, I thought we had settled this last night. You are not responsible for what happened to Elizabeth. As I said, I was expecting her to pass long before now. You did everything you could possibly do for her."

Sarah slowly nodded. She felt Daniel's reassuring caress on her hand a moment before he turned to go.

A few minutes later, he returned with a bowl of cool water and a cloth. Taking a seat on the bed next to Sarah, he began patting her brow with the dampened cloth. As Sarah studied him, she thought about what a handsome man he was. On top of that, he was also extremely kind, patient, and gentle. She then shook her head, attempting to rid herself of such thoughts. *If I forget myself, all too soon, George will be here to remind me that I have no place here with Daniel.*

Daniel glanced down when he felt Sarah's head move, wondering if the cloth was too cold on her hot brow. "Is this making you uncomfortable?"

Though Sarah knew what he meant, she had to smile at the thought that, yes, she was *uncomfortable* being so near Daniel; however, what she said was, "No…no. It's fine. But I believe I am much better now. There really is no need for you to take care of me. Having been gone from the house for a few days, you must have a great deal to do."

Smiling, Daniel responded, "Who is the doctor here?"

Sarah chuckled. "Perhaps it is best that I not tell you what to do."

Daniel was pleased that Sarah's mood seemed to be improving. Setting the cloth down, he said, "I shall fetch something for you to eat. You should stay in bed today. Since your fever is not as bad as it was last night, I expect that it shall soon pass."

◊◊◊

Daniel looked in on Sarah for about the tenth time. He was tired and ready for a little slumber himself. Reaching down, he said, "Your fever seems to be almost gone. I'll be in my bedchamber. If you need anything during the night, you need only call out and I shall come at once."

"I'm much obliged to you for looking after me yet again. I hope I shall not be so burdensome in the future. You really should have been resting today, not taking care of me."

"I had plenty of sleep last night, and I'm heading to my bedchamber now, so by tomorrow I shall be all caught up on my rest. And you have never been a burden to me," he said with a wink. "Goodnight, Sarah."

"Goodnight, Daniel."

Chapter 20

Daniel looked in on Sarah more than once during the night. When morning came, she was back to her usual self. Though they were both a little somber over the loss of their friend, while breaking the fast together, they spoke little about it.

Later that day, Zechariah came by with news of an appointed time to lay Elizabeth to rest. After thanking him, Daniel walked him out. When he returned, he observed Sarah right where he left her—at the table, sipping a cup of tea. Looking a little closer, he detected glistening upon her cheeks. The news had obviously brought her emotions back to the surface.

Seeing Daniel walking toward her, Sarah quickly turned away. But she soon realized he must have witnessed her tears, for he had come up behind her chair and had wrapped his arms around her.

When Sarah reached up and patted one of Daniel's arms as a sign that she was all right, Daniel released his hold.

She turned toward him and said with a smile, "If we are going to eat today, I better prepare something for us."

"I shall be in my study if you need anything."

The couple parted company for a few hours. Later, when the food was ready, Sarah called for Daniel. Hearing her call, he came to the kitchen and helped her carry the food to the table. Once they were seated, they thanked the Lord for the food and for what a blessing it had been to have Elizabeth as a friend. They would both miss her.

◊◊◊

Meanwhile, at Mrs. Findley's home, her son Simon had come for a visit. The kind woman had injured her toe. Although she could still walk, she had been having difficulty performing her chores, which hadn't bothered her nearly as much as not seeing Sarah, owing to her injury, since Daniel's brother-in-law had taken his leave. She wished that Sarah hadn't sworn her to secrecy regarding the nasty way in which Mr. Hoyt had treated her during his stay.

As Mrs. Findley sat with her son, she recalled the story he had told her about rescuing Sarah Thompson from a bear. She knew she shouldn't but she felt compelled to tell him what she had witnessed at the Thompson home.

Simon listened intently as his mother spoke. The more she said, the angrier he became at George Hoyt. "Mother, you should have said something earlier. I shall speak to Daniel at once."

"No! You mustn't! I promised Sarah I would not say a word to Daniel. She fears coming between her husband and his brother-in-law. Sarah explained to me that Joanna and George had been distant from each other and that

Daniel was very pleased that George seemed to have softened, at least enough to come for a visit."

"No matter. We cannot allow Sarah to be mistreated."

"Simon, I am quite serious! You cannot say a word. If George returns, we shall decide, then, whether or not to tell Daniel."

"I am at least going to call on Daniel and Sarah more often. That way, if he shows his face again, I'll put the fear of God into him."

"Well, that is fine, I suppose; but you must not tell Daniel unless it becomes necessary."

Simon reluctantly agreed to his mother's request. Later, on his way home, he stopped by to see Daniel and Sarah. Sarah greeted him and invited him in. Given that her countenance showed her pleasure at seeing him, he was happy he had come.

"Mr. Findley, I never had the opportunity to give you a proper thank you for saving me from that dreadful bear. I have attempted to speak with you at church on more than one occasion; however, you are usually surrounded by a group of rather eager, unmarried women. I hated to disturb you," she said with a grin.

Simon was pleased Sarah felt comfortable in his presence, which was certainly not the case when they first met. "Yes, well, having so many admirers can be rather wearisome," he answered with a wink.

Daniel heard voices and came to see who was with

Sarah. Upon entering the kitchen, he overheard the playful bantering going on between his wife and Simon. This made him smile, for Sarah wasn't always comfortable around men, especially of Simon's stature. As he approached he greeted his friend.

While responding to Daniel's welcome, Simon remembered the last time he had seen his friend. It had been when he was in town, following the incident with the bear. Daniel had thanked him, yet again, for having saved his wife. He recalled questioning why Sarah seemed so frightened of him, considering the fact that he had just rescued her. Offering little detail, Daniel had alluded to something in Sarah's past that caused her to be ill at ease around men. Sensing at the time that Daniel had said all he intended to regarding the matter, Simon had not questioned him further.

Not wanting to state the real reason for his visit—to look in on Sarah as well as to make certain Daniel's brother-in-law had truly left—he said, "I thought I would see how my favorite physician and his mischievous wife were getting on."

Daniel laughed out loud at Simon's description of Sarah. "Not many know what I have to put up with from this angelic looking woman," he said while patting the top of Sarah's head. His mind then went to Joanna and how, in this, she and Sarah were completely different. Joanna rarely disregarded his counsel, whereas Sarah had a tendency to ignore the guidance of others, which since their marriage had caused him some concern.

Even though Sarah knew Simon and Daniel were only teasing, she was aware that there was some truth to what they had said. She did have a tendency to get herself into trouble by not following the advice of others, and these two men were not the first to notice. Shrugging off such thoughts, Sarah trailed behind Simon and Daniel as they made their way to the parlor. Once they were seated, she stated that she would return in a few minutes with tea. Both men thanked her as she left.

Coming into the parlor a short time later, Sarah thought she observed a strange expression upon Simon's face when he looked her way. In seeing this, she had a discomfiting thought. *I wonder if Mrs. Findley has disclosed to Simon what she overheard when George was here.* That thought caused her to feel uneasy, not only from the humiliation of it all, but also for fear that he might inform Daniel.

Simon quickly schooled his face so as not to give away the compassion he was feeling for Sarah at that moment. When she was in the kitchen—while he and Daniel conversed—he had been tempted to tell his friend what a scalawag his brother-in-law was. Seeing Sarah and the questioning look upon her face made him remember his mother's warning.

Sarah poured the tea and then took a seat next to Daniel. With her eyes fixed on Simon, she listened as Daniel, after thanking her, continued on with their conversation.

Simon continued to study Sarah as Daniel spoke. He was certain she wondered what he knew of her situation with George. This was later confirmed when Daniel was called out to tend an injured woman, leaving him alone with Sarah. The physician had taken his leave with such haste that there wasn't time for Simon to first bid the couple farewell.

Though he knew he should not stay now that Daniel had gone, there were things he and Sarah needed to discuss privately.

He began the conversation. "Sarah, I ought to take my leave, but first I would like to talk to you about something."

With her heart racing, Sarah answered, "Indeed. What is it, Mr. Findley?" She hoped she was wrong about what he intended to discuss, and though she had no wish to hear, she forced herself to remain where she was in order to gain a promise that he would not reveal anything concerning George Hoyt to her husband, if indeed that was what his topic of conversation turned out to be.

"My mother, out of concern, shared with me what happened while George Hoyt was staying with you."

Shaken by the fact that she had accurately read Simon's expression earlier, Sarah responded, "I think she may have misunderstood the situation. We had a lovely visit with Joanna's brother."

Simon sensed that she spoke out of fear of Daniel

finding out. "Sarah, it is highly unlikely that what my mother overheard was merely a misunderstanding. I know you do not want Daniel to learn of this, but I truly believe he should be informed."

With her heart still beating loudly, Sarah tried to think of the best way to calm the situation. "Mr. Findley, even so, he is gone now. There really is no need to bother Daniel with this."

"Sarah, your husband would want to know."

"It is just that while Joanna was alive, she and George had a tumultuous relationship. And now, Daniel was so full of joy at seeing George, I simply cannot come between them, which is exactly what would happen if he were to hear of this. And having their uncle come for visits shall be good for the boys as well. After all, George is their flesh and blood. Moreover, Joanna was my dearest friend. I must do what I can for her family, including her brother."

"It is good of you to want to protect their relationship; nonetheless, you are a part of the Thompson family now. If they knew about this, they would want to protect you."

"That is precisely why you must not say a word about this, Mr. Findley. If I have to, to shield Daniel and the boys from knowing about this, I shall just go back to Amesbury."

Simon sensed that there was no convincing the determined young woman. Not wanting to make her run away to Amesbury, he responded, "I shall abide by your wishes, for now. But if he returns and continues to treat you cruelly, I will have no choice but to make the situation known to Daniel."

Sarah was grateful that for the time being Daniel would not learn of George's behavior.

With a heavy heart, Simon took his leave, still feeling as though he should not have agreed to remain silent.

Chapter 21

O ver the next couple of months, Sarah and Daniel were constantly together. She rarely stayed behind when he was out seeing to those in need of his services thus the bond between them had grown even stronger.

While breakfasting with Daniel one morning, Sarah thought about George and his inevitable return. The vicious man had not been far from her mind since his last visit. And with the knowledge that he intended to send her packing when he returned, she had been lying to herself with regard to her growing feelings for her husband. Just now, it was even more difficult, for as she looked across the table at Daniel, she was certain it was no longer purely friendship she was feeling.

As Sarah kept her focus on Daniel, their eyes met, causing her face to redden. Oh, she knew he could not possibly have known what she was thinking, but she wondered if her expression had given anything away.

Daniel noticed Sarah's face turning a deep red. "Sarah, is there anything the matter? You look rather flushed."

This made her blush all the more. She suddenly thought of Joanna and her uneasy feeling turned to one of shame. Hoping to avoid Daniel's question, she rose from the table, stating that she had a lot to do before they left. *If*

I could but think of an excuse to stay at home instead of accompanying him today, she thought to herself.

Since Sarah had not responded to his question, Daniel, still wondering if something was wrong, stood to help clear the table. They both remained silent while they straightened up the kitchen. When they had finished, Daniel stated that he would be ready to go as soon as he had collected his medical bag.

Eyes lowered, Sarah replied, "Very well." Once Daniel had left the room, she sighed with relief. *These feelings I am having for him shall not do.*

As Sarah expected, it was not more than a few minutes before Daniel called her name. Making her way to the door, she hurriedly scooted past him.

While they were on their way, Daniel looked over at Sarah a time or two, wishing he knew why things felt so awkward. He noticed that her eyes were roaming everywhere but in his direction. This was going to be a long day if he couldn't discover what was troubling her.

"Sarah." Seeing her entire body jolt at the sound of his voice, he couldn't hold back any longer. "What on earth is going on? All I did was speak your name and you nearly jumped out of the wagon."

In hearing his question, she realized she was going to have to answer for her strange behavior. Quickly thinking of an excuse, she replied, "Oh, I must have been half asleep."

Daniel knew she was not being truthful, but how to

call her on it, he didn't know. "To be frank, you do not seem yourself today."

"Oh…ah…well, I am not sure what you mean." Her hands then began to shake. How was she to explain without sharing that she had feelings for him? They had both promised this would never happen. She was certain it would only make him uncomfortable. He might even want to send her away, which would make his brother-in-law very happy.

It seems I am not to know what is troubling her. "Perhaps it is as you say; you are merely tired." Daniel spent the remainder of the day attempting to put Sarah at ease. By the time they were on their way home, she seemed more herself and he was glad of it.

Even though this time she had been able to hide the truth from him, she wondered how long she could continue to keep her feelings hidden. *Perhaps George is right and I should go back to Amesbury.* That night, Sarah tossed and turned as she thought about what to do. There were two reasons for her to leave, George and her feelings for Daniel, but when she thought about the boys, whether to stay or go wasn't as clear. She resolved to wait it out a bit longer. In time, perhaps her feelings for Daniel would fade, taking care of one problem. And as for George, maybe he would not return or, by some miracle, have a change of heart and allow her to stay. She knew the latter would be a miracle indeed.

With the week coming to a close, there was a knock at the door. To her utter chagrin, George Hoyt had returned. As he stood there looking contemptuously at her, she knew things between them remained unaltered, and the miracle she had been hoping for would likely never come.

When Daniel realized who was at the door, he knew there wasn't time to move Sarah's things into his room, as they had done on George's prior visit. As he thought about it, he wasn't quite as concerned as he had been the last time; however, he still didn't want his brother-in-law to learn the nature of his and Sarah's marriage. For that reason, he quietly made his way to Sarah's bedchamber and shut the door to hide the fact that someone was occupying the room. She could simply gather what she would need for the night when George wasn't looking.

After setting his belongings in the bedchamber he had previously used, George made his way to the kitchen, where Daniel and Sarah were waiting. Upon entering, he observed Sarah's troubled expression. Not wanting to give away the delight he felt at knowing how much he disturbed her, he began conversing with his brother-in-law.

Daniel hoped for another cordial visit. "George, it truly is wonderful to see you again. How long will you be with us this time?"

"I am not quite certain, but as long as necessary, I suppose."

Daniel found this to be a strange response, but

Sarah knew exactly what he meant. The vile man would stay until he had successfully forced her to leave.

That night as Sarah lay awake in Daniel's bedchamber, she silently prayed about what to do. Should she leave or stay? She had gone over all of this in her mind so many times, but had yet to make a decision. *Even if I decide that I want to stay, George will see to it that I do not, of that I am quite certain.* Peering through the darkness in the direction of the daybed on which Daniel was presently resting, her heart felt heavy at the thought of leaving.

Chapter 22

The following day was Sunday. The last time George had visited, Sarah had been unable to attend church because of her injuries. This time, however, she had every intention of going, for her injuries had long since healed. Of sound body now, she could simply go off with Daniel. This thought made her sigh with relief.

As she entered the kitchen to prepare breakfast, she silently prayed that God would give her strength, for who could know what George might do before the day was over.

The moment the food was ready, Daniel came into the kitchen. "Good morning, Sarah. Did you sleep well? When I awoke you had already left our bedchamber."

Sarah found it strange but also comforting somehow to hear him say "our" bedchamber. "Yes, I thought it best to rise early on this Lord's Day. I would not wish to be late for church."

Just about that time, George came sauntering in. He had yet to learn that this visit would be far different than his last. Sarah would not be left at his mercy this time. Not only that, but with the close of winter, his father and nephews would soon be arriving.

As George approached the table, Sarah invited him to go along with them to church. She had a twofold purpose; she wanted him to know that she would not be staying behind, but she also genuinely wished he would go. Despite their difficult relationship, she hoped he would come to a saving knowledge of Jesus Christ, for his sake as well as hers. She had seen for herself the change that comes over a person who surrenders their life to Christ.

She thought about the fact that the Bible calls it becoming a "new creation" when we are in Christ. *Besides his miserable existence here, there is eternity to consider. No matter his vile actions towards me, I would not wish for anyone to spend an eternity separated from our loving Savior.*

So caught up in her own thoughts was she, Sarah had not heard George's response. As her eyes went from George to Daniel, she noticed a smile on her husband's face. George, on the other hand, looked as though he were up to something.

Surmising that Sarah had not heard his brother-in-law, Daniel responded to George for her. "I hadn't anticipated that you would be agreeable to the idea, George, for it is a first for you; but I am delighted you shall be joining us."

George appreciated Daniel's honesty with regard to his response to Sarah's invitation. "My sister was always talking about church and how much she loved it—of course, in an attempt to get me to go. It is time I see for myself what all the fuss is about."

George spoke the truth about wanting to see what

church was about these days, wondering if it had changed since he had gone with his parents many years back; however, that wasn't his only reason he had decided to go. If Sarah was going along as Daniel's wife—to his sister's church—he was going to do his best to make it a miserable day for her. There was also a small part of him that wanted to honor his sister by going this one time.

Sarah's eyes widened as she listened to the conversation between Daniel and George. She was stunned George had said yes to going. Even though she knew he would make her as uncomfortable as possible for the remainder of the day, she silently prayed that God would speak to his heart through the pastor's message.

Before long, the three were on their way. Sarah kept her eyes focused on the road until they arrived at the meetinghouse, never glancing in George's direction. Daniel helped her down and they, along with George, made their way in.

Sarah stayed as close to Daniel as she could, hoping to scoot in first thus placing George on the other side of Daniel. She failed in this, as George grabbed her arm, holding her back for Daniel to be seated on the bench first.

With Sarah placed between the two men, the service began. Partway through, Daniel felt something touch his arm and looked down to find Sarah's head resting there. He glanced over at George, who looked vexed at the sight. Not wanting his wife to be caught by the tithingman, he gently nudged her.

Jolting awake, Sarah gasped. At this, George couldn't help but chuckle. Daniel also had difficulty in keeping his composure. Sarah, on the other hand, felt as if she could die of embarrassment. The tithingman soon strolled past, glancing back at Sarah with a look of disapproval. With her face turning a bright red, she lowered her eyes.

Daniel put his hand over Sarah's in an attempt to comfort her. He felt her shift around several times during the remainder of the service. When it was over, he whispered in her ear, "Sarah, you needn't be so upset over something so inconsequential."

Sarah looked up at him with appreciation. As she turned toward George, the relief she had felt only a moment ago at Daniel's words soon fled away. His look was one of utter contempt, which was nothing out of the ordinary for him.

Soon, some of their fellow parishioners approached to greet the Thompsons and the stranger standing with them. Daniel was delighted to introduce his brother-in-law, for many of his friends from church had been praying for Joanna's brother for years.

George was a little taken aback at the kind way in which everyone spoke to him. Those who had known his sister offered their condolences. Several of the ladies took the time to speak of Joanna's virtues and stated how much she had been missed since her passing.

Glancing in Sarah's direction, hoping to see discomfort on her face at all of the talk of Joanna, George was surprised to find that her countenance was one of joy. He wondered how she could endure hearing such praise of her husband's dead wife. All of this kindness, as well as Sarah's acceptance of the admiration for the former Mrs. Daniel Thompson, caused George's resolve with regard to his loathing of anything to do with church or the little woman standing near him to falter; however, the weak moment didn't last long, as the man, regaining his composure, slipped past the group and out the door of the church.

Sarah and Daniel quickly said their goodbyes and made their way out to the wagon, not wanting to make George wait too long for them. As the three in the wagon started for home, George, with an unsettled feeling, began teasing Sarah. At first he kept the conversation light, but that quickly changed, as his words became rude and insulting, at one point even questioning her reasons for attending church if all she was going to do was sleep through the sermon. He continued for a few moments, forgetting that Daniel was even there. As soon as he realized that he was showing his true feelings regarding Sarah to Daniel, he winked, hoping to make it as though the whole thing had been to amuse.

Daniel was about to admonish his brother-in-law when he noticed the wink. He could scarcely believe the meanness had all been done in jest. And as he continued to ponder the situation until they arrived at home, he remained uncertain about what had just happened between his wife and his brother-in-law, or to be more precise, what had happened to his wife, for she had had no part in the discussion.

George sensed that he had caused his brother-in-law concern over Sarah and decided to make up for it by treating the little woman with extreme kindness for the remainder of the day, or when Daniel was present, anyway.

Daniel kept a close eye on Sarah, hoping she had not been hurt by George's words. He still couldn't quite believe George could be so cruel.

Sarah apprehended that George had forgotten himself for a moment on the ride home, almost giving away his true feelings about her; consequently, she worked very hard not to show how unsettled the encounter had made her. When she could force herself, she even laughed with George when he attempted to alter the mood in the house with a little humor.

That night when they were alone, Daniel questioned Sarah to be sure she was indeed all right after all that had happened—what with almost stirring the ire of the tithingman and the seemingly mean-spirited words from his brother-in-law.

In another room, George was chiding himself for how foolish he had been in allowing Daniel to see his behavior toward Sarah. *I must be careful or I shall find myself thrown out of here before sending that woman on her way.*

Not a one rested much that night. When morning came, it brought with it a wonderful surprise.

Chapter 23

Soon after breaking the fast together the three occupants of the Thompson home heard a wagon pulling up in front of the house. Sarah quickly made her way to a window to see who it could be. To her great joy, she saw Mr. Hoyt and the young Thompson men. She nearly ran to the door. Quickly opening it, she called out a greeting.

Upon entering, Mr. Hoyt enfolded Sarah in an embrace, one she had longed for since he and the boys had taken leave of Boston for the winter.

Noticing his son—though a little apprehensive—Mr. Hoyt smiled. Yes, he was pleased to see George, but he was uncertain of how his son would receive him. He had tried so many times to find a way around his son's prickly nature, but up to now had met with little success. "George, I had no idea I would find you here."

By way of a greeting, George gave a slight nod. Oh, he was glad to see the family patriarch; however, he also knew their conversation would most likely be interspersed with lectures. He had always wondered if the man would have been so severe with him over the years if he had been his real son.

George's parents had lost their son to a premature birth. He had often wondered if he had merely been a replacement, one who never lived up to their expectations. While continuing to observe his father, George longed for the unconditional love the man had unceasingly offered his sister.

Dan and Joseph, after quickly hugging their father and Sarah, excitedly approached their uncle. Even though their visits with him had been few, they both adored their mother's brother. He had a way of making everything they did, including chores, enjoyable.

Although George was pleased to see his nephews, he felt a tinge of guilt over how little time he had spent with them over the years. But he quickly consoled himself with the thought that it was his sister who had made it difficult, given that most of his visits to the Thompson home had ended in a quarrel. Now that Joanna was gone, the anger he had previously felt toward her was all but gone, leaving him in a more reasonable state of mind. Truth be told, he knew it wasn't Joanna's fault that he was often asked to leave, for he was always making disparaging remarks about her faith in front of her sons as well as teaching them bad habits. In spite of this, she had always sent him on his way with the knowledge that she dearly loved him, and with never a word about the fact that they were not actually kin by blood.

As George surveyed his nephews, he noticed how

much they had grown. "Before you know it you boys will be taller than I." He pulled each in turn into his arms.

"When did you get here?" inquired Dan. He was old enough to comprehend that his mother, though she loved her brother, had found it a difficult relationship thus Dan was a little concerned over having his uncle there.

"Well, let me see," George replied while scratching his chin. "I have been here all winter, awaiting your return. What took you so long?"

Dan and Joseph chuckled. It was the same uncle—full of humor—they had always known. The boys led their uncle to the parlor for further conversation.

Sarah, Mr. Hoyt, and Daniel made their way to the table. Once the men were seated, Sarah set about fixing tea and something for the weary travelers to eat.

Mr. Hoyt, in a soft voice, questioned Daniel about how the visit with George was going and what had brought it about. He was aware that when his daughter was alive his son had rarely visited.

Daniel smiled at his father-in-law's questions, for on George's first visit he had been nearly as surprised as Joseph was now. "This is in fact his second visit since you and the boys took leave of Boston for the winter."

Mr. Hoyt's eyes grew large at the knowledge that his son may be beginning to make visiting the Thompsons a regular occurrence. It did his heart good to think George may finally be seeking to establish family connections.

Daniel continued. "As for how the visit is going, I

would say, overall, fairly well." Thinking back to the incident on the way home from church, he still wondered what that was all about, for to his knowledge George had been an ideal guest up until that point. Having no desire to upset his father-in-law, he decided not to mention the events of the previous day.

Mr. Hoyt sensed there was more to the story, but he allowed Daniel to continue uninterrupted.

"I only wish he had been so cordial whilst Joanna was alive. She carried a heavy burden in connection with him."

"Yes, she longed for a relationship with her brother. When they were young they were always close, but as adults their relationship was not what it ought to have been."

The two men looked up as Sarah approached the table. Daniel then stood to assist his wife. Once the tea and food were on the table, along with a place setting for each person, Sarah went to the parlor to inform the boys and George the food was ready.

As everyone conversed at the table, George observed Sarah. Watching how she interacted with his and his sister's family enraged him. As he thought about what to do next to try and force her out, he realized it would be much more difficult with his father there. The man had a knack, in nearly every situation, for uncovering the truth. When George was growing up he used to wonder if his father truly did have "eyes in the back of his head" as the older man had always joked.

Sarah caught a quick glimpse of the scowl on George's face and turned her head away. She would not allow him to ruin her visit with the three gentlemen she had greatly missed.

Just as his son had recalled only moments before, Mr. Hoyt, never missing a thing, observed the troubled expression upon Sarah's face, as well as the way in which she kept her head tilted so as not to look in his son's direction. He made a mental note to ask Sarah about it later.

When it was time for the boys to turn in, despite the fact that they were looking more and more like young men rather than boys, Dan and Joseph wanted Sarah to read to them, as usual. This time, since they hadn't seen their father in months, they asked him to come to their bedchamber as well.

Knowing it was rather late, Mr. Hoyt decided to wait and speak to Sarah the following day about what he had observed at the table that evening. As he lay in his bed, he recalled the moment he first set eyes on his beloved son. His pastor had introduced him—without exchanging names—to a young woman who had given birth out of wedlock, and as much as she wished to raise her son, she knew she could not, her parents would not allow it. He thought again about the sorrowful young woman with tears falling from her eyes as she placed her son in his arms. The last words she spoke to him were that he raise her son with love and in the faith from which she had temporarily strayed. For years, he had not been able to call to mind her face; however, just now—to his great surprise—he distinctly remembered. *How much she looked like our Sarah with her small stature, blue eyes, and sweet face.*

Mr. Hoyt felt sorrow at knowing the young lady's son had yet to accept the God she loved, and as much as he had tried to show her son he was treasured, George never seemed to fully accept it. *If only he would understand that I could not love him more, even if he were the son we lost.* He prayed yet again George would one day come to faith.

Chapter 24

Early the next morning, Mr. Hoyt found Sarah alone in the kitchen preparing breakfast. He loved the way her face always displayed great joy at seeing him. Thinking this a good time, with the boys—their uncle along—out in the barn doing chores, and Daniel having been called out, he began with a question. Leaning his back against the counter next to Sarah, he asked, "Sarah, you appeared troubled last night during the evening meal. Is there anything you wish to talk about? You must know that you may speak to me about anything."

Looking away, she continued preparing the food as though she hadn't heard him. "I am sure the boys will be quite ready to eat when they come in. I best finish this. May I get you something whilst you wait? Some bread perhaps?"

Mr. Hoyt would not be put off. He decided to be more direct. "Sarah, it is quite apparent that something is troubling you."

She could not fool Mr. Hoyt, who seemed to read her as easily as her father always had. "It's nothing, only a bit of trouble sleeping."

"Is there any particular reason you are unable to rest?"

"I believe it may be the heat. It has been rather

warm lately."

"Spring has scarcely begun. I have yet to see a day one would describe as warm. Are you certain it is heat that has been stealing your sleep?"

Sarah was ready for this conversation to end. "Mr. Hoyt, you needn't worry about me. As you see, I am in good health."

Seeing that he was not getting anywhere, the older man said, "Very well, Sarah, but you know you are welcome to come to me with any problem."

Nodding, she continued on with her work, never looking in his direction for fear he would discover that she had been untruthful.

Late in the afternoon, when Daniel was away and the boys had gone on a walk with their grandfather, Sarah, to her dismay, found herself alone in the house with George. How she had let that happen, she could not say. While kicking herself for not going with her husband, she tried her best to avoid eye contact with the hateful man.

George watched with delight as Sarah did her best to avoid him. While following her from room to room and taunting her at every opportunity, he observed her hands shaking with each task. Thinking this may be his only chance to continue on with his plan for chasing her from the home, he did not waste a moment.

"In watching you and Father, as it is with everyone else, I see that you have him under your spell."

While silently praying the boys and their

grandfather would soon return, she endeavored to ignore the spiteful words that were being spewed at her.

"Did you not hear me? Even if no one else in my family understands the kind of woman you are, I, for one, certainly grasp your true nature."

Mr. Hoyt and the boys returned to find that Sarah had laid out food for them before going to take a rest. The older man grew suspicious as to the reason Sarah had made herself scarce. If he had to guess, his son probably had something to do with it, for Sarah rarely rested in the middle of the day.

Hoping to see Sarah later that evening to ascertain what had gone on while she was alone in the house with his son, from his chair in the parlor, Mr. Hoyt kept glancing toward the doorway. When it was nearly time to turn in, his son-in-law returned from tending a broken ankle. The older man quickly informed Daniel that Sarah had been in her room since mid-afternoon.

Daniel was as surprised as his father-in-law by this. He decided to go straight to his room. As he entered, he noticed right away that Sarah seemed hesitant to look in his direction.

Sarah wished she could have fallen asleep before Daniel returned home, but that was not to be. The only thing she knew to do was keep her eyes focused on the mending she had in her lap as she reclined on the bed.

"Sarah, Joseph said that you have been in here for a good part of the day. Are you unwell?"

Remaining attentive to her task, she replied, "No, I simply had some mending that needed doing."

Daniel knew right away that what she had said was merely an excuse. He continued to wonder why she felt the need to close herself up in their room. Since he had already eaten while at his last stop, he readied himself for bed and then climbed in next to Sarah. She was a bit startled by his presence in the bed, for he had always slept on the daybed when she was in the room. While trying to appear calm, she set aside the mending and then rested her head against the pillow, facing away from her husband.

To gain her attention, Daniel placed his hand on his wife's shoulder and turned her toward him. "Sarah, you always do the mending in the parlor where you can take part in the conversation. Tell me, what is going on?"

Sarah had to think quickly so as not to be found out with regard to George and his treatment of her. "I...ah...you see...Father, yes, Father has been on my mind a good deal today, and...well...thinking of him made me a little melancholy." She hoped her answer would satisfy Daniel and the questioning would cease. She hated lying, but she knew no other way to keep the situation with George a secret.

As his wife had hoped, Daniel felt satisfied with her answer. He knew how much her father had meant to her. Wanting to bring her comfort, he slid his arm under her and drew her near.

While swathed in Daniel's arms, Sarah's resistance

to her own sentiments toward him weakened. As upset as she had been by George, feeling Daniel's reassuring embrace was just what she had needed.

Daniel had also had an emotional day. The child he had tended was the older sibling to an infant he had been unable to save the year before. In thinking of the infant that had died, he was reminded of Joanna and his own child. Thoughts of them then plagued him for much of the day; for that reason, holding Sarah resulted in soothing the torturous thoughts away.

When morning came, the couple had moved beyond mere friendship. Neither one had anticipated that the comfort they were receiving from each other would move them to consummate their marriage, and although there was nothing wrong with this, they had established before they wed that this would never happen.

◊◊◊

When the sun crept between Sarah's partially opened eyelids the next morning, she was startled to find Daniel's face, eyes closed, only inches from hers. As she stared at him, memories of the night before came flooding in like a storm. How would she be able to keep her feelings for him under control now? Nothing had changed with George and his intentions for sending her away, so before Daniel awakened, she thought it best to quickly dress and be gone from his bedchamber. While she finished readying herself, she felt desperate to go back to the way things had always been with Daniel. Even after the previous night, their marriage could never be anything more than a convenient arrangement. Truth be told, she now believed even that was too much to ask.

As Sarah was hurriedly finishing up with combing her hair, she heard Daniel stir. Darting from the room, she all but lost her footing. George happened to be passing by and caught her by the arm just before she hit the floor. Glancing up, she saw an agitated face glaring down at her. When she had gained her balance, he let go of his grasp and continued on his way.

As she made her way to the kitchen, she tried to force thoughts of Daniel and what had happened out of her head. Seeing George, as well as the guilt she was presently feeling, was little help in this endeavor. While preparing food for everyone, her heart felt heavy, for she knew the time had come for her to go. She began to form a plan for how she could take leave of Boston without having to reveal the truth, which was that she would not be returning.

In Daniel's bedchamber, he was just beginning to open his eyes. With his head still resting against the pillow, he thought about Sarah and what had taken place between them. He also remembered his promise to her that this sort of thing would never happen. He hoped last night meant that she was open to altering their agreement, for he now realized that though he had tried to fight it, for some time now he had not been thinking of her as only a friend.

Chapter 25

When Daniel came into the kitchen, he spotted Sarah chatting with the boys. Quietly leaning against the wall, he observed his wife and sons without causing a distraction. As he listened, he thought he detected a tremor in Sarah's voice. Without making a sound, he continued to listen.

Mr. Hoyt soon entered, humming a happy tune. Knowing Daniel and Sarah were sharing a bedchamber pleased him. He was aware, of course, that it was probably to show a united front for his son, but it still brought him joy to think Sarah felt comfortable enough to stay in with Daniel.

As with the other three in the room, no one seemed to notice Daniel's presence. After the boys had made their way over to the table, Sarah spoke in low tones to Mr. Hoyt, requesting to come along with him when he returned to Amesbury. She explained that she had yet to gather up her most precious belongings and that Mr. Swyndhurst had recently sent word of his intentions for returning to England. Without disclosing that he had also informed it would be several months before his journey would take place, she insisted that she had every desire to see him before he took leave of Amesbury.

Mr. Hoyt assured her that he welcomed her company on the trip.

Daniel's eyes grew wide at this new information. Sarah had not said a word about going to Amesbury. His heart sank at the thought that her decision may have had something to do with the previous night, and if it did, would she even return? He would never stop her from going, but he planned to take the situation to the Lord in prayer.

Sarah's heart felt as if it would fly out of her chest when she suddenly noticed Daniel. She wondered how much he had heard. With her eyes fixed upon him, she was once again overwhelmed by guilt. *How could I have done that to Joanna? Moreover, how will I ever tell Daniel and the boys I am leaving them, never to return?*

While continuing to make eye contact with Daniel, she noticed he was coming toward her. He suddenly had hold of her hand. He then led her from the room in the direction of his bedchamber. Once they had entered, he closed the door behind them.

Keeping her eyes lowered, Sarah's face began to heat. Daniel gently lifted her chin. He wanted to see her face as he questioned her about her reasons for going to Amesbury with his father-in-law.

Knowing she had to hide the truth that she would be staying in Amesbury, not to mention her embarrassment over what had occurred the night before, Sarah could not make herself look Daniel in the eye. "Well, as I was saying in the kitchen, I have not been back to Amesbury to collect my things. And there is Mr. Swyndhurst to consider. He shall be leaving for England very soon. And with no one there to oversee things, the servants will be at a loss as to what to do. I shall have to instruct them. And as you heard, Mr. Hoyt has no objection to the idea." She wrung her hands as she prattled on.

Daniel did not believe a word of it, but how could he call her on her lies when he himself had been untruthful in convincing her to marry him, assuring her at the time that he would never amend their agreement? In thinking about her sudden decision as well as her nervous demeanor, he was quite certain she meant to remain in Amesbury.

Sarah was relieved when Daniel appeared to have accepted everything she had said without question. When she dared a look up at him, she thought she detected an element of sadness in his eyes, or was it relief? She could not be sure, for his countenance did not fully betray his emotions.

Daniel patted Sarah's shoulder and then headed for the door. "Everyone is waiting for us. We best get back."

It was settled. She would be leaving. As Sarah slowly walked back to the kitchen, she felt tears threatening. She hoped when she saw the boys, the floodgates would hold.

George had joined his nephews and father at the table shortly before Sarah and Daniel returned. As he looked at his brother-in-law, he wondered what was wrong, for it was very apparent that something was. He then studied Sarah to see if he could discover if that something had anything to do with her. Unbeknownst to him, however, his questions were about to be answered.

With a sigh, Daniel stated that Sarah would be making the trip to Amesbury with Joseph. He went on to explain Sarah's reasons for going.

George could scarcely hold back a grin at the thought that Sarah would finally be leaving. And to look at her, he suspected she would not be coming back. He had won, or at least that was his hope.

Mr. Hoyt had a niggling feeling about the whole thing but decided to keep his thoughts to himself. The boys, on the other hand, both said they wanted to go as well—to which their father gave an emphatic no.

For the remainder of the day, Sarah wondered how she could manage being alone with Daniel when it came time to turn in for the night. Daniel, having similar thoughts, waited until he thought she would be asleep before going to bed. Without saying a word as he entered the room, he went directly to the daybed and sat down.

Sarah surreptitiously peered out from under the blanket she had tucked up almost to the top of her head so as to avoid eye contact with Daniel when he came to bed. She watched as he sat there on the edge of the daybed. She then heard him sigh. Though her heart felt as if it would break, she knew leaving was the right thing to do. Not only would it solve the problem of the progression in their relationship, it would also make way for George to continue coming for visits. He had promised to stay away if she remained. For everyone's sake, she felt it was best that she leave this family to themselves.

Chapter 26

Over the next few days, Sarah spent nearly every waking moment with Joseph and Dan. As these were the last moments she would ever have with them, being with them as much as possible was all she could think about. The togetherness, however, was a bit of a double edged sword, since the joy it brought was accompanied by profound pain.

Daniel made himself scarce over the days leading up to Sarah's departure. It was his wish to pretend everything would be all right, but whenever he saw Sarah, he knew he was probably fooling himself. He had seen this before. It was in her nature to flee from problems, and this time he had been the one to push her to it. He could only hope it was temporary and she would return, as she had said. But if she remained in Amesbury, he would have to learn to accept it. Presently, his heart was not at all prepared for that.

◊◊◊

It had been a few days since anything had been mentioned about Sarah leaving, so George took the first opportunity at finding Sarah alone to be certain she hadn't changed her mind. With his father and nephews in town and Daniel off doctoring someone, he knew he could say what he wished and no one would be the wiser. Without being purposeful in his quiet approach, George was stunned by Sarah's reaction when he spoke her name. She had all but jumped into the stream at the sound of his voice. He chuckled at the sight until he saw what could only be described as terror on the little woman's face a moment before she went limp and fell to the ground.

Sarah felt her knees go weak and then everything went black. The next thing she saw was George's silhouette against a blue sky. She blinked a few times while struggling to figure out what had happened. As she lay there, she remembered hearing George calling her name. It had sounded so much like Matthew Raymond's voice—not to mention this was just a few yards from where Mr. Raymond had captured her for the second time—she had immediately gone into a panic. That was the last thing she could remember before being confronted by yet another terrible man who was presently angling his head down to look at her.

Staring down at the tiny woman, George inquired, "What is the matter with you? Are you that frightened of me?" Part of him hoped she was, while his better nature felt a little ashamed.

Sarah struggled to stand without assistance, rather than take George's out stretched hand. "I am not the least bit frightened of you!" she responded forcefully. Though not exactly true, it wasn't the reason she had fainted. Sure he was vile and ill mannered, but she believed him better than to force his attentions upon anyone.

George watched as Sarah, still a little unsteady, shuffled by him. He decided not to press the issue of her leaving, but just as he had resolved to let her off easy this time, he heard her call back over her shoulder that he needn't worry, she would soon be gone. Even though he felt a pang of guilt over having caused her to faint, he couldn't help but be delighted that she still planned to leave.

Daniel came home late that evening after everyone had gone to bed. He had purposefully taken longer than necessary, hoping not to arrive home until Sarah was fast asleep. Though he wanted to discuss the matter of her going to Amesbury, he couldn't quite bring himself to do it for fear that Sarah would confirm what he suspected—she would not be coming back.

Sarah heard Daniel as he entered the room. Though she longed to hear his voice, she kept silent so as not to inadvertently say something that would give her plan away. Additionally, she was worried that having a conversation may test her resolve to leave.

Daniel knelt beside the daybed and silently prayed about his marriage. Then he quietly climbed into bed. When morning came, he was still awake. How could he allow Sarah to simply slip away from him? He had mulled over the situation throughout what seemed, to him, to be an exceedingly long night. In the end, he had decided to hope and pray for the best. She hadn't said she was leaving for good, he kept reminding himself.

Daniel closed his eyes when he heard Sarah stir. He then waited until she had left the room before rising to dress. While the family ate together a short time later, with his stomach in knots, he listened as his father-in-law and Sarah discussed their upcoming trip. Even though he hadn't been called out to tend to anyone as yet, he decided he would make a trip to town.

Upon Daniel's arrival in town, he spotted his friend Simon Findley. As they talked, Simon mentioned that he would be going to Amesbury in a few days. On occasion, to earn a little extra income, his friend had conducted individuals or even entire families to towns not more than two to three days' journey. Daniel then informed him of his father-in-law and Sarah's upcoming travel plans, to which Simon suggested he and his traveling companions go along with them. Daniel stated that he was pleased at the idea, for it was always safer to travel in a large company.

"Very good, Daniel. I shall call a little later at your home to go over the particulars with Sarah and Mr. Hoyt."

"I am much obliged to you, Simon. Knowing they shall travel with you settles my mind immensely."

The two men then parted company. As he had said he would, Simon arrived at the Thompson home late in the afternoon. Daniel had only been home for an hour or so. He ushered his friend into the parlor. Everyone in the room listened as Mr. Findley suggested he go along with Sarah and Mr. Hoyt to Amesbury. The boys begged to go but to no benefit; their father had not changed his mind.

George little cared how Sarah went, or with whom. He just wanted her gone. This time, when he took his leave a few days hence, he could do it without a care, for his sister's home would finally be safe from this female intruder.

Not once during the conversation did Daniel's wife look in his direction, which heightened the sinking feeling he had already been experiencing.

Once everything was settled, Simon took his leave, promising to return early the morning they were to set off.

Sarah bustled about, keeping busy right up until the day of her departure. When it was time to go, Simon and Daniel loaded up Mr. Hoyt's wagon with supplies while Sarah gathered up the few belongings she planned to take along. Rather than bring everything, she took only what was necessary so as not to draw attention to the fact that this was to be her final day in Boston. The boys helped her carry her things out to the wagon. Fighting back tears, she hugged Dan and Joseph before turning to Daniel.

Daniel looked down at Sarah as she approached. Without saying a word, he pulled her into a long embrace. Before letting her go he whispered, "You come back to me, you hear?" He knew he shouldn't burden her with his request, but he couldn't help himself.

Sarah's eyes grew wide at the knowledge that he suspected her. Pretending that she hadn't heard him, she slowly pulled away and hurriedly went to the wagon. Simon lifted her up beside Mr. Hoyt, who was already settled on the bench. He then climbed on his own wagon and they were off.

On their way out of town they would be stopping off to collect the family that would be traveling with them to Amesbury. Daniel, with tears in his eyes, waved them on. As for Sarah, it was taking every bit of strength she had for her not to cry; consequently, she couldn't make herself look back at the family of which she had temporarily been a part.

Chapter 27

As Mr. Hoyt observed Sarah fidgeting on the bench beside him, he recalled another time they had traveled together not many years earlier. At that time, the poor young woman was fleeing town after having been harmed in the vilest of ways. Although these were different circumstances, the older man—wondering if she had in mind to run away again—still felt uneasy about having her along. Just to look at her, he knew something was amiss.

Sarah passed the time with light conversation as they rode along. Besides Mr. Hoyt, there was Mr. Findley to consider. Either man might guess her true intentions for making the trip if she was not extremely careful. If that happened she would be pressured to explain herself, which she could not do.

Simon glanced back at Sarah and Mr. Hoyt many times the first day of the journey wanting to be certain they had not fallen behind. He was also thinking about Sarah. Knowing George had returned made him question whether the ill-mannered man had been bothering her again. This line of thought caused him to grow angry at himself for keeping silent.

That evening everyone stiffly alighted from the wagons and settled in for the night at the home of an acquaintance of Simon's, one he had often stopped off to see when traveling. The home was spacious enough to accommodate the lot of them.

In order to prevent an inquisition, Sarah avoided Simon as much as possible, biding her time until they were again in separate wagons, where there would be no opportunity for conversation. Every time she was nearly cornered, she found a way to elude him.

When morning came, Simon awoke to find everyone up and prepared to set off. He grabbed a couple of pieces of bread and some water before following the group out to the wagons. Looking over at Sarah, he decided that during the trip, with strangers about was probably not the best time to question her about George.

Simon Findley traveled along the road from Boston to Amesbury rather slowly, as was his habit; thus they reached their first destination on day three. Upon their arrival, Mr. Hoyt assisted Sarah in climbing down from the wagon while Simon collected her belongings from the back and then made his way to the house, taking in his surroundings as he went. He had no idea that Sarah had been living at such a large estate before moving to Boston.

Sarah led Simon and Mr. Hoyt into the house. Before she could call out to the occupants of the home, someone had wrapped their arms around her from behind. Glancing back over her shoulder, she saw her beloved friend, Martha Fowler. Sarah quickly whirled around to hug her. By now, everyone in the house, including Mr. Swyndhurst, had come to find out what all the noise was about.

Once Sarah Thompson had made the introductions, Simon explained that he needed to take his leave for now. He had yet to convey the family that had come along with them to their destination. "Sarah, I shall be staying on in Amesbury for a few days. If it is satisfactory, I'll call again before leaving town."

Sarah reluctantly agreed. *I shall keep Esther by my side to ward off a private conversation when he returns.*

Since Mr. Hoyt was more than ready to rest his weary body, he said much the same about returning another day and soon took his leave as well.

Once the other travelers had gone, Martha and Esther began questioning Sarah about why she had not sent word of her coming. In a scolding tone, Mr. Swyndhurst instructed them to allow Sarah to settle in for a few days before bombarding her with questions. He then took Sarah by the arm and led her to the parlor, while Peter, one of the servants, carried her belongings up to her bedchamber.

Mr. Swyndhurst sensed right away that something was wrong. Having no desire to press her, especially since he had just chastised the servants for doing much the same, he simply sat there with his arm around her.

Sarah leaned into his embrace. Her first husband's father had always made her feel cared for and safe, just as his son had. Being back in this home, sitting here with her father-in-law caused her emotions to rise to the surface. Unexpectedly, tears came trickling down her cheeks.

Still, Mr. Swyndhurst remained silent. *Tomorrow,* he thought, *she will tell me what is troubling her tomorrow.*

As Sarah lay in her bed the next morning, a bed she had not been in for some time, she studied the room. Though much had changed in her life, the room had remained virtually the same as when she had first arrived at Alexander Swyndhurst's estate some five years earlier. There were still fluffy, lace covered pillows on the bed, the same soft, blue quilt, a small settee by the window facing the front yard, and an alcove containing a maple-wood washstand, as well as a low to the ground wooden cabinet with the concealed chamber pot within.

Sarah turned over on her stomach and as was her habit when staying in this room, began tracing the rose-petal carvings on the oak bedstead with her finger. As she thought about her life, she realized yet again that nothing other than God was certain. *When you least expect it, change inevitably comes,* she thought. Exhausted from all that had happened, Sarah fell back to sleep.

When she awoke a little later, she found her maid-friend, Esther, hovering over her with a smile that stretched almost to the width of her face. Seeing this caused Sarah to chuckle.

Esther plopped down on the bed next to her friend. "I have missed you so," she said, a little tearful. Paying no heed to Mr. Swyndhurst's admonishment to wait before questioning Sarah, she asked, "How long can you stay? No, no, don't tell me. Knowing will only make me fret rather than enjoy the time we have."

Sarah was glad Esther had not pushed for an answer. She had no desire to give an account of what had happened that led to her decision to come.

Esther helped Sarah ready herself for the day. Martha was not to be excluded from this happy occasion; consequently, there soon came a knock at Sarah's bedchamber door. Letting herself in before anyone had answered, the older woman entered carrying a tray of food.

Sarah grinned at the sight. Martha would, of course, wish to prepare food for her. She expected no less from her faithful friend. "Martha, I have missed you so."

Setting the tray aside, Martha responded, "Not more than I. Even as I look at you, I cannot believe you are actually here." Sitting herself down on the edge of Sarah's bed, she watched as Esther pinned Sarah's hair.

Sarah smiled at her two friends. *It shall be as though I never left. Now to keep myself busy so as not to think of Daniel and the boys.*

Esther and Martha saw Sarah's countenance change to one of sadness, if only for a moment. They knew their mistress well enough to comprehend the instant she had schooled her face to appear happy once again. While glancing at each other, the younger woman gave a little tilt of the head to the older, who then returned the gesture.

Sarah, none the wiser, stood to her feet and said, "Let us go down to the kitchen." Gathering up her tray, she made her way from the room, then down the stairs, with Martha and Esther close behind.

Martha and Esther, already having had their breakfast, joined Sarah at the table. When the ladies had all taken a seat, Mr. Swyndhurst entered. "If there is no objection, I should like to join you."

"But of course," responded Sarah, who was delighted to be surrounded by familiar faces, faces she had dearly missed. The conversation was kept to trivial matters. For this, Sarah was most grateful. But later that evening, when she and her elderly friend were alone, Martha urged her to explain what was going on.

"Martha, I never should have agreed to marry Daniel. All I shall say for now is I shan't be returning to Boston."

Having knowledge of the marriage between Sarah and Mr. Thompson for some time now—as she had attended church with the Thompson boys when they wintered with their grandfather in Amesbury—with eyes wide, Martha gasped. "Sarah, you are married to him now. You cannot abandon him. And what of the children? Have you not a care as to how they shall feel about this?" She had greatly missed Sarah and would love to have her stay, but she knew this was wrong.

With her hand pressed against her forehead, Sarah responded, "I know, but you do not understand the situation in which I found myself. There are things I cannot divulge to you. And Daniel is quite capable of looking after the boys."

Martha could see that Sarah was upset. "Will you not tell me what happened to cause you to leave?"

"No, Martha, I cannot. Please, trust that I know what I am doing."

Mr. Swyndhurst overheard part of the conversation. Even though he was in England the last time Sarah had left home, precisely as Mr. Hoyt had thought, this all seemed a little too familiar to him. When she had run away before, he had left his home in England and had come to Amesbury to be with his son.

Calling to mind something Sarah's father had shared in confidence about his wife having had a son before their marriage and his wish that he could have located him, Mr. Swyndhurst now found himself wishing the same. He then remembered the wooden box Sarah's father had left in his care—stating that, amongst other things, it contained a journal his wife had written. The journal held the entire narrative wherein the woman had been forced to give her son away. Mr. Goodwin had also shared with him that he had always wondered if he should have told Sarah about her brother—adding that there may come a time, after his passing, when his daughter should be told.

I wonder if the time has come to hand the box over to Sarah, not that she would be able to do what her father never could, that is, to find her brother. If I could but locate the young man myself before I leave for England.

Lacking any helpful information with which to

begin a search—since there had been no exchange of names between his friend and the young woman—per her parents' orders—Mr. Swyndhurst shifted his thoughts in another direction. *Should I go to Boston to speak with Sarah's husband? he silently questioned*

The thought of leaving Sarah devoid of a man's protection, be it husband or brother, disturbed Mr. Swyndhurst a great deal.

Chapter 28

Sarah had been gone for eight weeks. Before she left, Daniel had been concerned she might be fleeing to Amesbury rather than going for a simple visit and to collect more of her things, as she had said. He was beginning to think he had been correct as to her intentions of never returning. Unlike Alexander, however, he would not be going after her, for he believed he was to blame for her feeling the need to go. He should never have allowed what had happened between them, not after making promises to the contrary.

Dan and Joseph had asked their father over and over when Sarah would be coming home. As much as it pained him not to run after her, if only for his boys, he knew he could not. They would all have to learn to get along without her. Still, he was hesitant to inform his sons that Sarah most likely would not be returning. Even with the certainty of the situation growing with each day Sarah stayed away, he kept telling himself there was hope yet.

One morning as Daniel was fixing breakfast, Mrs. Findley knocked at the door. After ushering her in, he led her over to the table and placed a cup of tea in front of her. While he carried the food he had just finished preparing to the table, the neighbor inquired as to how his wife was faring. Unbeknownst to him, since the kind neighbor had not seen Sarah in quite some time, she wanted to see for herself that all was well. He bristled at the thought of exposing the truth that his marriage was probably over; not in the formal sense, but for practical purposes it was.

"Well, as you may know, Sarah joined the boys' grandfather on his trip to Amesbury. She had not been to her old home in quite some time, so she felt the need to go."

"Indeed, that was several weeks ago, was it not?" Mrs. Findley disliked prying, but she had to know. Similar to her son, she had been having regrets about not telling Mr. Thompson about his brother-in-law's cruelty toward his wife.

"I was, in fact, not expecting her to make a hasty visit." He was feeling a little put out with Mrs. Findley's questions. He had never taken her for a busybody.

Sensing Mr. Thompson's irritation with her, Mrs. Findley left off with the inquiries about Sarah. Moreover, she wasn't prepared as yet to break Sarah's confidence regarding George.

Dan and Joseph came into the kitchen about this time. They were pleased to see Mrs. Findley. After listening as their kindhearted neighbor offered her assistance to their father for while Sarah was away, the boys both wondered, yet again, when Sarah would return.

Daniel calmed upon hearing the neighbor's generous offer. As he thought about it, she had always been a great help to his family. He began to feel a little ashamed of his indignation over her questions. "That is good of you, Mrs. Findley. I am much obliged to you for continuously looking after my family."

Having no desire to become a bothersome neighbor by staying too long, Mrs. Findley smiled and rose from her chair to go. "Well, I shall be going now."

Dan escorted the neighbor out to the yard and waved her on her way. When he returned, he inquired again about Sarah and when his father expected her home. Having Mrs. Findley offer to come to their house had given him pause.

Daniel's steadfast attitude not to go after Sarah diminished a little upon hearing the desperate tone in his son's voice. Having no wish to discuss the matter again, he said, "Boys, it is time to do your chores."

Both boys nodded and took the last couple of bites of their food before heading out to get started. Once they were alone in the barn, they talked of Sarah, wondering what was keeping her so long in Amesbury and why their father had not answered their questions. When she left, they were under the impression that she would be gone no more than a couple of weeks—just long enough to allow for travel as well as a couple of days at her house in Amesbury before returning.

While Daniel straightened up the kitchen, he prayed once more for God's will with regard to his marriage. He thought again of Alexander and how his heart must have broken over Sarah's disappearance. At least this time her location was known, for all the good it was doing him.

◊◊◊

When Daniel and his sons arrived at the meetinghouse on the next Lord's Day, unaccompanied by Sarah yet again, many eyes were on them. It had been a little over two months since anyone in Boston had seen the new Mrs. Thompson. Daniel wondered if he was only being sensitive, or were people actually whispering about them.

When they were seated, with some difficulty, Daniel tried to focus on the message. When the service finally ended, his friend, Simon Findley, approached. Daniel noticed that he seemed to be looking for someone. Sighing, he prepared himself for the usual questions about his wife.

"Daniel, is Sarah unwell? Do not tell me she is yet in Amesbury." Simon, with little time for visiting, had not been to see Daniel, nor his mother, since his return from Amesbury. Having been to call on Sarah before returning to Boston, he had been satisfied she was truly there to gather up more of her belongings, as well as to have a short visit. They had even talked of George, and she had reassured him that George's annoyance at her presence in his sister's home had somewhat subsided.

"She has not as yet returned, but I expect her home any day now." Feeling bad about perhaps misleading his friend, Daniel quickly ended the conversation with the excuse that he had a patient to see on his way home, which in fact he did. As they walked toward the door, the concerned husband eased his mind with the thought that he may not have spoken falsely to his friend, for who could know; Sarah may yet return.

After walking the Thompsons out, Simon patted his friend on the shoulder and promised to visit him later in the week. As he watched them set off down the road, he wished that his next scheduled visit to Amesbury wasn't so long away—that is, unless someone else hired him in the meantime. He needed to speak with Sarah about her prolonged stay in Amesbury. If George Hoyt had anything to do with it, he had every intention of telling Daniel about his brother-in-law's contemptible behavior toward Sarah.

Chapter 29

Sarah lay there, unable to make herself move. She had been feeling exhausted for weeks, and her desire for food was almost nonexistent. Truth be told, lately she found the smell of certain foods odious. She wondered if it was merely the turmoil going on within her over having left Daniel and the boys, with no plans of ever returning.

Martha knocked on the door moments after Sarah had decided to sit up with the intention of forcing herself out of her oh so comfortable bed.

Sarah smiled in her servant-friend's direction as she made her way into the room. As weak in body and spirit as Sarah was feeling at that moment, seeing Martha somehow gave her strength. "Good morning, Martha."

Martha noticed right away that Sarah appeared as though she lacked the strength to even climb out of her bed. "Sarah, are you unwell?"

Sarah disliked causing Martha any concern thus she responded, "No need to worry, Martha. I shall be just fine once I haul this slothful body out of bed."

Martha had yet to ask any questions of Sarah pertaining to her time in Boston. If she could ask but one it would be about the sort of relationship her mistress and Mr. Thompson shared. She had worked for Sarah's first husband, Alexander, long before he married Sarah. It had taken two years for Sarah and Alexander to live under the same roof. In this marriage with her young friend and Dr. Thompson, Martha had not been present to witness how the couple interacted, and the longer her mistress stayed on, the more she wished she knew more about Dr. Daniel Thompson.

Later, after breakfasting together with Mr. Swyndhurst, feeling ill Sarah had returned to her bed. Her maid, Esther, had been in to see that she was all right several times throughout the day, each time offering Sarah something to eat.

By late afternoon, Sarah felt she could attempt taking in a bit of food. After making her way to the kitchen, as she had expected, she found Martha. Her elderly friend was more than happy to prepare something for her. She had in fact already made Sarah's favorite sweet bread with the hope that it might entice her.

While her mistress ate a small portion of the sweet bread she had set before her, Martha could not help but stare. She had been around more than one expectant mother in her day. If she had to guess what was wrong with Sarah, she felt certain it was that there was likely a baby on the way. She then recalled something she had heard some time back about Sarah's chances of having another child following her injuries from tumbling out of a wagon and giving birth prematurely. *No, barring a miracle, I suppose it could not be that she is with child.*

Sarah caught a glimpse of the questioning expression upon Martha's face. "Martha, you seem to want to ask me something. What is it?" *What am I doing? I have now left myself open.*

Shaking her head, Martha replied, "Oh, it is really nothing, nothing at all."

Sarah sighed with relief that she had escaped any probing questions; but in thinking about it, she realized it wasn't like Martha to keep silent. Before her friend changed her mind and began asking questions, Sarah quickly ate a few more bites of bread and then excused herself.

As she rose from the table, she noticed that the little she had eaten was already causing her stomach to feel as if it were warring against her.

While making her way to the parlor—unaware that Martha had been having similar thoughts—she recalled the last time she had felt this way and shook her head. *It could not be. We have only been together once, and Daniel told me when I was injured that it was very unlikely.* After reassuring herself that what she had thought couldn't possibly be, she calmed a little. Thinking about the intimate time she had shared with Daniel made her feel ashamed all over again. Though she was no longer amongst the living, to Sarah, Joanna was still Daniel's wife.

Mr. Swyndhurst looked up from his book when Sarah came into the room. Rising from his chair, he said with a smile, "Well, it is good to see you up and about." He had stepped out for a short walk and had not seen her come down from her room. Still standing, he waved her over to him.

Having this man whom she dearly loved continue to care about her, even though his son was gone, warmed her heart. She stepped into his open arms and stood there for a moment. Her life was so uncertain at this time, his embrace somehow made her feel as if everything was going to be all right.

The following day Mr. Hoyt came to call. He had been there a time or two since Sarah's arrival a few weeks before. Like his son-in-law, he was beginning to believe the young woman intended to stay on indefinitely. He was not exactly sure when it would happen, but he planned to speak to Sarah about her reasons for having left Boston. He also wondered why Daniel had not come for her. With all of this on his mind, with a heavy heart, he followed after Martha to the parlor to see Sarah.

Though Sarah was delighted to see him, she knew the visit might be awkward considering the fact that it was now three months since she had taken leave of Boston. She had avoided the question up to now, but this time she felt certain Mr. Hoyt would ask why she was yet in Amesbury.

"Mr. Hoyt, I am so glad you have come," she said as she stood up from her chair to properly greet him. After embracing each other, Sarah guided him over to the chair next to where she had been sitting.

Mr. Hoyt began the conversation with a question.

"Sarah, though I am happy to see you as well, I have been wondering when you plan to return to Boston."

There it was, the exact question she was hoping to avoid. She was not ready to reveal the fact that she would not be going back, so she had to think quickly. "You see...I simply have so much left to see to here that I cannot possibly make the journey at this time. And since Mr. Swyndhurst shall be setting off for England soon, I wish to stay on with him a little longer, for this may be the last time we shall ever be together."

Mr. Hoyt had been wondering if anything had occurred between Sarah and his son. He would not be at all surprised to learn that his son had upset her in some way. But as he listened, he felt certain that Sarah had only been longing to see her father-in-law and her home. Even though Daniel and his grandsons were surely missing her, she obviously needed this time in Amesbury. *They'll be fine for a little while longer*, he told himself.

Sarah was happy Mr. Hoyt had accepted her answer. They could now visit comfortably. A few hours had passed when Mr. Hoyt stood up to go. He thanked Sarah for a wonderful afternoon and offered to escort her to church on the next Lord's Day. She had in fact gone a couple of times with Mr. Swyndhurst since she had been back. Her old friend Reverend Edmund March had been delighted to see her, as were Jonathan and Hannah Bleasdell. She had yet to see her friends, Susanna and William Pressey, who had been away since her arrival. She wondered how long it would be before everyone realized she was back to stay.

Chapter 30

Midsummer, the year 1736, Amesbury, Massachusetts Bay
Colony

Sarah had successfully concealed her true reasons for
staying on in Amesbury for over three months. She had
received one missive from Daniel and the boys. As she had
expected, there were no pleas for her to come home. They
were getting on just fine without her.

Although Daniel and the boys had been on her mind
a good deal of the time, Sarah had other concerns. She had
not been feeling well most days—very similar to an earlier
time—a time when she was awaiting the birth of the child
she later lost.

Martha had instructed everyone in the house to
keep silent about the length of Sarah's stay. For whatever
reason, the young woman needed to be there, so she
determined not to press her about Daniel and his sons
again, nor would she allow anyone to make their mistress
feel uncomfortable. Martha was also growing concerned
about Sarah, for she was more certain than ever there
would be a child in a few months. Until Sarah was prepared
to discuss the matter, the head-servant was determined
not to speak about it. This stance was becoming more and

more difficult.

One morning while Esther was helping Sarah dress, she finally broke down and told her what she suspected— that she was with child.

"Are you certain?" the maid asked. Seeing Sarah nod, Esther squealed, "What happy news!" In hearing the loudness of her own voice, the maid quickly covered her mouth. Her mistress had spoken so softly she was sure this was for her ears only.

Sarah responded with less enthusiasm, "I was told this would not be possible. You mustn't say a word about this, Esther. You see, I have no plans of returning to Boston."

To Sarah's last remark, Esther gasped, recalling another time Sarah had asked her to keep such a deep secret; that time had not ended well; therefore, she had always regretted not speaking up. "But why? Was Dr. Thompson unkind to you?"

"No, it is nothing like that, Esther. Come over here next to me," she said, patting the bed. "I need to tell someone, and you and Martha are my dearest friends. I cannot tell Martha, however. You know how she worries."

Esther shook her head yes while waiting patiently for Sarah to enlighten her regarding her reasons for leaving Boston.

When Sarah had finished explaining what had happened with George Hoyt, as well as her feelings over what had occurred with Daniel, she saw tears in her friend's eyes. "What is it, Esther?"

"I had hoped you were happy in Boston, and after what you went through with Matthew Raymond, I cannot believe you have had to face yet another scoundrel. Sarah, what are you going to do if you really are carrying Dr. Thompson's child?"

"When I decided to come home to Amesbury, I had no idea of my condition. Still, in the circumstances, I might have made the same decision, had I known."

Though she thought Sarah was making a mistake in not returning to her husband, Esther said not a word to her mistress.

"In finally telling someone, it seems more real, somehow. I never thought myself capable of carrying a child, so part of me had been refusing to believe it."

Esther leaned in and hugged her friend. "Sarah, everyone here will help you. You know that."

Sarah nodded. "Remember, Esther, for now not a word to anyone. I expect that very soon everyone shall know, for it cannot be concealed for long."

Esther wished Sarah had not sworn her to secrecy about the baby. She felt Martha should be told, for she would surely know what to do. Keeping her thoughts to herself, the maid replied, "If that is your wish."

"It is."

Once Sarah's hair was pinned and she was ready to start the day, with a deep breath she led the way out of the room and down the stairs. Esther stayed with her until they arrived in the kitchen, where she left her mistress in the capable hands of the head-servant.

Martha smiled at the sight of her mistress entering the room. She could still scarcely believe Sarah was home. As she set a cup of tea on the table for her, she hoped she would at last tell her what was going on, for something surely was. The exact moment she was about to prod the younger woman a little to see if she would offer any explanation for why she had graced them with her company for so long, Mr. Swyndhurst came into the room.

"Good morning, ladies. And what a lovely day it is." Taking a seat next to Sarah, Mr. Swyndhurst continued, "What are your plans for the day, young lady?"

Sarah had not thought that far ahead. "Well, do you have any suggestions for what I might do today?"

"Now that you have asked, I plan on making a trip to the Bleasdell home. Would you like to come along with me?"

"Indeed I would. When I last saw them, they inquired as to when I might come."

Mr. Swyndhurst hoped Sarah might be more likely to talk if it were just the two of them. "Very good. We shall set off within the hour."

With their plans settled, Mr. Swyndhurst sent Peter out to hitch up the wagon.

Chapter 31

As Mr. Swyndhurst and Sarah arrived at the Bleasdell home, Jonathan came out of the barn to greet them. He was delighted to see Sarah had accompanied Mr. Swyndhurst, whom he had spoken to on the previous Lord's Day about coming for a visit.

"I hope it is all right that I have come with Father." Sarah had continued calling her former father-in-law "Father"—as it had quite become a habit when Alexander was alive.

"To be sure," replied Jonathan as he helped her down from the wagon. "Hannah shall be so pleased to see you, as am I."

Mr. Swyndhurst took Sarah's hand and slid it through the crook of his arm as they walked toward the house. The Bleasdells had an expansive farm. Their son, David, and his wife, Abigail Colby, lived on the homestead, too. David Bleasdell had set up shop on the property for making clocks and surgical instruments, as well as repairing guns. He and his father, amongst many other things, were also blacksmiths; and as if that did not keep the men busy enough, David had to be away from home from time to time as a representative to the Court, and both men were present at every town meeting—the father as moderator, and the son as one of the selectmen.

Hannah opened the door to the house to find Sarah and Mr. Swyndhurst approaching. She quickly led them in and gave them each a hug. Jonathan and Hannah's young daughter, Elizabeth, greeted them as well. Sarah was surprised to find her at home since, in the past when she had come, the youngster was frequently off at one of her older siblings' homes. Her parents indulged her in this because they hoped all of their children would have a strong connection with each other.

When an hour had passed, Hannah quietly whisked Sarah from the room, hoping to learn what was troubling her, for she knew Sarah well enough to sense when something was wrong.

As the ladies entered Hannah's bedchamber, Sarah felt ill at ease. Hannah was certain to ask difficult questions that she would not be able to skirt around as easily as she had with everyone else. Hannah was much too clever for that.

Making themselves comfortable on the settee that was situated on the farthest wall from the door, Hannah took hold of Sarah's hand. "Sarah, what is troubling you?"

Sarah lowered her eyes. "Not a thing, Hannah."

"We are friends, are we not?"

The younger woman knew where that question was leading. "Yes, of course, Hannah."

"As your friend, I am here to help."

Sarah studied Hannah for a moment. Knowing all

her friend had suffered, she hated to trouble her, and said as much.

"You have never been, nor shall you ever be a burden. Now tell me what is going on."

Sarah decided to include Hannah in her secret, which of course would be known by everyone soon enough. Over the next few minutes, the younger woman told the older everything, including her plans for remaining in Amesbury.

Hannah was left speechless. When words finally came, she offered a suggestion. "Sarah, at this point, I shall not try to talk you out of what you have made up your mind to do. If you are certain this is your wish—remaining in Amesbury—why not stay here until the baby arrives? With the townsfolk believing you had returned to Boston, you would be left to yourself."

Sarah had already decided she would not be leaving her home even to attend church when it became obvious she was with child. Staying with Jonathan and Hannah would end the questioning that was sure to continue at her home. As Hannah had suggested, everyone would believe she had returned to Boston. But what would she do after the baby was born, she wondered? She could not hide out forever.

Hannah sensed Sarah's hesitancy. "I know this will not solve everything. If you plan to stay in Amesbury with the baby, people will eventually know; however, you will have several months of calm before having to face everyone. And if you find that coming here won't suit your needs, I could send word to a cousin of mine in Ipswich. I am certain she would be delighted to have you."

The more Sarah thought about getting away, either to Hannah's or the cousin's, the more the idea appealed to her. "Since I cannot disclose my reasons for leaving Boston, I have been uncertain as to how to explain things to everyone. As you say, being away may be more tolerable."

Hannah smiled, knowing she had been some help to her troubled friend.

When Sarah recalled the difficulties Hannah had been through—with her grandmother having been accused as a witch and put to death, and on top of that losing a child—she looked over at her friend. "Hannah, I really should not be bothering you with my predicament, you have been through so many trying times of your own."

"Sarah, we each have our own troubles to bear, yours are no less burdensome for you. Thankfully, no matter how big the problem, God is bigger yet."

Knowing this to be true, Sarah nodded.

Chapter 32

Joanna's brother arrived at the Thompson home early one morning. Daniel welcomed him—oblivious to the part the man had played in Sarah's decision to leave. Also always joyous at seeing their uncle, Dan and Joseph both came running at the sound of his voice.

As Dan and Joseph gathered up their uncle's belongings, they asked their father to which room they should convey his things. Sarah had taken most of her belongings with her, so the bedchamber she had occupied was virtually empty, other than the furniture.

"Boys, take his things to Sar...that is to say, the room with the window that overlooks the backyard." *Sarah's bedchamber is a little larger than the guest bedchamber. There is no reason he cannot stay in there. It is not as if she shall be returning any time soon,* he thought.

Unbeknownst to Daniel, George fully comprehended what it meant for his brother-in-law to allow him use of that specific bedchamber. With that knowledge, a deep satisfaction settled over the pitiless man.

Later, while the family was at the table, the boys expressed their concerns about Sarah and her delayed return to their uncle. As he listened, he felt a little uncomfortable, for it seemed his nephews were quite unsettled by her absence.

Daniel attempted to change the subject a few times, for this topic caused him even more discomfort than it did his brother-in-law. Not wanting to silence his boys on the subject of Sarah, however, he allowed the conversation to continually drift back to his wife's absence.

◊◊◊

Over the next few days, George heard more and more about Sarah from his nephews, including the close relationship between their mother and the new Mrs. Thompson. They also shared that her husband, Alexander, had been killed right in front of her when he was run over by a wagon. All he had known of the tiny woman that had caused him so much grief was that she had barged her way into his sister's family. The last thing he wanted to feel for her was pity, which might easily turn to guilt over how he had treated her.

Daniel listened intently to his sons' discussion with his brother-in-law; after which, his heart grew even heavier at the remembrance of what Sarah had been through. He hoped the boys would not mention her capture and subsequent loss of her child, for he couldn't bear to hear any more about Sarah's darkest days, not with the guilt he was presently feeling over adding to her burdens.

When George set off for home at the end of the week, the glee he had felt over Sarah's absence from the Thompson home had diminished, for he had not been able to stop thinking about all Dan and Joseph had shared with him concerning Sarah. His nephews obviously loved her and were missing her terribly. His brother-in-law had also not been his usual happy self. And when he recalled what the boys had said about what a help Sarah had been to his sister, the unease he was experiencing was almost overwhelming. This woman he could little tolerate had been better to Joanna than he had been. Just now, he wondered what his sister would think of his treatment of her friend, if she had indeed loved Sarah as much as his nephews had said.

◊◊◊

The day after George Hoyt left, Simon Findley arrived at the Thompson home. His mother had divulged that Sarah was still away. As he hopped down from his wagon and started for the house, Daniel came strolling toward him from the direction of the barn.

"It is good to see you, Simon." It had been a few weeks since the friends had been in each other's company.

"And you as well, Daniel. In another month, the weather will put a halt to my travel and you shall be seeing me so often you are certain to grow tired of me."

Chuckling, Daniel responded, "Not likely. You are welcome here any time."

"I hear Sarah has not yet returned. She ought to make the journey home soon, or the roads shall not be fit for travel."

"Yes, well...Sarah has not been to Amesbury in some

time. She has my blessing to stay as long as she wishes."

Simon moved his foot around in the dirt while searching for a way to tell his friend what his wife had endured at the hands of George Hoyt. "I heard that George was staying with you."

"You heard right. He left just yesterday."

"Oh, I see. I do not recall Joanna's brother visiting her whilst she—"

"As you say, we saw him but rarely before Joanna's passing. I am not certain what brought about the change. Perhaps after losing his sister, he came to a better understanding of the importance of family."

At that moment, Dan came running to tell his father that Joseph had been kicked by one of the horses. The boys' father and Simon hastily followed after Dan as he led them to his brother.

Finding his son on the ground holding his stomach, Daniel knelt down next to him. Joseph could scarcely talk as his father questioned him about where he was hurting.

After evaluating the situation, Daniel decided his youngest son had only had the wind knocked out of him. "Joseph, I think you will be just fine once you catch your breath."

Joseph soon began to breathe easier. "I...th...think I am all right now."

Dan helped his brother to his feet and offered to finish the chores by himself. "You go in and rest."

Joseph, his father and Simon then made their way to

the house. As they approached, Simon stated that it may be best if he visited another day. Daniel and Joseph waved him on and continued on their way.

While on his way home, Simon wished he had not missed the opportunity to speak with Daniel about his brother-in-law. Though Sarah would likely be angry with him for disclosing what had happened, he was now certain, as she had not yet returned, it was the right thing to do.

Chapter 33

Sarah had been considering Hannah's offer for her to stay with them. It would give her more time before her situation became known. She decided to talk to Esther about it.

Esther listened as Sarah informed her of the invitation by Hannah Bleasdell to lodge with them for a time. The maid then stated that Martha should be told about the baby.

"I am not yet prepared to inform Martha. I need a little more time, Esther."

In hearing Sarah's firm response, Esther spoke not another word.

The next morning, Sarah informed everyone that she would be setting off for the Bleasdell home at the end of the week. She asked that Peter convey her there when the time came. Martha privately questioned her about her reasons for going. Sarah's vague answer left the head-servant confused.

There are times of vexation in every marriage; as for Sarah and Daniel, I cannot fathom that being the reason she came to Amesbury.

Mr. Swyndhurst took Sarah aside one day to ask her what was going on. He had been patiently waiting for her to tell him, but to no benefit.

Sitting there next to him in the parlor, Sarah felt she had no way of escaping his questions. Not knowing where to start, she hung her head and sighed.

Mr. Swyndhurst reached over and grabbed Sarah's hand. "You can tell me anything, my girl."

"It seems so strange to be talking to you about my marriage to Daniel. I am not sure how to even begin."

"You are like a daughter to me, Sarah. You know that. Alexander is gone. You're Mr. Thompson's wife now, so do not concern yourself with injuring me by speaking of your new husband."

Sarah leaned against Mr. Swyndhurst's arm and began, "I never expected to be married to Daniel, but it was the only way for me to remain in Boston to care for the boys."

"I am aware of that, Sarah. There is no shame in taking another husband now that Alexander is gone."

Sarah knew that to be true, but to reveal her present circumstances still felt wrong somehow. "If you will allow me a little more time, I shall tell you the whole story. I would first like to go and see Hannah for a time."

With that, Mr. Swyndhurst ceased from questioning her. He pulled her close and whispered that he would be there waiting to hear when she felt ready.

As for Martha, she suspected that, like her, Mr. Swyndhurst wished to get to the bottom of what was going on; for that reason, she hovered near the parlor, hoping to hear the conversation between Sarah and Mr. Swyndhurst.

Sarah thanked Mr. Swyndhurst for his concern and then went to her bedchamber to gather up what she would require for her stay at Hannah's.

Martha came into the parlor and spoke to Mr. Swyndhurst. "I apologize for eavesdropping. I was hoping Sarah would reveal what is troubling her."

"That was my hope as well, Martha. There is something going on, that is for certain."

Up in her bedchamber, Sarah was sitting on the edge of her bed, wishing she had the answer for her dilemma. The only thing she knew for sure was that those who care about her would strongly encourage her to return to Daniel and the boys if they knew she planned to stay on permanently, especially if they had knowledge of the baby.

Knocking on Sarah's door, Esther called out, "May I come in?"

Sarah rose and walked over to the door. "Come in, Esther."

"I thought you might need some help packing for your visit with the Bleasdells."

"You are such a dear, always thinking of me. Yes, I could use some help. Truth be known, I am feeling rather weary at the moment."

"You sit yourself down and direct me from there."

As Esther worked, Sarah told her of her conversation with Mr. Swyndhurst. She also said that she was still reluctant to disclose the news of the baby. Esther completely understood but still wished they could consult Martha, for she had nearly always taken the head-servant's advice in everything.

"I know what you are thinking, Esther, but you know as well as I that Martha will want to tell Daniel about what happened with George Hoyt and that there is a baby on the way. At least I am fairly certain there is. I still can scarcely believe it."

"You are right. Do not worry. I shall not say a word."

Chapter 34

Hannah rose early to prepare for Sarah's arrival. She wanted the room in which her friend would be staying to be as cheerful as possible; consequently, she placed her most colorful quilt at the foot of the bed and a bouquet of dried flowers on the little table by the window. Jonathan helped his wife set the room in order. They both loved having a home that was so peaceful others felt it a refuge in times of trouble. Sarah wasn't the first to accept their invitation to stay.

Peter conveyed Sarah to the Bleasdell home. Upon their arrival, Jonathan Bleasdell came out to greet them. He grabbed Sarah's satchel from the back of the wagon and then came around to help her down.

Sarah thanked Peter and then followed Mr. Bleasdell to the house. After meeting her younger friend at the door, Hannah ushered her to the kitchen while Jonathan took her belongings to the guest bedchamber.

The ladies made small talk over tea and cake. Finally, Hannah broached the subject of Sarah's child. "Sarah, from what you have disclosed, it would seem you intend to stay on in Amesbury. Are you certain this is the right choice now that you are aware of the baby?"

"Hannah, I am not certain of anything." Knowing

that she was carrying Daniel's child had shaken her determination to stay away.

Hannah sensed the turmoil within Sarah. "Sarah, let us pray about all of this, as well as that God will move on George's heart so that you might go home."

Sarah lowered her head and the ladies prayed for the next few minutes.

Later that night, snuggled in her bed at the Bleasdell home, Sarah patted her stomach. "Little one, what am I to do? I never planned on having that kind of a relationship with Daniel, one from which you emerged, and now I may be raising you alone; nonetheless, I am glad God saw fit to allow me this opportunity, especially since it seemed certain I would never have another child."

In Hannah and Jonathan's bedchamber, they spoke of Sarah and her circumstances. Sarah had said Hannah had her permission to tell Jonathan as long as he kept her secret, for now. Jonathan wisely suggested to his wife that they pray about the situation. They had seen their young friend act impulsively before, believing she was making the right decision. That time, it had been the wrong choice. Jonathan then said that if Sarah did not tell her husband about the baby, he would.

The following morning, Sarah decided a bit of distraction would be of benefit, so she made her way to David Bleasdell's shop, which was on his parents' property. As she entered, David Bleasdell welcomed her. He then proceeded to show her the clocks he was either repairing or building. Besides the many clocks, he also made surgical instruments, tin ware, and repaired guns. She looked on with great interest. David's clocks were well known even in Boston, and she had never before taken the time to see his shop.

Just as Sarah was leaving the shop, David's wife, Abigail Colby, arrived. Sarah remembered meeting Abigail at church some time ago. "Good day to you, Abigail."

"And to you, Sarah. Hannah mentioned she had asked you to come for a visit. I am sure we will see a lot of each other whilst you are here."

"Indeed. Well I best return to the house." While strolling along on her way back, Sarah thought about the many children Jonathan and Hannah had raised. Two were yet at home, Elizabeth and Hannah. The couple had suffered the loss of more than one child—two after they had grown, and the other at a young age. Their daughter, Mary, had in fact passed shortly before Sarah returned to Amesbury. For all Jonathan and Hannah had been through they were still some of the happiest people among her acquaintances.

Upon entering the house, Sarah was met by a jubilant Hannah. Her friend stated that it might be great fun if they each made a blanket for the baby. Sarah was delighted at the idea, and before long the ladies were comfortably seated in the parlor, both working on their own creations.

Hannah's daughters came in to watch. As they

observed Sarah and their mother, they questioned them about what they were making. Sarah was a little hesitant to reveal that what they were making was for her baby. And Hannah merely said that they had decided to fashion baby blankets, as there was always a need for such things. Young Hannah and Elizabeth never caught on to the fact that the blankets were actually for Sarah.

Over the next few days, whenever Hannah and Sarah had time on their hands, they worked on the little blankets, both completing them within hours of each other.

As Sarah held them up, one at a time, to admire them, she beamed with delight. Somehow looking at blankets her baby would be using made the fact that she would soon be a mother seem more real to her.

As she observed Sarah, Hannah was glad she had suggested making the blankets, for her friend was clearly pleased at the finished work.

Jonathan came into the room in time to see a happy Sarah holding up the blanket she had made. "It seems you have finished, and from what I see, you both did marvelously."

Hearing the compliment, Sarah glanced over at Jonathan. Her face suddenly turned a deep red. Feeling the heat in her cheeks, she turned her gaze toward Hannah, who appeared amused at the sight. All three erupted in laughter at Sarah's embarrassment.

"Sarah, you were not anticipating praise for your work, I take it." Jonathan was still chuckling as he said this.

"I expect not, Jonathan. If you compare mine with Hannah's, you will quickly see why my needlework has never received much praise."

To this, the laughter began again.

Moving toward her friend, Hannah picked up Sarah's blanket for closer inspection. "I see nothing wrong with your work. You did a fine job."

Even though the blanket had flaws, Sarah felt a sense of accomplishment at making it for her own child.

That night Sarah decided to put aside her thoughts of Daniel and her future and think of the baby and no one else. She closed her eyes, hoping to quickly fall asleep. That was not to be, for she lay there wide awake for many hours. She knew she was doing the right thing for Daniel and the boys in staying away so that George could finally be a part of their family, as Joanna had always wanted, but what of *her* child. Staying away would mean he or she would be fatherless. The decision had been easy when she only had herself to think about. Feeling restless, she began to pray, asking God to show her His will.

When the sun shone through the window the next morning, bringing comfort as it warmed her face, it reminded her of the many times God had comforted her during difficult times. She needed to trust Him with her current circumstances as well. She had always loved the Bible verse in I Samuel 7:12, "Then Samuel took a stone, and set *it* between Mizpeh and Shen, and called the name of it Ebenezer, saying, 'Hitherto hath the LORD helped us.'"

In fact, she had once carved it on a piece of wood, and from that time forward kept it in her room as a reminder that God had never failed her. Not having seen it in a while, she decided to look for it when she returned home.

Chapter 35

While George Hoyt arranged his schedule that he might return to Boston to see his family, he thought again of Sarah and what his nephews had disclosed concerning her life before her marriage to Daniel. He had been plagued with a niggling guilty feeling ever since.

Two days later, while on his way to Boston, George conversed with his friend, John Littlefield, who had decided to ride along, both having family there. As George listened, he thought he heard John mention Sarah's name in connection with an incident that occurred a few miles from John's childhood home.

"Did you say the woman's name was Sarah, Sarah Swyndhurst, and that something had happened to her near the home in which you were raised?" George questioned his friend to be certain he had heard correctly. He was acquainted with Sarah's family name since his nephews had made mention of it.

"Yes, I believe that was her name. From the account given at the time, it seems it was a rather tragic event for the young woman. I am not sure of all of the particulars, but it was rumored that she lost the child she was carrying and that the driver had been killed."

George's eyes grew large as he continued to listen. The more he heard of Sarah's heartrending story, the more guilt ridden he became. Not wanting to hear anymore, he began to talk of something unrelated.

After finally letting his friend off at his intended destination, George was relieved he would be traveling the rest of the way alone. When the Thompson home came into view, he wished he had planned his visit for another time. The stories he had heard about Sarah had been just too unsettling.

Daniel, with a troubled look upon his face, came strolling toward George's wagon. George instantly knew Daniel's dejected countenance had everything to do with Sarah.

Climbing down from his wagon, George then patted his brother-in-law's shoulder. "It is good to see you. How are the boys faring?"

With such a heavy heart over Sarah's prolonged absence and how deeply his boys had felt the separation, it was difficult for Daniel to answer. "Let me help you with your satchel," he said, leaving George's question unanswered.

George said not a word about his brother-in-law disregarding his inquiry. The two men then quietly made their way to the house where the boys, who were presently watching out the window, were eagerly awaiting.

That evening, while the family enjoyed time together in the parlor, George listened to his nephews go on about Sarah. This time, Joseph mentioned several events with not only Sarah, but also his sister. *As the boys have previously intimated, my sister thought a great deal of Sarah; however, I am certain she would have been displeased to learn that her friend had married Daniel, particularly with such haste.*

George then silently refuted every warm mention of Sarah. He could not allow himself to believe he had misjudged her, not after every hateful thing he had said to her.

From where Daniel was sitting, he observed George's countenance as it changed with every story his sons recounted. It seemed that whenever Sarah's name was mentioned, there was a scowl upon his brother-in-law's face. *What might he be thinking? To look at him, one would think he despised Sarah.*

George caught Daniel studying him while he was listening to his nephew's stories. He then forced a smile at the warm accounts of the little woman he had driven away.

"Dan, Joseph, it is time to turn in. We should get an early start tomorrow. With only a few more weeks of summer, we must be certain there is enough feed for the horses. I have a meeting pertaining to the poor house that will be opening soon, so I shall be away for part of the day." Unbeknownst to his sons, until now the physician had been asked to assist in overseeing the care of the sick at the poor house.

Knowing it would be too much for his sons to manage alone, Daniel was thankful for his farmhand Zechariah, who would be helping the boys when he left for his meeting the following day.

Once Dan and Joseph were no longer in the room, Daniel inquired, "George, is something troubling you?"

Knowing Daniel had seen his reaction to all the talk of Sarah, in a calm manner he shrewdly responded, "Whatever do you mean? What could be troubling me, here with my favorite brother-in-law and nephews?"

Relaxing a little in hearing George, Daniel chortled, "You mean to say, your only brother-in-law."

The two men lingered for a time in the parlor, enjoying the conversation. The next morning, everyone in the house was up with the sun, ready to work. George worked alongside the boys when their father left for his engagement. As the three labored along with Zechariah, George felt he could relieve himself of the guilt that had been pervading his thoughts. *The boys are very content just to have their father and myself here. I shall make it a point to come to see them regularly.*

George stayed on for a few more days. When it came time to take his leave, his heart again felt heavy at the thought that he had run off the woman his family dearly loved. Even so, he had no intention of returning things to the way they were before, with Sarah keeping house in his sister's home and mothering her sons. As for his brother-in-law, George was quite certain the marriage to Sarah was merely for convenience and that Daniel would be just fine without her. While observing his sister's sons waving him on, he took a deep breath and resolved to forget all about Sarah.

Chapter 36

Back at the Bleasdell home, Hannah and Jonathan were in their bedchamber, once again discussing Sarah's dilemma. While they understood her rationale for leaving Boston, neither thought Daniel would have wanted it that way had he been privy to what had happened with George. They also shared the belief that he had the right to know about the child.

"Have you given any further thought to making a trip to see Daniel?"

"I do not believe the time has come for that, as yet, Hannah. Let us be patient a while longer. I am quite confident Sarah shall eventually feel the need to tell Daniel. If not, then as I said before I shall see to the matter myself. Ever since she arrived, I have been thinking of Alexander and the many months he searched for her. There was a child involved that time, too. It is truly astonishing the similarities in Daniel's and Alexander's circumstances with regard to Sarah's need to run from certain situations."

"Indeed. The similarities have crossed my mind a time or two as well. I best get to the kitchen. Everyone will soon be up." Hannah hugged her husband and kissed him on the cheek before leaving the room.

Jonathan smiled at his wife as she showered him

with affection. Things had not always been easy for them in the many years they had been married, but their love for each other had never waned.

◊◊◊

Later that afternoon Martha and Esther came to call. Hannah showed them into the parlor to visit with Sarah. She then returned to the kitchen to prepare tea for her guests.

Though a little apprehensive at seeing Martha, Sarah was happy they had come. After directing them to where they might be seated, she waited to hear why they were paying her a visit.

"Sarah, my dear, how are you?"

"I am well, Martha. I have been having a wonderful visit with the Bleasdells."

"That is very good to hear."

Esther kept silent for a time for fear of saying something she shouldn't.

Before long, Hannah returned with tea. Once everyone was served, she took a seat next to Sarah and quietly listened to her younger friend conversing with their guests.

"How is everything at home, Martha?"

"It has been rather busy with Mr. Swyndhurst making preparations for returning to England."

"What? So soon? It cannot be. I must come home, then." Sarah was nearly frantic over the news of Mr. Swyndhurst's forthcoming departure.

Martha was glad to hear Sarah intended to come home, which was exactly what she had expected once Sarah learned of Mr. Swyndhurst's plans. Looking over at Esther, she gave a slight grin. The maidservant returned the pleased expression.

"When shall you go, Sarah?" Hannah inquired.

"I should like to go along with Martha and Esther, if that meets with everyone's approval."

Martha quickly responded, "But of course, dear. Why don't you go and gather up your things? In the meantime, Esther and I shall visit with Hannah."

As Sarah stood, she looked over at Hannah. "I do apologize, Hannah. You have been such a wonderful hostess, and here I am, running off without warning."

"You mustn't worry about that. Now go and collect your belongings."

Hannah's daughters came into the room a few minutes after Sarah had gone. They questioned their mother about the reason Sarah was packing up her things. Their mother explained that Sarah would be going home with her friends, when it came time to leave. Elizabeth then reminded her mother about the blanket Sarah had made, wondering if she might like to take it along. Before her mother could stop her, Hannah's other daughter and namesake went to fetch the little blanket from the kitchen. When she returned, blanket in hand, Esther's eyes nearly popped out of her head.

Endeavoring to distract Martha, almost choking out

the words, she said, "Martha, should we inform Peter we will be leaving soon? I am sure he has not gone very far. He said something about going to the barn."

Martha knew in an instant Esther was attempting to draw her attention away from the baby quilt, but she would have none of it. "Well, is that not the most precious thing you ever saw?" She reached out to the young girl, who then placed the little treasure in her hand.

Sarah came into the room in time to see Martha admiring her handiwork. "Oh...ah...I...thought I would try my hand at something small. My knowledge of needlework is so lacking, Hannah and I thought something this size would be best."

Sensing now was the time for Martha to be told, Hannah sent her daughters to the barn to inform Peter the ladies would soon be ready to go. With only the adults in the room, Hannah gave Sarah a look to convey her belief that it was time. She then said, "Sarah, Martha is much too clever for that questionable story."

Feeling ashamed for having lied, with her head low, Sarah revealed the truth to Martha.

Martha simply said, "Well, it's about time. I have been waiting for you to tell me."

Stunned, Sarah's head popped up and her eyes darted in Martha's direction. "What did you say?"

"I said that I have been waiting for you to tell me."

"You knew, then."

"I was quite certain, yes."

Hannah and Esther began to snigger at the exchange between Sarah and Martha.

Sarah and her head-servant looked over at the other two women in the room, and seeing the amusement on their faces, they began to laugh as well.

Sarah was glad for the lighthearted moment; however, she and the other women in the room knew it really was not a laughing matter.

Martha's mood had changed as quickly as Sarah's. "Once we get you home, I want to hear the whole story, including why you are in Amesbury instead of with your husband in Boston."

Hannah stood to walk her guests out. At the door, she hugged Sarah and told her she was always welcome.

Sarah thanked Hannah and then followed after the other two ladies. As she approached the wagon, she noticed that Peter, having already been informed that the time had come to take their leave, was seated on the bench, reins in hand. Jonathan assisted all three ladies, in turn, onto the back of the wagon, where they made themselves comfortable on two large blankets. The occupants of the wagon waved to Jonathan, Hannah, and their two daughters—who were now standing next to their parents. Peter then set the wagon in motion and they were off.

Jonathan and Hannah were sorry to see Sarah leaving so soon. But now that Martha had been made aware of Sarah's situation, they were certain she would manage everything well.

Back at the Swyndhurst estate, Mr. Swyndhurst was finishing up his last bit of packing. Although he knew he would miss everyone, especially Sarah, he felt it was best that he take his leave, for he had come to believe that Sarah might be hanging on to her past with his son even more with him there as a reminder. As for Sarah and seeing her before he left, he was also certain that once Martha made his plans known, she was sure to come. Since it was likely to be the last time he would see her, he would not leave until she returned, even if it took some time for her to come home.

He soon heard a wagon arriving. Assuming it was Martha, the others, and he hoped Sarah, the older man made his way down to greet them.

As soon as Sarah entered, she fell into her father-in-law's arms, weeping. Pulling her close, he said, "Now, it is not as bad as all of that. Perhaps you and Daniel will make a journey to England one day."

Sarah cried all the more as he spoke. "You cannot go. We would all miss you too much. We are your family. There is no one there for you to return to."

Weakening a little in his resolve to be gone from Sarah's life, Mr. Swyndhurst fell silent for a moment. *Am I doing the right thing? Yes, yes, I must do this if Sarah is to ever move on with her life.* "Sarah, I have been in Amesbury much too long. My home is in England."

As he led Sarah to the parlor to continue their conversation, Martha and Esther, looking sorrowful, dried their eyes and went about their business.

Later, without having had to disclose the primary reason he was returning to England, Mr. Swyndhurst felt satisfied he had settled Sarah down and she now seemed to accept the idea that he would no longer be living there; however, his heart's desire would be to have seen her back in Boston before taking his leave. He also knew he was leaving the whole business of Sarah's brother unresolved. Since he hadn't a clue where her brother was, all he could do was hand over the wooden box Mr. Goodwin had left for his daughter and hope the news did not come as too much of a shock.

Chapter 37

Mr. Swyndhurst had been gone for two days. Sarah had yet to accept that she may never see him again. She had put on a brave front that had not lasted beyond seeing the door close behind him the day he left.

As she moped around the house, she thought about the last conversation she had with the man who had been like a father to her. She had revealed that there was a child on the way and he had all but told her to go back to Boston to be with her husband. She knew he was right, but she remained perplexed with regard to what to do about George. And then there was Daniel. She knew it would feel strange being around him after what had happened, as it had been before she left.

Sarah was mindful of the fact that Martha had been waiting to speak to her about the child. As she was not prepared for yet another person telling her to go back to Boston, she had been avoiding her friend. On this day she sensed that she would not be let off so easily as Martha came toward her with a determined look on her face.

"Sarah, it is time we had a conversation about your plans. I poured us some tea. Let us go to the kitchen."

As her elderly friend led her to the kitchen, Sarah swallowed hard. What could she say? She had yet to sort out all that had transpired in Boston with George as well as her relationship with Daniel. How could she return, knowing what had happened between them? Though she knew there was nothing wrong with a married couple sharing an intimate night, in her view, this was still her friend's husband. This train of thought was never far from her thoughts. She also wondered what the boys would think of her if they knew, for she had promised the marriage would be in name only.

After taking a seat, Sarah observed Martha studying her from across the table. "Martha, I can guess what is on your mind. Very soon I shall be prepared to answer your questions, but not today."

Not wanting to press her, Martha responded, "Very well, Sarah, but you have me greatly concerned. I have seen you do this before."

"This is not at all the same." She had no desire to disclose all that had occurred.

"What is more, I cannot fathom a man not following after his wife."

"Do not think poorly of him, Martha. He has his reasons."

Martha softly muttered something unfavorable about Daniel. She could not help herself. The man knew where her mistress was and yet had not come to fetch her.

"Martha, there is no need to place the blame for my being here on Daniel. It is not his fault! Do you hear?"

Though she was angry with Sarah's husband,

Martha was delighted the younger woman was so forceful about defending him. *That must mean that she truly does care about him,* she concluded.

"Let us talk of something else," Sarah said with great annoyance at her friend's complaints about Daniel. *At times like this it might have been better to have kept my relationship with the servants at a distance. If I had, Martha would not have felt so free to involve herself in my affairs.* But in thinking on it a little longer, she knew her life would have been very lonely without Martha's friendship.

"Yes, let's do. How are you feeling about becoming a mother?"

This Sarah could answer. "Martha, I am beside myself with joy. I never thought it possible." No matter what happens with Daniel, she would love this child.

"God be praised that He has seen fit to allow this. Just think, in a few months we shall be greeting a new life in this home, or better yet, in Boston."

The younger woman scowled at Martha, causing her to close her lips tightly and gesture with her hand that she would not take the conversation in that direction.

Sarah could not help but smile at the sight of her friend biting her lip to keep from speaking things she oughtn't.

"Tomorrow I will begin making your little one some clothes. You did a marvelous job on the baby blanket."

Sarah beamed at Martha's approval of her handiwork. "I cannot quite believe I managed it mostly by myself. I hope to make two or three more before the baby arrives."

Esther came sauntering into the room in time to hear the conversation about making things for the baby. "This baby shall want for nothing with all of us seeing to its needs."

Sarah was grateful for her friends. They had seen her through some difficult times, and the current situation, though joyous, had also proven to be yet another trial.

"Sarah, have you any plans of returning to the Bleasdell home now that Mr. Swyndhurst has gone?" Martha secretly hoped Sarah would stay there with her, for she planned to try and persuade her younger friend to return to Boston. She could not be certain the Bleasdells were of the same mind.

"As yet, I have not decided, Martha. It was comforting, being there with Hannah and away from...well, there are sure to be questions as time goes by."

Martha understood that with Sarah living apart from her husband there would be inquiries, particularly the closer the time came for the birth of the child.

The older woman, rising from the table, silently motioned to the younger maid that it was time they go, leaving Sarah to herself to think over what to do about whether to return to the Bleasdell home. On her way out, she placed her hand on Sarah's shoulder for a moment.

Once her servant-friends had gone, Sarah sat there, mulling over the situation. By the time she was ready to turn in for the night, she had decided against returning to the Bleasdell home. She would remain at home and send her servants to town for her needs, which would keep her away from inquisitive eyes.

Chapter 38

Early autumn, the year 1736, Amesbury, Massachusetts Bay Colony

Daniel had not set eyes on Sarah for nearly five months. He was more certain than ever she would not be returning. At times, he wondered if he should have gone after her; but uncertain as to whether his wife would receive him, he had decided against it.

Later that day, without having had to make any house calls, as Daniel worked at home finishing up the preparations for winter, Simon Findley arrived. He had one more trip to make, and as providence would have it, it was to Amesbury he would be traveling.

Slapping Daniel on the back when he came out from the barn to greet him, he asked, "Daniel, my friend, how are you?" With the hollow eyes staring back at him, he could guess the answer.

Daniel attempted to appear cheerful as he strolled, along with Simon, back to the barn, but with Sarah's absence weighing heavily upon him, he could not quite manage it. "Truth be told, Simon, Sarah is on my mind a great deal."

"Well then, my friend, you may be pleased to learn

that I am off for Amesbury in a couple of days. While there, I shall call upon Sarah."

Daniel's eyes lit up at the mention of Sarah and the possibility of his friend paying her a visit. "Would you tell her for me that we miss her terribly?"

"You may depend upon it. And if my powers of persuasion are as good as ever they were, I may just convince her to come back to Boston."

◊◊◊

Daniel's mood seemed lighter than it had been in weeks after his visit with Simon. The boys even took notice of the transformation in their father's countenance. They both wondered what had brought about the change.

Daniel's farmhand, Zechariah, had overheard part of the conversation between Simon and Daniel, so he had no doubts as to the reason for Daniel's improved mood. He hoped and prayed the concerned husband would not be disappointed by distressing news when Mr. Findley returned from seeing Sarah. *If only the young lady would come home. If she could but see what her absence is doing to her husband, I am certain she would.*

Mrs. Findley called at the Thompson home several days after her son had visited there. She was aware that Simon would be seeing Sarah while in Amesbury. Neither she nor her son had disclosed to Daniel his brother-in-law's ill treatment of his wife. Simon had tried but had been interrupted thus she decided it was now her responsibility. If Sarah returned with her son, as was his

233

hope, Mrs. Findley had no desire for her to face the dreadful man again.

Upon Mrs. Findley's arrival, Mr. Thompson ushered her into the parlor where his sons were presently sitting, chatting with each other. Once she was seated, she asked if they might speak privately. Mr. Thompson then sent his sons out to the barn to get an early start on their afternoon chores.

"What is it, Mrs. Findley?"

"I really should have told you about this long ago, but Sarah would not allow it."

Daniel felt uneasy at the tone of the conversation. "Do go on, Mrs. Findley."

"I truly dislike speaking ill of anyone but, in this case, it seems I have no choice. Mr. Thompson, your brother-in-law used Sarah very ill whilst visiting with your family."

Daniel's heart sank. Had Sarah had yet another man force himself upon her? Hoping he was wrong about the nature of the offense, he questioned her further. "Please tell me what you know, Mrs. Findley."

The woman felt awful about upsetting Mr. Thompson, considering all that he had suffered, but she forced herself to go on. "One day, after setting off for home, forgetting something, I had to turn back. As I came into the kitchen, I heard Mr. Hoyt speaking appallingly to Sarah. Though she tried to deny it, I am of the opinion that your brother-in-law had been treating her terribly all along.

From what I overheard, it seemed the root of it was that he resented her for marrying his sister's husband."

Daniel could not believe what he was hearing, for George had seemed so cordial toward Sarah whenever he was present. Rubbing the back of his neck, his heart racing, he asked why Sarah had refused to allow her to tell him.

"I heard him say that as long as she was living in his sister's house, he would not be coming to see his family. You know how tenderhearted she is. It is my belief that she must have felt it was more important for George to be a part of your family than it was for her to be. She dearly loved Joanna, and I am certain that, in leaving, she thought she was doing right by her friend as well as you and the boys."

After listening to all that had happened to Sarah, Daniel had grown so angry at his brother-in-law he could scarcely contain himself. Bolting from his chair for the third time, he sighed several times while pacing around the room. When at last he returned to his seat, no less upset, he said, "I am much obliged to you, Mrs. Findley. Despite Sarah's wishes to the contrary, you may be sure that you did the right thing in telling me."

When Mrs. Findley had taken her leave, Daniel began pacing around the room yet again, grumbling to himself about his brother-in-law. He was also angry at himself for trusting that George would have been good to Sarah while he was out on his calls.

What was he to do now? With this new information

he began to doubt Sarah had left merely because of the change in their relationship. It now seemed more likely his brother-in-law played a major role in her decision to leave. If that be the case, should he go after her, or should he first go and have it out with George? The more he paced, the more upset he became.

When he had calmed down a little, he realized this was something he needed to take to God. After he had prayed to be rid of his rage toward George, with a clearer head he decided to wait until Simon returned before setting off after Sarah. No matter what, he would not allow George anywhere near his wife until the duplicitous man had a change of heart and apologized.

Chapter 39

As curious as Sarah had been about the little wooden box Mr. Swyndhurst had given her before setting off for England—the one her father had asked him to hold onto until he felt the time was right for her to know its contents—she had yet to have a look. With the baby, Daniel, and the boys constantly on her mind, she hadn't been in the right frame of mind for what was sure to be a moving experience. With a heart now prepared to endure whatever emotions the contents of the box might bring about, with immense excitement she peeked inside. The first thing she came upon was a missive in her father's hand. Holding it with great care, she began to read.

To my dear Sarah,

You are likely to be quite shocked by what you are about to read. Let me first say that your mother was one of the godliest women I have ever known, and remember—we all have sinned, so please do not judge her too harshly. What happened was long before our marriage, when your dear mother was very young. If I had known her then, she would never have had to give up her child.

You see, Sarah, you have a brother. Your mother's parents forced her to give up the child and warned her never to try and make contact with him or they would turn her out. Later, while considering whether to try to find him, she decided against it, for she had no desire to disrupt his life, especially not knowing whether or not he had been made aware of her existence.

When I learned I was not long for this world, I agonized over whether to take this secret with me to the grave. In the end, I could not allow the news to die with me, so I left this missive and your mother's journal in the box that I entrusted to Mr. Swyndhurst.

Even after receiving this news, you must believe that your mother was still the loving, godly woman who raised you. I love you, my girl, and I hope one day you and your brother are reunited, though I feel the chances of that are slim since I do not even

have the name of the family who took him;
however, with God all things are possible.

When Sarah had finished reading the missive, she felt faint; she had a brother, her mother's child. If only her father had shared this with her while he was still living she might have been able to learn more. She then scanned the missive again to be certain she had not misunderstood.

Then, setting it aside, she quickly riffled through the box in search of her mother's journal. Beneath a couple of her father's ledgers and what appeared, by its size, to be a baby's blanket, she found her mother's tattered journal. By the shape it was in, her mother had obviously handled it many times. Sarah's heart began beating faster at the thought that not only was this something her beloved mother had written in, it likely also contained further news of her brother.

Before she opened the journal, she glanced back at the blanket. She had not given it much thought upon seeing it, but she now wondered if her mother had made it for her brother. *Perhaps her parents would not allow her to give it to him.* A wave of sadness swept over Sarah as she allowed herself to feel what her mother must have gone through over such a loss.

Just then, Esther knocked on Sarah's door.

Quickly covering up the journal, blanket and missive, she called out for her servant-friend to enter. As Sarah observed Esther making her way into the room, she knew she could not share her mother's secret. She did not want anyone looking down on her dear mother. No, this she would have to keep to herself.

Esther had come to tell Sarah that Martha wished to speak with her about having Mr. Hoyt over for a meal. The elderly servant wished to show him her appreciation for his friendship to her mistress.

Sarah followed Esther down to the kitchen where she and Martha decided on the menu for what would be served to their friend, Mr. Hoyt. Sarah felt she had been neglecting the man that was much like a father to her, similar to Mr. Swyndhurst, so she was pleased at the idea of having an evening with him. She also felt it was time she told him about the baby, for he would know soon enough. She could hardly stay on in the same town without him finding out, and she knew it would be better if it came from her. Now to just convince him that this was where she needed to be without letting on that it was his son who had forced her to leave Boston. But how was she to convince him that she needed to remain in Amesbury when she herself was not certain it was the right thing to do?

Throughout the remainder of the day, all Sarah could think about was returning to her bedchamber to read her mother's journal. Not wanting to be disturbed once she began, she decided to wait until it was time to turn in for the night.

Esther sensed that something was amiss with her friend; therefore, she kept a close eye on her for the rest of the day. With Sarah, one never knew what might send her running. Esther could not bear to have that happen again.

When at length curiosity, as well as concern, got the better of her, she finally asked, "Sarah, whatever is the matter? You have been unable to concentrate on a single thing all day. Twice, I found you picking up a book, only to return it to the shelf moments later."

I should have known Esther would find me out. Why was I not more careful? To protect my mother's reputation, I must keep her secret. "It really is nothing, Esther. In fact, from what I have been told, it is quite common for expectant mothers to be a little muddled in their thinking."

"Ah, that is true. I had not thought of that." With the realization that her friend's behavior was related to the baby, Esther felt more at ease.

Sarah disliked being untruthful with her friend. She consoled herself that it was for her mother's sake and therefore necessary.

When it came time for Sarah to turn in for the night, she nearly ran up the stairs to her room, then hastily donned her nightgown and flew to her bed. Grabbing the journal, with great anticipation, she opened the cover. Once she had read the first page, it seemed to her that her mother began the journal at the very time she learned she was with child. As she continued to read, she sensed her mother's immense shame, as well as fear of having to inform her parents.

Over the next few hours, through her tears, Sarah managed to read the entire journal. She was so caught up in what she was reading, she could almost see her mother, as a young woman—barely sixteen—sitting at her desk agonizing over what had happened and what to do about it. *If only my grandmother had been more understanding. How could the woman force her daughter to send her child away?*

Sarah's grandparents had both passed before she was yet five years of age. She could scarcely remember them, and after reading how they had treated their daughter, she was glad of it. *My poor, dear mother loved her son so very much. The least they could have done was get the name of the family that adopted him. They obviously wished to prevent her from ever finding him.*

As Sarah lay back against her pillow, completely exhausted, she recalled how her mother at a certain time every year, had seemed withdrawn, even sad. Her father had warned her during those times to leave her mother be. Until now, she had never understood her mother or what she was feeling on those occasions. *I wish I had known so I could have comforted her somehow.*

Sarah turned toward her pillow and wept until she fell asleep.

Chapter 40

Just after breakfasting with Martha and Esther, Sarah heard a knock at the door. As she rose from her chair to greet whomever it was, Peter escorted Simon Findley into the room.

Before Sarah could conceal the fact that she was with child, Simon's eyes became fixed upon her midriff. In a panic, Sarah quickly turned and again took her seat at the table. Then, with a tremor in her voice, she called for Simon to join her; after which she directed Martha to prepare tea for her guest.

While sitting at the table across from Sarah, Simon searched for something to say. His friend's wife was obviously with child.

Sarah decided to ignore the fact that the man was now aware of the full extent of her predicament. "I had no knowledge of your being in Amesbury, Mr. Findley. When did you arrive?"

"I came to town with the son of one of Boston's residents late yesterday. I thought it was a good idea to call upon you before starting for home. When visiting with Daniel not long ago, I learned that you had not yet returned to Boston."

Sarah had no wish to speak about Daniel, for it was

too painful. "Yes, well—"

When Sarah Thompson offered no explanation for her continued presence in Amesbury, Simon—hoping his words would influence the young woman—decided to bluntly describe what he had witnessed when visiting Daniel. "Sarah, your husband looks like a walking dead man. Besides his hollow cheeks, when last I saw him, his countenance was one of utter despair."

At this news, Sarah's heart felt as though it would break. She thought she had done the right thing in leaving. *Have I misjudged Daniel's ability to go on without me there, looking after things?*

Simon continued, "And what of the boys? They ask after you daily. Is pleasing George worth ruining the happiness of your family?"

Sarah had already been considering what her separation from Daniel would mean for her child, and now, in hearing Mr. Findley, she couldn't close her eyes to the fact that she had made her husband, Joseph, and Dan miserable.

Simon detected that Sarah was troubled by what he had said and was happy for it. If he could but push her harder, she might just give way. "In fact, I am not going back to Boston without you. I shall stay right here in this house until you agree to go."

Sarah's eyes darted at the man. By his expression, she knew he meant it. "Mr. Findley, I need more time to think about what it would mean if I were to return." She had much to consider. She had to come up with a way around George's threat, and too, her relationship with Daniel had become uncomfortable. If Daniel and the boys weren't doing well without her, then none of that would matter, for she would not see them unhappy if she could prevent it. And there was also her child, who deserved to have a father present. And after reading about all that her mother had gone through, could she deprive Daniel of having his child? If she did, she would be no better than her grandparents. The longer she pondered, the more she was leaning toward traveling back to Boston with Mr. Findley.

Though Simon remained silent to allow Sarah to think about what he had said, he smiled, for he was certain she would return with him now that she was aware of the difficulty her family was having in her absence.

Martha listened on the other side of the doorway. She hated the idea of Sarah leaving, but she knew it was for the best. As she continued to listen, she heard a light rap. Turning, she made her way over to the door. It was their good friend Mr. Hoyt that awaited entrance.

"We were just speaking of you, come in, come in." Martha ushered him in with her finger to her lips as a sign that they speak quietly. "We hoped you would join us for a meal, and here you are."

"I happened to be passing by on my way back from town, and as I hadn't been to see you all in some time, I thought I would call unannounced. I hope it is not too much of an inconvenience."

"You are always welcome. And as I said, we were hoping to have you join us for a meal, when you had the time." Martha then pointed toward the kitchen and whispered that Simon Findley was in with Sarah trying to convince her to go back to Boston with him.

Mr. Hoyt nodded and smiled. The two then inched their way over near the entrance to the kitchen to listen. As they approached, they heard Simon's voice.

"How do you think Daniel will feel when he learns of his child and that you have been keeping the news from him?"

"When I took leave of Boston, I had no way of knowing I was carrying his child. I am aware that what I am doing is not right; however, there is much to consider if I am to return."

On the other side of the doorway, just out of sight, Mr. Hoyt's brows rose with the news of the child. "Well, I guess things had indeed progressed with my son-in-law and Sarah," he said with a chuckle. He then remembered what Daniel had said about Sarah not being able to have another child. *Although I have a very intelligent son-in-law, he cannot speak for our Creator. If God wills it, it shall happen,* he thought to himself.

Even though she was amused by Mr. Hoyt's comment about the progression in Daniel and Sarah's relationship, Martha had no desire for the two in the kitchen to catch her listening thus she reached out to cover the elderly gentleman's mouth.

Mr. Hoyt grasped the hand that was presently covering his mouth and led the older woman, who was meeting with little success at attempting to hold her ground, into the kitchen where Simon and Sarah were conversing. Sarah looked up as Mr. Hoyt and Martha entered the room. The older man sat himself down next to her, while Martha—not knowing what to do—picked up a wet cloth, attempting to appear busy.

"Go on, Simon. Do not let me stop you," the older gentleman said. Simon had often interacted with Mr. Hoyt whenever he was in Boston visiting his family; therefore, they were on quite friendly terms.

Looking over at Sarah, Simon shrugged. "We were making plans for Sarah to return with me to Boston."

Sarah knew she had not actually agreed to go as yet, but she made no objection.

"Well, then, I should like to go along, too," interjected Mr. Hoyt. "To make it all proper, you know." Mr. Hoyt glanced down at Sarah's round middle to see for himself that the young woman was actually with child. "Is that not like our God, reminding us He is still in control?"

Sarah smiled at her elderly friend's joyous expression at seeing her swelled middle. She was relieved that he was genuinely happy. Though he was Joanna's father, not hers, he had never treated her as anything less than a daughter. "Mr. Hoyt, I had every intention of telling you the next time I saw you."

"I am certain you were planning to do just that, my girl. We must get you home before you are any further along—not to mention, it shall not be long before the first snow."

Simon was pleased that Sarah appeared to have accepted the idea of returning to Boston. "Let us set off by the end of the week."

"Yes, indeed, and you shall stay with me until then," stated Mr. Hoyt with a wink.

Simon was grateful for the offer and quickly thanked Mr. Hoyt.

Later, when her visitors had gone, Sarah talked over the whole business with Martha. By the end of the conversation, both ladies were a little weepy at the thought of having to part from one another once again.

Chapter 41

Sarah's head was spinning with all of the changes that had occurred over the past few days. She had learned of a brother she never knew existed, and she had somehow been convinced to return to Boston.

Today was the day the gentlemen would be coming to collect her. She had packed up the things she wished to take along—the most important of which was her mother's journal and the blanket she had assumed was intended for her brother. Peter had carried everything down by the door, ready to be loaded onto the wagon.

Esther and Martha were waiting in the kitchen for Sarah to join them. It would be a sad day for the entire household. They all dearly loved their mistress and hated to see her go. Sarah had assured everyone that she intended to keep the Amesbury home for the time being. Now that Mr. Swyndhurst was gone, there really was no need for her to keep the estate, but she could not bring herself to part with it, for not only did it hold precious memories for her, it was also comforting to know she had a place to return to if the need arose.

When Simon and Mr. Hoyt arrived, Sarah lavished hugs on each of her servant-friends. Leaving Martha to manage the house and servants, she promised to come for a visit in the spring.

"We really must be going, Sarah," said Simon as he pulled her hand through the crook of his arm in order to escort her out.

Sarah waved as the wagon pulled onto the road. She was seated in the rear of the wagon on several pillows with blankets nestled all around her. Simon and Mr. Hoyt had made certain she would ride in comfort, especially considering her condition.

In the days Mr. Hoyt and Simon were together at his home, while Sarah was at her estate preparing for the journey, Simon had shared with him what his mother had said about his son George. Mr. Hoyt, though he felt terrible for Sarah, was not at all surprised by his son's actions.

When it came time for Sarah and the two gentlemen to take leave of Amesbury, Mr. Hoyt had decided to ride next to Sarah rather than up on the bench with Simon. His heart felt heavy as he observed Sarah, for his thoughts were focused on all she had suffered owing to his son. He had seen signs that something was amiss when last he visited. If only he had acted on his intuition, perhaps Sarah would not have had to leave Boston.

When they had bumped along for almost an hour, Mr. Hoyt leaned over to Sarah to see what had her so captivated. He had been observing her as she read from what appeared to be a journal of some kind. While glancing at the page, he read something his young friend had not intended for anyone to see. Wishing he hadn't meddled, he quickly sat back and turned his gaze elsewhere.

Though she had already read the journal from cover to cover, it still held her attention as she read it for a second time. In fact, with her eyes so fixed on the journal, she never noticed Mr. Hoyt peeking over her shoulder. All at once, she let out a yawn and stretched her hands up over her head. She then remembered Mr. Hoyt and turned her head toward him. "Oh, I do apologize. I've not been very good company."

As stunned as he was at the few lines he had read from her journal, he could scarcely speak. Seeing the questioning look on her face, he forced himself to answer, "Not to worry. I have been enjoying the ride, no need for conversation."

"Nevertheless, I should not have neglected you so."

"Please do not concern yourself, child. We should be quite unable to speak by the time we reach Boston if we converse the entire way." He patted her shoulder to reassure her he had not been put out by their lack of conversation.

Feeling satisfied that he was not vexed with her for taking no notice of him, Sarah leaned back against the mound of pillows, once again, and then set the journal in her lap. She noticed her friend was eyeing the journal with a rather strange look upon his face. "This was my mother's journal," she explained. "My father left it with Mr. Swyndhurst to give to me at his discretion." All at once, her face flushed for having divulged that last bit of information. She wondered how she would account for her father not giving her the box himself without disclosing its contents. But to her surprise, Mr. Hoyt did not question her about it.

"I see. You must treasure having something written in your mother's hand." Not for the world would he let on what he had read while looking over her shoulder.

"Indeed. I simply cannot stop myself from rereading every page." The young woman realized she could talk of the journal in general terms without revealing the secrets within.

The two then fell silent. With what he had just read, Mr. Hoyt thought of a time long ago, the day George's mother placed her son in his hands. *Sarah's mother must have felt much the same as that young lady for having to give her child away. I wonder how long Sarah has known about her brother.*

While pondering what he read in the journal, Mr. Hoyt felt something press against his arm. Looking down, he saw that it was Sarah. She had fallen asleep, leaning on him. He slowly lifted his arm over her head and pulled her into his chest so she might rest more comfortably. He then gathered the blanket up around her to keep her warm.

Simon took a look in the rear of the wagon to see how his traveling companions were faring. He smiled at the sight of Sarah asleep on Mr. Hoyt's chest. They had a long way to go, but he was grateful he had met with success at convincing Sarah. Mr. Hoyt looked up at him and winked. Simon understood that Mr. Hoyt was as pleased as he that Sarah and Daniel would soon be reunited.

Chapter 42

Daniel heard a wagon approaching and, with great haste, went out to see who it was. Simon had taken longer in Amesbury than the worried husband had expected. He hoped this was his friend arriving.

As the wagon pulled up in front of the house, Sarah felt panicked at the idea of seeing Daniel. How was she to explain her long absence? Additionally, she remained confused regarding her marriage. Now that she and Daniel were to have a child, was their marriage still for merely convenience? What bedchamber would she now occupy? Her thoughts and emotions were in such an upheaval, she felt like crying.

Mr. Hoyt felt Sarah's tight grasp on his arm and knew she must be nervous about seeing Daniel. He thought she might also be thinking about his son and what to do about him. Wrapping his arm around Sarah's shoulder, he whispered, "Not to worry. Everything shall be all right."

That was all it took for the floodgates to open. By the time Simon had made his way to the rear of the wagon to help Mr. Hoyt and Sarah down, Sarah's face was a mess with tears. Both gentlemen said not a word as they helped

Sarah onto her feet. Daniel came toward her the moment she had steadied herself with the assistance of the men on either side of her.

Sarah quickly wiped at her face when she noticed Daniel coming her way; but try as she might to hide the fact that she had been crying, she could not, for the tears just kept coming.

The boys had heard the sounds out in the yard as well and were rapidly approaching. When they caught sight of Sarah, excitedly, they both yelled out her name.

Their father, not wanting them to make Sarah uncomfortable about crying in front of them, gently turned his wife's head toward him. He had yet to notice her swelled middle with her cape covering almost to her ankles. As he walked her in the direction of the house, he motioned for his sons to follow quietly behind.

Not knowing the reason the woman they dearly loved was upset, they complied with their father's wishes.

Once the husband and wife had entered the house, Daniel escorted her to his bedchamber where they might talk privately, but that would come after she rested.

The relieved husband helped his wife out of her cape, and said, "Sarah, you rest now. We shall talk later." Just having her home was enough for now.

Acquiescing, his wife made her way over to the bed and sat down. Daniel bent down to undress her feet. Suddenly, he noticed her round middle. He then slowly lifted his head to see her face. When he saw her cheeks instantly flush, he checked his emotions so as to put her at ease.

Allowing the reality of the child to settle in for a moment, he smiled at his wife. "Once you have rested, it seems we have much to discuss."

Her husband's warm smile put Sarah at ease. She still had to figure out how to explain her absence without revealing George's part in it, but if nothing else, the news about the child was out and her husband seemed happy about it.

Daniel covered his wife with a quilt, bent down and kissed her brow, and then left her alone to rest. Leaning against the closed door to his bedchamber, Daniel could hardly believe his wife was home. As he thought about how many months she had been gone, he calculated how far along she was. He had thought the chances of Sarah having another child after her extensive injuries—which led to the premature birth and death of her son—were slim. *Her recovery is more complete than I had previously thought possible.*

As he thought about George and that he had been the reason his wife had been away from his care when she needed him most, his anger toward his brother-in-law intensified. This was a dangerous time for his wife, given her previous injuries, and he had not been afforded the opportunity to look after her. *How shall I broach this topic with Sarah in a way she will understand her importance over George to this family?*

Taking a deep breath to calm himself, he decided it was best not to focus on all of that and appreciate his time with her now. "Once she is up, I shall see for myself that she and the baby are well," he stated aloud as though speaking to someone.

Daniel's eldest son, having come from his room, was passing by when he heard his father say something about a baby. "Father, is Sarah going to have a baby?"

Unaware that Dan was there before he spoke, Daniel's eyes shot in his son's direction. *Everyone will know once Sarah is up,* he told himself. "Yes, Dan, she is."

Dan smiled with delight. He was old enough to understand what this actually meant about his father's relationship with Sarah. He was happy for them but even happier about having a new sister or brother.

"I shall rely on you and Joseph to see that Sarah does not exceed her limits. Sarah was not expected to be able to carry another child after losing her last, which may make this a precarious time for her and the baby."

"I understand, Father. We shall see to it that she gets plenty of rest."

Daniel gave a gentle squeeze on his son's arm and then went in search of Simon and Mr. Hoyt. Finding them in the parlor, he conveyed them to a private place to talk. As the three men were cloistered in his examining room, they discussed Sarah and the situation with George. It was decided amongst them that at the first opportunity, Mr. Hoyt and Daniel would make a trip to see George. They hoped they could convince him to have a change of heart; however, if he did not, he would not be invited to the Thompson home again.

After settling on the best strategy for managing the situation with George, Daniel thanked Simon and Mr. Hoyt over and over again for bringing his wife home.

Then, with peace in his heart that his friend would no longer be suffering over his wife, Simon took his leave.

Mr. Hoyt had brought along enough of his belongings to stay for the winter, if he was permitted. He felt Sarah and Daniel needed him, for just as Daniel had understood, he also was aware that this was sure to be a challenge for Sarah, both bodily and emotionally.

Still not quite able to believe his wife was really home, Daniel looked in on her several times. She must have needed the rest, he decided, for she never stirred when he climbed in the bed next to her later that evening. As he lay there, he reached over to pull the covers up over her shoulders. Before long, he heard his wife move about. When she climbed out of bed and began searching around in the dark for something, he suddenly realized she needed to make use of the chamber pot. As she continued to search, he heard her sigh when she found what she had been looking for.

Daniel remained silent until he heard his wife sigh once again, this time with relief; at that point, he couldn't help but laugh, but since he had covered his mouth, his wife was unaware that he was awake. Once she had washed her hands in the basin next to the bed and climbed back in bed, he let her know that he was awake. His wife started at the sound of his voice. The two laughed together for several minutes. Then Daniel reached over and caressed her cheek.

"I am so happy you have come home. As for my brother-in-law, you leave him to me. I never should have left you alone with him."

Sarah was shocked that Daniel knew about George. "Who told you?"

"You should have been the one to tell me, Sarah. Did you truly believe we would wish for you to leave so George could have his way?"

"George is Joanna's brother. Of course I would want him to be able to see his family, for her sake as well as for you and the boys."

"Sarah, Joanna loved you dearly. She would never have allowed her brother to send you away. If he wants to force us to choose, we, all of us, choose you. Do you hear?"

Sarah continued to feel regretful, knowing George would probably never return; then again, she now had her own child to consider.

"Would you really have stayed away forever if Simon had not convinced you to return, even knowing you were carrying my child?"

"No, I suppose not. I was not aware of the child, though, not until I had already gone. Lately, I had been pondering a way to come home without causing a rift with George."

"I'm glad to hear it. Tomorrow I shall have a look at you to see if everything is progressing as it should. You do know this is rather a miracle—you having a child, I mean to say. I really did not think it was possible."

Though her husband could not see her pleased expression through the darkness, Sarah's face beamed at the thought that God had allowed her to have another child. "Yes, Daniel, our child is a little miracle."

Chapter 43

The next day, while Daniel was helping his wife put her things away in *their* bedchamber, he picked up the tattered journal to inspect it.

Sarah, seeing the journal in her husband's hand, quickly snatched it away. Then, catching sight of the look of shock upon his face, she attempted to explain her actions without disclosing anything about the journal. "Oh, I do apologize, Daniel. It is just that it is such an old journal, it ought to be handled with care."

"Between the two of us, I would say that I was the one handling it with care; whereas you—" Observing his wife, he noticed her lower lip beginning to quiver; as a result, stopping midsentence, he changed the subject. "We really ought to leave the rest of this for later. You should rest now."

Sarah was angry at herself for being so emotional. "Very well, Daniel. I do apologize about the journal."

"I took no offense," was his reply as he walked her over to the bed. After fluffing her pillows, he helped her slide back against them. He then decided to climb in next to her. The pair, hand in hand, soon fell asleep.

Daniel awakened from their nap before Sarah. As he lay there, he thought again of the old journal his wife had seemed unwilling to allow him to see. With all of the secrets between them of late, he felt a strong temptation to sneak a look at the journal. He decided he might just do that, but later, when Sarah was somewhere other than their bedchamber lest he be caught.

That evening, while Sarah was conversing with his sons and father-in-law in the parlor, with the journal still on his mind, Daniel crept back to the couple's bedchamber to read from the tattered, old journal. Sarah had hidden it somewhere, which only bolstered his desire to take a look. He finally located it under her side of the bed, up next to the wall.

After lifting the cover, he quickly scanned the first few pages. He grasped enough to understand why Sarah had wished to keep it from him, surmising it was to protect her mother's reputation. *She has never said a word about having a brother. I wonder if she has ever laid eyes on him.*

Suddenly, a missive fell out, landing on the floor. Daniel reached down to pick it up. As he read the signature at the bottom, he found that it was penned by Sarah's father. His eyes then went to the top to see to whom it had been written. Seeing that it was intended for Sarah, though he knew he shouldn't, he read the missive. "Well, that answers my question," he said as though speaking to Mr. Goodwin. *Before this missive was penned, along with the journal, she apparently had no knowledge of a brother.*

Having no wish to be discovered snooping, Daniel swiftly stuffed the missive in the journal and then put it back where he had found it. He knew he would have to tell Sarah what he had done. *If I expect her to be forthcoming, I must do the same, but it will have to wait for another day,* he told himself.

In the parlor, Sarah was enjoying spending time with Dan and Joseph, as well as Mr. Hoyt. She had dearly missed the two young men. She thought she was doing the right thing when she left, but now she felt sorry she had ever allowed herself to be run off by George. Oh, she knew she could not blame him entirely, as she had been having mixed emotions about Daniel, which also influenced her decision to return to Amesbury.

Mr. Hoyt enjoyed watching Sarah and his grandsons interacting. He believed he had made the right decision about staying for the winter. As he observed Sarah, not for the first time did he think her appearance was quite similar to his son's real mother. He had not taken note of the similarities until recently. He guessed it was because, while reminiscing about the day George became a member of his family, the image of his son's birth mother had come to mind.

Sarah glanced up while Mr. Hoyt was studying her. Noticing a strange expression upon his face, she wondered what was on his mind.

Having been caught staring, Mr. Hoyt decided to inquire about Sarah's parents, asking how they met and where they were living at the time.

"I believe they met at our church in Cambridge

shortly after Mother moved to town," she responded. Sarah dared not say too much for fear of giving away her mother's secret. Sarah wondered at that moment if her mother and father's marriage had been arranged, given the difference in their age. *I surely could see her mother marrying her off to an older man. Thankfully, my father, though he was much older, was a kind and loving man and theirs was a good match.*

"Oh, I see, and do you know from where she hailed before moving to Cambridge?"

Sarah found Mr. Hoyt's questions rather peculiar. Considering he was not at all connected to her family, she wondered what interested him. "I believe she was born in Boston."

To this answer, Mr. Hoyt's interest in Sarah's mother intensified. It was to Boston his minister had sent him to meet his new son. Before he could learn more, his son-in-law came into the room.

Neither man knew the other had come upon Sarah's secret thus they would not speak a word about it to each other, not even in private. As for Sarah, the news of a brother had not been far from her mind. She wished she could discuss the contents of the journal with her husband but was reluctant to do so. She had dearly loved her mother and had no desire to cause others to think badly of her.

Later that evening, after Sarah and the boys had gone to bed, Mr. Hoyt and Daniel discussed when they would make a trip to see George, as was planned when Simon was there not long before. It was decided they would leave by week's end.

When morning came and Sarah learned of their plans, she felt ill, for it was sure to be a confrontational visit with Joanna's brother. "Once he learns that I have returned, he is certain to detach himself from all of you," she told her husband and Mr. Hoyt.

"Not to worry, Sarah. Leave everything to us," the elderly gentleman said reassuringly.

"Zechariah shall be on hand if you require anything whilst we are away," stated Daniel. He loathed leaving Sarah so soon after her return, and the fact that she was with child made the upcoming separation even more worrisome for him. He decided, in order to set his mind at ease, he would ask Mrs. Findley to look in on Sarah and his sons.

With everything settled, the two men set off a few days later.

Chapter 44

As he traveled with Daniel to his son's home in Salem, Mr. Hoyt thought about Sarah's mother and the possibility of her being his son's real mother. He mulled over what he knew for certain; the girl had lived in Boston, which was where he was sent to meet George's mother. Additionally, the girl looked astonishingly similar to Sarah. Shaking his head, he thought, *No, it could not be!*

Daniel peered over at his father-in-law. "What is on your mind, Joseph? Something appears to be troubling you."

Mr. Hoyt continued in his silence regarding Sarah's mother. "Thinking about George, I suppose. He is sure to be upset over being confronted by the two of us."

"Though I was extremely angry, and still am to a certain degree, I intend to handle him gently."

"I have never known you to be anything but gentle, my boy. Even so, my son is just the opposite. He is likely to reveal a side of himself the likes of which you have never seen."

Daniel's brow furrowed at Joseph's words. He had not considered his brother-in-law's wrath as something to be feared, that is until now.

By the time the two gentlemen arrived at the

younger Mr. Hoyt's home, since they had benefitted from a time of prayer while traveling there, they felt a little more prepared for what was to come.

Hearing a wagon approaching, George opened his door to look out. Seeing his father and Daniel, he felt a sudden wave of dread. Daniel and his father were not the sort to leave the boys behind if this were just a cordial visit. As he slowly walked out to the yard, he attempted to muster up courage for what the men might say. He assumed it had something to do with Sarah. *The woman must have informed them about the things I said to her*, he told himself.

"It is good to see you, Father...Daniel," he said while approaching.

"Let us go in, George. Daniel and I have something about which we need to speak to you."

George led his visitors into his home. They left their belongings in the wagon, knowing they would not be invited to stay, and quite certain they would have to seek shelter for the night elsewhere.

After offering his callers something to eat, George took a seat at the table with his father and Daniel. "Now what is this all about? By the looks on your faces, this is not merely a friendly visit, I take it."

Daniel began by reaffirming his love for his brother-in-law. He then went on to explain that he had been made aware of his treatment of his wife, but he made it clear that she had not said a word.

George knew, if not Sarah, it had to have been the meddlesome neighbor. "What would you have me do, dear brother-in-law? Welcome her with open arms, and so soon after my sister's death? Could you not have waited a decent amount of time before moving on with your life, completely forgetting my sister?"

Even though he had known the truth for a while now, Daniel's heart still sank. The wonderful visits with George had been a complete pretense. He had fully expected his brother-in-law to react this way upon hearing the news of his marriage to Sarah and had been astounded when George seemed to have accepted the idea. At this moment, he was wondering how he could have been so foolish as to believe Joanna's brother had truly acknowledged Sarah as his wife.

Mr. Hoyt broke in, "George, have a care. You know very well how much Daniel loved your sister; what is more, the boys needed looking after. And it was your sister's suggestion, after all."

George had heard somewhere before that his sister had wanted Daniel and Sarah to marry, perhaps from one of his nephews, but had not believed it. "Do you actually trust that Joanna wished for this, Father? I think not!"

"Indeed I do, and if you took a moment to consider, you would, too. Your sister loved her family. She also loved Sarah; consequently, in making the suggestion that Sarah be a part of her family when she was gone, she knew everyone would be well looked after."

"No matter. I cannot bear to have that woman in my sister's home."

"'That woman' is going to have my child in a few months."

George's eyes grew wide upon hearing the news of the child. He knew he would never be able to push her out now. This enraged him even more. "There has never been a place for me in this family, starting with Father, and now with you and the boys."

Mr. Hoyt spoke up. "George, you have never accepted the fact that you were wanted and very much loved when you joined our family. I have loved you from the first moment I saw you at the church in Boston. And as for your mother, there could be no doubt as to her love for you. In fact, both of your mothers adored you. If you could have but seen your real mother's sorrowful face when she handed you to me. She was not much more than a child herself, at only sixteen. I believe she was forced to give you up. She even made a little blanket for you; however, her mother snatched it from you. You see, my boy, from your birth mother to your adopted parents, you have been treasured."

Daniel listened to the entire account of George and his birth mother, taking in every detail. He thought about how old George was now in relation to the year of his birth. Thinking back to Sarah's mother's journal, he realized the years matched exactly. His eyes grew wide as the full meaning of what he had read, as well as what Mr. Hoyt had just said, struck him. *There was even a little blanket amongst Sarah's things.*

George had listened carefully to his father, wanting very much to believe him. Glancing at Daniel, he noted that his countenance was one of utter amazement.

Still stunned after putting all of the pieces together, Daniel stated, "Joseph, I have never heard this narrative of the day you became George's father."

"No, I suppose you would not have, seeing as I rarely speak of it as George has been my real son since the day we brought him home."

Daniel decided he could no longer keep the account in Sarah's mother's journal a secret. "I am not quite certain how to tell you this, Joseph...and...you too, George, but I believe Sarah may be George's sister."

George began to laugh. "Have you gone mad, brother-in-law? My sister? Wherever did you get such a notion?"

Joseph was a little stunned that Daniel had come to the same conclusion, at which he himself was slowly arriving. "You have seen the journal, then?"

"Wha...when...when did you—"Daniel could not complete his question he was so dumbfounded at the whole idea; and as guarded as his wife had been over her mother's journal that Mr. Hoyt had found an occasion to view it, surprised him not a little.

"I stole a look when Sarah was reading from it on our journey from Amesbury to Boston."

George had no idea as to what the two men were referring. "You are not making a bit of sense. What journal? And why do you believe I am...Sarah's brother?" It was too absurd a notion for George to even entertain.

George listened intently as Daniel and Joseph went over the details of what was known between the two of them, which included his father making mention of a baby blanket. His face went pale when his brother-in-law revealed that Sarah kept a baby blanket along with the journal. Although the conversation was causing him to feel uneasy, he continued to listen.

Mr. Hoyt asked for more details about the blanket. When his son-in-law described the squares that had been stitched together, which were likely from the mother's old discarded gowns, Joseph knew it had to have been the one he had seen years ago.

"It must be the very one the baby's grandmother would not allow him to have, which caused a great deal of grief for the little mother. She had obviously sewn every stitch with all the love she would never be able to bestow upon her son. As it was made of a lady's garments, it was not like any I had ever seen. She must have later retrieved it from her mother."

As George hung on every word his brother-in-law and father shared between them, offering proof of his origin, he began to tremble. "This cannot be! Sarah...my sister? I cannot believe it. But with everything you have said, it has to be true. Here I was thinking I was being loyal to my sister, Joanna, by running Sarah off. Now you say that Sarah is the one who is actually my sister?"

Daniel and Joseph were as astonished as George at the unforeseen development. Even with his recent suspicions, the older man had not fully grasped the truth of the situation until now.

Over the next two hours, George's anger reached its peak regarding the matter. Up to now he would have said that what he felt for Sarah came close to hate. Having to settle in his mind that she was his sister was not an easy task. And if he believed this, he now had much about which to feel guilty concerning Sarah.

With George in a better frame of mind, after talking for hours, he invited his father and Daniel to stay for the night. Before turning in, though, they decided on the best course for revealing the truth to Sarah. George would follow along when his visitors returned to Boston; at which point together they would inform Sarah of her connection to the younger Mr. Hoyt.

Chapter 45

With her husband and Mr. Hoyt on their way to Salem, Sarah spent some time praying for them concerning their meeting with the younger Mr. Hoyt. She also prayed for the brother on whom she had never before laid eyes and wasn't even certain was still amongst the living.

Just as she was about to go to bed on this the third night since her husband and Mr. Hoyt had set off for Salem, she heard a wagon pulling up in front. Quickly throwing a blanket around her shoulders, she made for the door, anxious to learn how the talk with George had gone.

Entering first, Daniel leaned down and kissed his wife's cheek. He was followed into the kitchen by Mr. Hoyt. She motioned for them to take a seat at the table and then went straight to work fixing tea and slicing bread. She wanted to hear everything but knew they were probably hungry.

As she turned toward the table with a tray loaded down with bread, she nearly dropped it when she caught sight of George. The last thing she had expected was for him to return with her husband and Mr. Hoyt. She had in fact wondered if any of them would ever see him again. Slowly moving toward the table, with eyes lowered, she set the tray down. Daring a glance in George's direction, she was stunned to see a serene expression upon his face, for she was sure he would despise her for returning. *Is this all for show? What else could it be?*

While traveling to Boston from Salem, George had come to accept the idea that Sarah was very likely his sister. Somehow the hate he had previously felt for her had all but melted away. He had a blood relative. Knowing this brought joy to his heart, for he had never believed it possible that he would ever make the acquaintance of a member of his birth family.

George came toward her, gently took hold of her arm, and led her to the table. "Sarah, there is something I need to tell you that is beyond belief." Taking a seat in the chair next to his sister, he reached over and put his hand atop hers. Scarcely able to believe it himself, he wondered how she would react to the news.

Daniel and his father-in-law remained silent, allowing George to inform his sister himself. When his wife glanced at him with a bewildered expression upon her face, Daniel gave her a reassuring look.

All at once, Mr. Hoyt spoke up. He had to be very sure what his son was about to tell Sarah was in fact true; consequently, he asked Sarah if he might have a look at the little quilt her father had left for her. Seeing a blank look upon the young woman's face he further described the quilt, stating that it was the one her mother had made for the child she was forced to give up.

If Sarah was confused before—owing to George's actions—she was even more so now. "Ho...how did you—"

"Let's just say that every now and then, my curiosity gets the better of me." He would tell her all about it later, but for now he needed to confirm that the quilt was the one he had seen.

Hands shaking, Sarah rose and went to fetch the blanket. As soon as she returned, blanket in hand, Mr. Hoyt nodded in affirmation that this was definitely the creation George's mother had made for her beloved child.

Noting his father's confirmation, George's countenance was one of awe. He asked Sarah if he might have a look as well.

Given their history, Sarah was reluctant to allow her mother's handiwork to be held by a man who had so mistreated her ever since she joined the Thompson family. *What might he do to it?* she asked herself.

"I promise to hold it carefully, Sarah," George assured. With a questioning look, his sister placed it in his hands. As he inspected the tiny creation, he could no longer hold back the tears.

Stunned at the man's reaction to her mother's quilt, still standing, Sarah took a step back. She then glanced over at her husband and Mr. Hoyt. "What on earth is going on? Why is everyone crying?"

Mr. Hoyt spoke then, for he could see that his son was too emotional to finish what he had started. "Sarah, many years ago I made the acquaintance of a young lady who had wrapped her baby in that very quilt before bringing him to me—his new father. Her mother, your grandmother, seized the quilt from the child."

Sarah's eyes grew large as she listened to Mr. Hoyt's story.

"You see, Sarah, the child about whom I am speaking is George."

"What! How can this be?" By now, her complexion was white as a sheet.

"It is all true, Sarah. As I said, I was there that day to collect my adopted son."

Sarah's eyes shot in George's direction. Observing a tilt of the head to validate his father's words, she inquired in a frantic voice, "Does this mean...you...and I are—"

So there would be no doubt, Daniel answered for his brother-in-law. "Yes, Sarah. George is indeed your brother."

The tiny woman slumped down in the chair next to George, which was the closest empty seat. She suddenly felt a hand encompassing hers. Knowing it to be George's, she quickly pulled hers from his grasp.

"Sarah, I have treated you contemptibly. I hope with all of my heart that you will allow me to make it up to you." Glancing down at his sister's swelled middle, the tears started to flow once again. He had forced her from her home at a time when she needed her husband more than ever.

As she stared at the man, she sensed he was in

earnest. Her heart then melted a little as she observed tears streaming down his face. She remained silent for what seemed an eternity, listening to her brother's mournful cries. With a heart as big as the ocean, she could not remain silent any longer. Wanting to lift his mood, she chuckled and said, "Thankfully, you do not take after Mother in stature or your nephews would already be towering over you, as is the case with me."

Hearing Sarah's lighthearted words, George allowed himself a glance in her direction. To his great surprise, she was smiling at him. "How can you be so forgiving of such a despicable man? I have never once spoken a kind word to you."

"How can I do otherwise, when God has forgiven me much?" Although she was yet a little dubious, never one to sit idly by while watching the suffering of another, she continued to comfort him. "Besides, you are my...brother, are you not? What kind of a sister would I be if I did not forgive you?" She faltered on the word "brother" —for not only had she been stunned by the news of having a brother, but that it was this man, made it all the more shocking. For now, she would accept the news for the benefit of everyone else, but she would remain watchful to see if what she had observed of his behavior was for appearances only. She half expected that by tomorrow he would have returned to his usual taunting ways.

All three men breathed a sigh of relief. Sarah had taken the news better than anyone could have hoped.

Mr. Hoyt looked beside him at his son-in-law, who nodded to indicate that, yes, everything would now be well with these two.

Chapter 46

Elated at the notion of having a sister and the possibility of learning more about the woman who gave him life, George was sitting in the kitchen, anxiously waiting for his sister to emerge from her bedchamber.

When Sarah came into the kitchen to prepare breakfast, the first thing she spotted was her brother, his countenance one of immense joy. Unbeknownst to her, before first light, George had prayed to receive Christ as his Savior. The weight of what he had done to not only one, but both of his sisters, had been too much for him. He had been taught that God was merciful, always ready to forgive; however, up to now he little cared about such things. As his bedchamber became illuminated by the sun after a long night of struggling with what a wicked man he knew himself to be, he finally surrendered to a loving God. And as the darkness was chased away by the sun, his heart, once dark, was now illuminated by God's glory. Now, so overflowing with love, he scarcely remembered the ill feelings he had once had for his sister.

"My dear sister, what shall we do today?" He hoped she would suggest spending the day together.

Still unable to completely accept that the change was permanent, Sarah looked around and found that they were alone. He could easily have gotten away with his usual behavior towards her, she realized. Perhaps his being her brother truly meant he now accepted her.

George sensed the turmoil within his sister and knew right away he was to blame. "Sarah, it shall not be easy for you to trust me, but I hope you shall, in time. In fact, I was in hopes of having you all to myself today. Perhaps after a day together, your apprehension, where I am concerned, will have lessened."

Observing her brother, she decided to give it a try. "Very well, let us—just the two of us—spend the day together. If you like, I could show you our mother's journal." *That sounds so strange, "our" mother.*

"I would like that very much. Are you sure you do not mind?"

"I only recently had a look at it myself. Father left it in the care of my father-in-law, Mr. Swyndhurst, so I know to a certain extent how you feel about having the opportunity to read something in mother's hand that also reveals her most private thoughts."

In hearing his sister speak of a father-in-law he had never heard of before, he comprehended how little he really knew of her life before Daniel.

"As soon as you have had something to eat, I shall go and fetch the journal. You may wish to read it in the privacy of your bedchamber."

George smiled warmly at his sister. Before he could properly thank her, his nephews joined them. They had overheard a little of the conversation between Sarah and their uncle while making their way to the kitchen.

"What is this journal you mentioned?" Dan inquired of his uncle.

"It is a journal our mother penned long ago."

Dan's brows rose when he heard his uncle say "our mother" in relation to the journal. "Whatever do you mean?"

"Sit down, boys, there is much to tell," their uncle replied.

By the time the boys' father and grandfather arrived at breakfast, the young men had learned the astonishing truth about their uncle and Sarah.

The talk at the table became more than a little confusing, the boys bursting out with questions every couple of minutes, making any discussion between Sarah and George nearly impossible. The news was just too exciting for the Thompson brothers who had to have their part in the conversation.

Daniel had to tell his sons more than once to quiet themselves and finish eating. His sons at last complied. Their questions would have to wait.

Once the kitchen was set in order, George followed his sister to her bedchamber. While handing him their mother's journal, she told him there would be no doubt as to her love for him once he read it. With a grateful heart, he turned and went to his room, where for the next few hours he read, wept, and read some more.

That evening when the boys had gone to bed, the adults conversed in the parlor. Mr. Hoyt was heartened at the change in his son. Daniel was also in a rather good mood at having his wife home, for not long before he had wondered if she would ever return.

George revealed much of what was in his mother's journal to Daniel and his father. They were so happy that at last the younger Mr. Hoyt seemed to be at peace.

When Sarah and Daniel were alone in their bedchamber a short time later, she stated that she wished Joanna could have seen her brother so happy. "Would she not have been amazed at the turn of events in this family?" For the first time since her marriage to Daniel, Sarah had not been plagued by guilt at having married her friend's husband.

Daniel smiled at his wife. It was good to be married to someone who had also loved Joanna. "Yes, she would have been quite amazed. Sarah, I know I have said it before, but I am so glad you have come home." He reached over and put his hand on her middle.

They both began to laugh when Daniel started at the movement under his hand. Until now, he had not had the opportunity to feel his child move. "I say, be careful, little one; that is your mother you are kicking."

It would not be long before the Thompson family would be joined by yet another member.

Chapter 47

O ver the next several weeks, Sarah received more than one missive from her brother. He had become quite the protective sort, always asking if she was eating well and getting enough rest. Sarah hoped that one day he would live close by.

Mr. Hoyt had very much enjoyed wintering in Boston with his family. The thought of returning to Amesbury displeased him, for he would be, once again, separated from everyone he loved. One afternoon, he mentioned to Daniel that he was thinking of selling his home in Amesbury and coming to Boston to live.

"Joseph, I would not do that just yet. You see, I have been contemplating a move myself. To Amesbury."

The two men laughed at the thought that, if they had not spoken to each other, they may have merely swapped towns.

"But what of the folks who depend on you here in Boston?"

"I am certain they shall be all right in the care of another. My family has to be my first concern. We are soon to have another child in this house, and Sarah's Amesbury home is much larger. More importantly, there would be servants to assist Sarah in rearing the children and taking care of the home."

"When you put it in those terms, I see your point. Well, then, it seems I shall not be moving."

Daniel smiled and then warned his father-in-law not to mention a word to anyone until he had spoken to Sarah.

Once Sarah and Daniel were settled in bed that evening, Daniel told his wife what he had been considering. "The house in Amesbury is much larger, and there are servants there to help out with keeping the house and caring for the children. Furthermore, a move to Amesbury shall put a halt to your tendency to flee from difficulties, for you shall have no place to run." This he said with a wink.

Sarah pretended to be affronted by Daniel's comment about her propensity to run from trouble; however, with an expression that showed she was clearly amused, she asked, "When would we go, Daniel?" Living with Martha and Esther again suited her just fine.

"Well, there is the house to sell, and winter is not exactly the best time for moving. I would say, not before spring, anyway."

"We should speak to the boys about this. I would not wish to go if they have any objections."

Daniel adored his wife, particularly when she so unselfishly put the needs of others above her own. "We shall discuss it with them; however, we have the final say. When they are grown, they may decide where they wish to live."

Sarah merely nodded. She loved the boys and had no desire to upset them.

"Sarah, I was speaking in jest about you running off, but the possibility of it happening, if something were to upset you again, is not far from my mind."

Sarah felt ashamed at hearing her husband's concerns. She knew he had good reason to fear she would do that very thing. "Daniel, I do apologize; I should not have gone off like that."

"If you have a concern, you must come to me."

"I shall, Daniel, from this moment on."

It eased his mind a bit just hearing her say that. Leaning in close, he kissed her brow. "Rest now. Morning shall be here before we know it."

"Very well, but if I could have but one wish it would be that George would move to Amesbury as well. In the past, I could not be far enough away from him, but now I miss him dearly when he is not here."

"Indeed, what a miracle of God that the two of you should find each other and the unbearable relationship mended to this degree," he replied while leaning over to blow out the candle.

◊◊◊

When morning came, Sarah could hardly contain her excitement over moving to Amesbury, her beloved home. Impatiently, she made it through breaking the fast with her family, all the while hoping Daniel would speak to Dan and Joseph about removing to Amesbury.

Daniel had observed the rushed manner in which his wife had prepared and served breakfast. He chuckled to himself, knowing he had made the right decision about moving. He rose from his chair and teasingly stated that he had to call upon a few people and would be gone until nightfall. In truth, things had been quiet and he was not needed anywhere, other than at home with his impatient wife.

Sarah looked for all the world like a little child pleading with a parent over a supposed need when she asked, "Do you not have time to first speak with Dan and Joseph?"

With his back turned to her to hide his laughter, he replied, "It shall have to wait."

Dan and Joseph spoke up then, wondering to what Sarah was referring. Looking at each other, they silently questioned whether they were about to be reprimanded.

Observing their worried faces, Sarah reassured them they were not in any trouble. All at once, she heard her husband break into laughter. Realizing he had only been jesting when he said he had to take his leave and would be gone until late, she stomped her foot. "I do not see what is so amusing!"

Seeing the tiny woman stomping her foot, the boys began to laugh as well. Once they settled themselves, the eldest inquired, "What is it, Father?"

Daniel then rejoined his family at the table. Over the next hour, he discussed the move with his sons. In the end, everyone had agreed to a move to Amesbury. It was an easy decision for the Thompson boys since they would be living closer to their grandfather

Chapter 48

Sarah was awakened in the middle of the night by an unexpected and extreme pain. Her physician husband had indicated their child would not arrive until late December. This was only the final week of November. She was thankful when it passed as quickly as it came. Soon, she fell back to sleep.

The next morning, once her husband had set off to see a child under his care for a broken leg, the pains began again. This pattern continued for a time.

Scarcely able to stand, with much difficulty Sarah made her way to the kitchen, hoping to find Mr. Hoyt. As she entered, she found Dan sitting at the table.

"Have you already finished in the barn?" she inquired while grimacing from pain that was waxing just now.

"Yes, I had trouble sleeping so I began early." Dan then noticed the difficulty Sarah was having. "What is the matter?" Making haste to assist the doubled over woman, he led her over to a chair. "Is it the baby?"

"I believe so. I hope your father returns soon."

Then Mr. Hoyt came into the kitchen. In seeing his grandson's worried expression as he hovered over Sarah, the elderly man's eyes shifted to Sarah. "Have your pains begun?"

As Mr. Hoyt approached her, she replied through clenched teeth, "They have indeed, but it is too soon. The baby should not be coming for another few weeks."

Observing the worried look upon Sarah's face, he replied. "Everything is going to be all right. Let us get you back to bed, and then see what can be done about locating Daniel." Mr. Hoyt helped Sarah back to her bedchamber while Dan went out to the barn. Within minutes the eldest Thompson son, atop their fastest horse, went to find his father. He was pretty certain he knew where to look.

Upon his arrival at the home he had rightly suspected as being the one to which his father had gone, he spotted his father's horse. He hastened toward the house.

When the physician learned of Sarah's condition, he hurriedly gathered up his medical bag and followed his son out to the yard, where both Thompson men hopped on their horses and were off.

Daniel and his son arrived at home a short time later to find Mr. Hoyt sitting beside Sarah's bed, holding her hand. Joseph, looking fearful, was seated by the window on the far wall. Daniel suspected his youngest son was thinking about his mother and that she had been lost to them shortly after giving birth. Wishing he had the time to comfort his son, Daniel sent him from the room, with his older brother right behind him. He would speak to them at the first opportunity, but for now Sarah required his full attention.

As Daniel approached the bed, he asked Mr. Hoyt how long it had been since the pains had begun. After hearing how many hours it had been, he sent his father-in-law from the room so that he might examine his wife. When it was only the two of them, Sarah shared her concerns about the baby coming too soon. Daniel reassured her that, in his experience, it was common for mothers to go a little early. He suspected his wife's earlier injuries had something to do with the child coming sooner than expected.

With her physician husband there, Sarah's concerns subsided a bit. Looking carefully at him, she wondered if Joanna and the child they lost were on his mind, as they were hers.

As his wife had suspected, his thoughts were also on Joanna and the day he lost her and their child. Not allowing fear of losing Sarah as well to distract him, Daniel forced himself to focus on the here and now. For hours he successfully pushed all worries aside; however, that ended when Sarah began hemorrhaging. As he had thought, her previous injuries were most likely the reason the child had come this early as well as for the excessive blood loss.

Finally, the baby made its entrance. Daniel whispered to his wife, who was in a weakened condition, that the child was a girl. His wife smiled as he placed the child next to her. Not long after, he heaved a sigh of relief when the excessive flow of blood had subsided. It now appeared that Sarah would be all right.

As Daniel stood there looking lovingly at his wife and new daughter, he silently thanked God for allowing him to have another daughter. The daughter that went on to heaven with her mother could never be replaced, but having another to hold would ease the loss, if only a little.

◊ ◊ ◊

Over the next few days, Daniel had no worries about his wife overexerting, for the other men in the house had not allowed her to set foot out of her room while taking care of her every need. The girl child's siblings also relieved Sarah of much of the care of their sister, as they could not get enough of her.

When Sarah's strength had returned and she felt well enough to venture out, the family made plans for when they would go to the meetinghouse for the baby's christening. Father and mother had bestowed the honor of naming their daughter upon Mr. Hoyt, who loved her as a granddaughter. The older man was moved to tears at the thought of naming his grandchild.

Mrs. Findley had asked if she might make the silk gown for the occasion. As soon as mother and father saw the gown, they were astonished at the impeccable flowered embroidery along the edge of the sleeves, down the front, and across the bottom. When the day of the blessed event arrived, Simon conveyed his mother to the meetinghouse.

Another very welcomed guest at the christening was the baby's uncle. When he was last in Boston, he paid a visit to Mrs. Findley and her son, apologizing for all that had happened. The Findleys also learned that day about George and Sarah's connection and were amazed at the news. The three stood together on this joyous occasion, observing the ceremony.

George was overjoyed at seeing his new niece. In the moments before the formalities were to begin, the younger Mr. Hoyt whispered suggestions to his father for what to name the child. The Findleys, who were standing next to the jubilant uncle, chortled at the sight of the younger and older Mr. Hoyts bantering back and forth.

Mr. Hoyt had kept his decision about the child's name to himself right up until the minister requested it of him; at which point the proud grandfather replied, "Abigail. Her name shall be Abigail, for she has brought so much joy not only to her father, as the name implies, but also to the rest of her family. Additionally, the Abigail in the Bible—who was married to Nabal—was wise enough to make good decisions and strong enough to see that they were carried out despite what ramifications she might face. I pray that our little Abigail grows up to display such wonderful qualities."

Beaming, Sarah thanked Mr. Hoyt for giving such a suitable name to her child. She had been praying for her daughter to grow up to be wise and strong—both spiritually and physically—so it would seem Mr. Hoyt had chosen the perfect name.

Chapter 49

It had been several months since Abigail joined the Thompson family. Never had a child brought so much joy to one family. For Sarah and Daniel—where they once had been merely friends—she served to strengthen their relationship as husband and wife.

With the close of spring, the Thompsons would soon be removing to Amesbury. They had found someone to purchase their home, and the physician had informed the town of his impending departure.

The family's excitement grew as the day for the move approached. Their church had surprised the Thompsons with a picnic on their final day to worship with them. With all the fuss, there was no doubt they would be missed. To Sarah's great surprise, many of the ladies who had previously slighted her for marrying Joanna's husband so soon after her death made it known that she would be missed as well.

Knowing the day of their departure would be very soon, Sarah sent a missive off to Martha so she would be prepared for their arrival. As pleased as she was about the move, she was certain her elderly friend's joy would surpass her own.

As she gathered up her daughter's belongings, she thought about her Amesbury home and her first husband. Her marriage to Alexander had been arranged by her father. The plan had been for her to live with only the servants while her husband resided in England, which was the case for nearly two years. Alexander had returned to Amesbury in hopes of having a real marriage with her. She then recalled how stunned she had been when she learned he had changed his mind and wished to have a traditional marriage. In the end, she too thought differently about her marriage. As Daniel and Joanna had, they had loved each other dearly. If anyone had told her after his tragic death she would love as deeply again, she would not have believed it; but here she was, not many years later, very much in love with Daniel.

It is better not to know these things ahead of time, she reasoned. Just as her mind went to Daniel and how much her life had changed, he came sauntering into the room.

"I have been looking for you. The boys are ready to begin loading yours and Abigail's things on the wagon."

Thinking about how much God had blessed her in giving her yet another wonderful husband, she smiled at him and said, "You are a blessing from God, and I love you so very much." Then, having no desire to become overly emotional, she directed her attention back to the task at hand. "I am almost done."

"If you believe you are simply going to finish

packing after a statement like that, you are very much mistaken." Leaning down, he lifted her into his arms and then slowly twirled her around. As he snuggled her close, he chuckled at her protests. All at once, he heard someone coming and placed her back down next to the satchel she had nearly finished filling. Just as his youngest son came into the room, the amused husband cleared his throat. "You are through, then. Very good," he said to his wife.

Pretending he had not been aware of his son's presence, he stated, "Oh, Joseph, here you are. I believe this is the last of Sarah's things. You may load them, if you wish." Once Joseph had gone, Daniel bent down and kissed the top of his wife's head. Then, spinning on his heels, he left the room.

◊◊◊

A few days later, the Thompsons arrived in Amesbury with their first wagonload of belongings. Daniel and his sons would return to Boston in a couple of days for the remainder of their things. They were planning to leave a good deal behind—in the way of furnishings—for the new owners, as the Amesbury home was well supplied.

Martha was delighted to see Sarah and her family, but when her eyes caught sight of little Abigail, there was no holding her back. She quickly reached out and gently took her from her mother. After kissing the child on the cheek and giving her a squeeze, she turned toward the house. Other than when she needed to be fed, Abigail was not in her mother's arms for the remainder of the day.

Martha had reluctantly passed her off to Esther when the young maid insisted it was her turn to hold the child. Even Peter had gathered the child in his arms a time or two that first day.

Sarah had sent Peter to inform Mr. Hoyt—who had returned to Amesbury a couple of weeks after the final snowfall of the season—they had safely arrived. As she had expected, the elderly man was not long in coming, in fact only minutes behind Peter.

The first person he wished to see was Abigail, who seemed to grow and change by the day. As he lifted her, she pulled on his beard. Laughing loudly, he drew her close.

As was common for siblings, though rare for the Thompson boys, there had been jealousy between them when it came to vying for attention, but not once had they felt anything of the kind for their sister thus they both smiled at the sight of their grandfather hugging their baby sister.

As Sarah observed the sight, she realized there was one missing from the happy reunion, Mr. Swyndhurst. Saddened at the thought that she may never see him again, she determined to send off a missive to him as soon as possible. Perhaps he would return if she made it known that he was greatly missed. When she had mentioned the idea of Mr. Swyndhurst coming to live with them to her husband, he had encouraged her to do what she could to convince him.

Later that night, once his wife had put Abigail to bed, Daniel watched as she composed a missive to Mr. Swyndhurst. He knew it would mean the world to her if her elderly friend returned. Leaning back against his pillow, he glanced around the room. Knowing it was the one Sarah had occupied before Alexander returned from England and not the one they had shared as husband and wife, caused him to feel more at ease. Other than in this room, he had found many of Alexander's belongings still in the home, which had served to remind him of Sarah's life before her marriage to him. The thought then came to him that Sarah must also at times have felt uncomfortable in the home he had shared with Joanna.

Seeing that she had finished writing, he said, "Sarah, I believe I now understand a little of how you must have felt living in the home I shared with Joanna for so long."

"Oh, Daniel. I do apologize for being so insensitive. This must be difficult for you, being here in this home where you are surrounded by Alexander's books, keepsakes, and such."

Daniel had not brought up the subject to gain that kind of a response. "Sarah, though being in this home is somewhat of a reminder of your life with Alexander, I shall be perfectly fine living here."

"Are you certain, Daniel? Perhaps we should sell this home and look for another here in Amesbury."

"That will not be necessary. I shall grow to love this home, I am certain of it. It suits our needs perfectly. We should rest now. Abigail is sure to be up long before we wish her to be."

Sarah nodded and then blew out the candle. The next morning, Hannah and Jonathan came to call. Mr. Hoyt had seen Jonathan in town and had informed him of the Thompsons' arrival. Though they knew they should wait a little longer before coming to call, Hannah could not wait. She was anxious to see Sarah's child.

Martha led them into the parlor where Sarah and Daniel were presently sitting in the middle of the floor, on a blanket, enjoying time with Abigail.

Sarah looked up as Hannah approached. After jumping to her feet, she quickly embraced her friend. "It is wonderful to see you, Hannah, and you as well, Jonathan."

Daniel stood then. Before he could properly greet either of the Bleasdells, they had both plopped down on the blanket with Abigail. He glanced over at his wife and found her smiling at the pair now taking turns squeezing their daughter.

Hannah and Jonathan became better acquainted with Daniel as they conversed over dinner. The Bleasdells had adored Sarah's first husband. When it came time for them to take their leave, they were sure Sarah had made as good a match with Daniel.

When Daniel walked them out, Jonathan promised to take him to call on the town's surgeon by week's end. The two medical men had met in Boston on more than one occasion at events related to their occupation. Daniel hoped he might lighten the work load for the surgeon who attended folks not only in Amesbury but, from time to time, in the surrounding towns as well.

As Daniel watched the wagon disappear into the night, he felt a peace about having moved to Amesbury. If the Bleasdells were any indication of the kind of people living there, he was certain he would form deep and lasting attachments.

Chapter 50

Sarah hoped that any day now she would receive word from Mr. Swyndhurst regarding her invitation to return to Amesbury. To her dismay, the reply to her missive was long in coming. When at last it arrived, she discovered the reason for the delay. Mr. Swyndhurst had been unwell, as the letter from his head-servant, Robert Hamilton, informed.

She hurriedly studied the communication for further information concerning Mr. Swyndhurst's condition. Towards the end, she learned he had been struck down by apoplexy but, thankfully, had been slowly regaining the use of the left side of his body; however, with his right leg incapable of moving, he was rendered unable to walk.

Tears came spilling from Sarah's eyes at the thought of what her dear father-in-law had suffered. Hearing a sound, she looked up and saw her husband coming into the room.

Seeing his wife's wet face and red eyes, Daniel quickly made his way over to her. "What has happened?" Sobbing, Sarah handed him the missive. Once he had read it, he took hold of her hand and led her over to the settee by the window. "Let us pray for him." They did just that for the next few minutes.

Sarah felt more at ease after praying. "I know it shall not be very long before he joins Alexander and Joanna in heaven, as he is not a young man, but I wish I could see him once more."

While caressing his wife's hand, Daniel thought to himself, *Perhaps we shall make a journey one day.* "From what Mr. Hamilton offered for information, it sounds as though Mr. Swyndhurst may yet recover."

"Oh, that he would. He has yet to see our little Abigail."

Martha knocked on the door at that moment. Hearing Sarah call for her to come in, she entered. "Our little miss is in need of her mother." While handing Abigail to Sarah, Martha noticed her red, puffy eyes. Not wanting to meddle, she turned and left the room. As she made her way down the stairs, she prayed that all would be well, whatever the trouble may be.

Seeing Abigail's smiling face lightened Sarah's mood. Once Sarah had seen to Abigail's needs, she and Daniel decided to take her out for a walk. As it was a rather windy day, Daniel wrapped his child in a quilt and the three were off.

As they neared the home Matthew Raymond had formerly occupied, Sarah became agitated and asked to return to the house. Daniel had seen her countenance change from one of joy to what he would describe as almost fearful. Peering over at the house that seemed to have upset his wife, he rightly guessed to whom it had belonged. He knew full well the injury his wife had suffered at the man's hands, as she had come to his home not long after. Not only had she suffered the worst kind of injury for a woman, she also later lost the child conceived at the time of the attack. Daniel pulled his wife close, turned, and started for home.

When Sarah was safely home, she felt foolish for having become so emotional, for the man was dead and could no longer be a danger to her. Deciding to take a rest, she asked her husband to see if Martha could watch Abigail for a little while.

Once he had placed Abigail in Martha's care, Daniel made his way up to his bedchamber, where his wife was currently resting.

After quietly closing the door behind him, Daniel glanced over to see his wife lying on the bed, awake. "Are you well, Sarah?"

Mortified at her earlier show of emotion, Sarah responded, "Yes, of course. Just a little tired."

Daniel came toward her. Taking a seat on the bed next to her, he touched her hand. "Sarah, the house we passed by belonged to Matthew Raymond, did it not?"

"Ho...how did you—"

"It was not all that difficult to guess what had unnerved you so."

Turning her head away, she muttered, "I thought I was over it. When I was last in Amesbury, I believed I had put it all behind me."

"Sarah, you have been away for a time. Coming back was sure to bring up old memories. These feelings shall pass as they did before; however, I dare say, not completely. The kind of thing that happened to you is not easily forgotten." Daniel stood and walked around to the other side of the bed. Once he had climbed in, he slid his arm under his wife and pulled her into his arms. The pair soon fell asleep.

Over the next few days, Sarah did not venture out. Knowing the young woman's love for walks where she could enjoy the out of doors, Martha wondered at the reason.

Finding a moment alone with Mr. Thompson, she inquired, "Is there something amiss with Sarah? She has not set foot out of the house in days, which is very unlike her."

Having now been acquainted with Martha's great love for his wife, Daniel freely responded, "She seems to be afflicted with unpleasant memories following our walk a few days ago."

"I see, and in which direction did you walk?" She was certain she knew the answer.

"Yes, Martha, we went by Matthew Raymond's former home. Had I known, I would not have led us by there."

"Oh, I had hoped she would not think of that despicable man ever again; but of course one does not forget—" Even after all this time, Martha still could not bring herself to speak aloud what had happened.

"Indeed, she could not. Since you asked in which direction we walked, would she have been all right had we gone the other way, or is it your opinion that returning to Amesbury is going to be problematic for her?"

"When she was living here, after Alexander's passing, she went out for strolls on a regular basis, but each time I noticed it was not in the direction of that particular house."

"I am happy to hear it. I shall keep her attention away from that home in the future."

After his conversation with Martha, Daniel made his way to the parlor. Selecting a book from Sarah's stack on the little table by the window, he took a seat. Opening the book, his eyes went to the first page. Unable to focus, his mind wandered to the time when he had first met Sarah. The small woman was as white as a sheet except for the bruises she had acquired at the hands of Matthew Raymond. At that time, she had also had a great fear of going out of doors. To his amazement, though, she had quickly overcome her fears.

I have married a very brave, albeit little woman, he thought to himself. *She has been through so much.* Just then, Sarah came into the room. Turning his head in her direction, Daniel smiled and came to his feet.

"I thought I should like a walk and wondered if you would wish to join me." She knew she could not let her fears take over, or she might once again be self-confined to her home.

"Indeed I would," Daniel replied. *Yes, I have married myself a very courageous woman.*

Chapter 51

Late spring, the year 1737, Amesbury, Massachusetts Bay Colony

To the great delight of everyone in the Thompson home, Uncle George arrived, prepared to take his nephews out on a hunt. A bounty had been established for wolves once again at fifty shillings per animal, as they had become bothersome to the sheep. He had sent word of his coming and that he was to stay a few days.

Sarah was possibly the most overjoyed of the group at seeing her brother. As he entered, he hastened toward her, scooping her up, nearly squeezing the breath out of her. "George, I am so glad you have come. I have missed you so, and the boys are anxious for the promised hunt."

George, so different than he once was, appeared quite peaceful and happy. Nudging his brother-in-law, he asked where he might find little Abigail. His sister then informed him that the child was down for a nap. Feigning a pout, George gathered up his satchel and followed after his sister to the room in which he would be staying.

Once settled, he went in search of his nephews. It was time they set off on the hunt. They were to meet up with a few of his father's acquaintances.

Late in the day, the threesome strolled toward home. They had killed two wolves during the hunt and had already collected their reward, to be split between the two young men. Truth be told, it was their uncle who had made the precise shot for each kill.

As they were passing by Matthew Raymond's home, their father came strolling out. He was there attending the new owner, who had burned her hand while cooking. The boys were surprised at seeing him. Once they had greeted him, their father sent them on ahead.

Daniel explained to George why he had held him back. As they stood in front of the home once owned by Matthew Raymond, Daniel disclosed the entire account of the terrible event that had happened there. George had already heard a little of the story, but he had not, until now, heard it in its entirety. His eyes filled with tears at what his sister had endured. He was also, yet again, overwhelmed by guilt at what she had suffered at his hands as well.

"George, I know what you are thinking. Sarah has long since forgiven you."

With his head hanging low, George responded, "I know. I do not deserve such a sister." Then, growing angry at the dead man, he burst out, "If Matthew Raymond was still alive, he would feel my wrath."

Daniel smiled at his brother-in-law. "Spoken like a true older brother."

"I shall spend the remainder of my days looking out for my sister. I only wish our relationship had begun as it is now. I have much to regret when it comes to my sisters. I used them both abominably."

"As I said, Sarah never thinks of such things, and you know Joanna loved you dearly."

The men then continued on towards home. Sarah greeted them as they came into the parlor. She instantly knew something was amiss with George, for when he looked at her, his eyes were tear-filled.

Later, when they were alone, after everyone else had gone to bed, her brother stated once more his regret at his earlier treatment of her. With a fierce tone, she replied that she never wanted to hear him say such things again.

To see his sister's stern countenance caused George's mood to lift. "Sarah, if you could but see yourself. You are too adorable."

A little frustrated that he was not taking her seriously yet still glad to see her brother's mood had altered, she replied, "I am in earnest. I never wish to hear that kind of talk again. You are a blessing to me."

"Sarah, as long as I am around, I mean to see you happy and protected."

Hearing his words brought joy to Sarah's heart. She had a brother looking after her now. How good it felt.

By the time George was ready to take his leave a few days later, he and his sister had grown an even deeper bond.

Daniel stood with his wife by the door, waving as George's wagon set off down the road. "He has become the best of brothers, has he not?"

"Yes, Daniel. I could not wish for a better one. In fact, I have several wonderful men in my life."

Teasing, Daniel tried to appear hurt at her words of having *several* men in her life. Not taking the bait, his wife poked him.

"No matter the men in my life, you are the most treasured."

Daniel glanced downward at his wife's smiling face. Unable to resist, stooping, he kissed her. There was a time he believed he could never look upon this tiny person as a fully grown woman. But in seeing her strength of character and her perseverance in the face of adversity, he had come to see her not only as a woman, but one of great worth.

The couple began their union as merely friends, but in the end their marriage had blossomed into one of deep and abiding love.

Postscript

The first poor house was established in Boston in 1735.

Hannah and Jonathan Bleasdell are part of the authors' family history, including certain details about the children and Jonathan's and David's occupations.

The Sack Posset recipe was taken from *The Yankee Chef: Feel Good Food for Every Kitchen*, by Jim Bailey. Jim Bailey's ancestors journeyed with the authors' ancestors on the Angel Gabriel in 1635. http://theyankeechef.com/

Genealogical outline provided by:
http://www.blaisdell.org/

Epilogue

Sarah had welcomed the arrival of her brother's first child. George had married a lovely, Christian woman a year after learning he and Sarah were siblings. It had been two months since the child's birth. Her brother and his family would be arriving in Amesbury on this day. When the wagon pulled into the yard, little Abigail toddled alongside her mother as they made their way out to greet their guests.

Daniel and his sons came strolling out of the barn to receive George and his family. Mr. Hoyt would be joining them as soon as Peter went to fetch him. The family spent a lovely evening conversing together in the parlor. Everyone adored George's new wife, Rebecca, and their baby son, Mark.

Later, after everyone had gone to bed, Sarah read the missive she had received from England to her husband. Mr. Swyndhurst had passed and, as Joanna and Alexander, he was now with the Lord. The couple then talked about the fact that, because of God's great love and sacrifice, they would one day all be together again. They then thanked the Lord that George had become the "new creature in Christ" the Bible talks about in 2 Corinthians 5:17.

"Therefore if any man be in Christ, he is a new creature: old things are passed away; behold, all things are become new."

Other Books by Bryant and Dorman

Lost Love and Shipwrecked
Madeline Pike Finds Hope in the New Land

Grandmother's Namesake

Sarah Anne's Expedient Marriage

http://www.bryantdormanbooks.com/